AGAINST THE COUNTRY

AGAINST THE COUNTRY

A NOVEL

BEN METCALF

RANDOM HOUSE NEW YORK

Published in the United States by Random House, an imprint of The Random House Publishing Group, a division of Random House LLC, a Penguin Random House Company, New York.

RANDOM HOUSE and the HOUSE colophon are registered trademarks of Random House LLC.

LIBRARY OF CONGRESS CATALOGING-IN-PUBLICATION DATA
Metcalf, Ben.
Against the country : a novel / Ben Metcalf.
pages cm
ISBN 978-1-4000-6269-0
eBook ISBN 978-0-8129-9653-1
1. Family life—Fiction. I. Title.
PS3613.E8783A53 2014
813'.6—dc23
2014002175

Printed in the United States of America on acid-free paper

www.atrandom.com

2 4 6 8 9 7 5 3 1

FIRST EDITION

Book design by Barbara M. Bachman

For Linda, who knows full well that there could not possibly exist, in Virginia or elsewhere in our nation, a county with so preposterous a name as the one given here.

BOOK ONE

Town

I was worked like a jackass for the worst part of my childhood, and offered up to climate and predator and vice, and introduced to solitude, and braced against hope, and dangled before the Lord our God, and schooled in the subtle truths and blatant lies of a half life in the American countryside, all because my parents did not trust that I would mature to their specifications in town. That their plan busted would be of some comfort to me could I find fault in its formulation, but these two were not stupid: I have spoken at length with the both of them and judge each one to be of the highest wit. Nor were they cruel: my brother and sister will no doubt attest to the fact that our makers never left us hungry and that they seemed, on the whole, at least partial to us. Nor may I safely argue that their verdict on town life, whatever torments I might ascribe to the sentence, differed in any large part from my own, so negligent was town in its attitude toward us, and so sorry a welcome did our line receive there after nearly three centuries spent adrift in the New World's vast and terrible wilderness.

Town (by which I mean the middling depots of Southern Illinois, though from what I have seen of such places elsewhere they might have served just as well) was where a former farmboy's peers led him with little effort to conclude that scholarship money was best put toward Scotch whiskey and unfiltered cigarettes; where in the resultant fog he resolved that only marriage to, and abrupt procreation with, a woman met some eight weeks prior could plausibly avert commerce with the Vietcong; whereupon he watched a single child swell with remarkable ease into three and then learned from his town wife that an enormous effort would now be required to feed them all; whereupon in a panic he fell prey to what the French call a nostalgia for the mud and contrived thereafter to work only with his hands, sure that these hands would not betray him as the brain had; whereupon he discovered that town tended to confine such people to jobs concerned primarily with the assembly of prefabricated homes, whose authors balanced the monotony of their craft with a fast loyalty to amphetamine; whereupon an insipid despair left him open to, but deprived him of the imagination to accept, proposals from more motivated coworkers to help rob area fast-food establishments and drive tractor-trailers full of marijuana down into these United States from the fabled nurseries of western Canada.

Town was where a young woman, confident of her sophistication despite only a slim generation's remove from the trees herself, married the farmboy to amputate herself, fashionably, from the trunk of her own family; and bore not the first of her children but certainly the subsequent two so that she might cauterize the wound, or else salt it; and soon enough grasped the illogic of union to a man unfamiliar with affluence and beholden to the dirt for his self-esteem and his sanity. Who was then clotheslined in her effort to aid the brood materially when, the aforementioned fine mind notwithstanding, no better task presented than secretary at the local rock radio station, WEIC, which position she would lose anyway at a time roughly concurrent with the loss of her husband's job at UniBuilt.

Town was where this woman beheld the great locust wave of in-laws come in search of money she did not have or could not possibly spare, where out of empathy, or embarrassment, or guilt, or a confluence of these ills, she took it upon herself to provide the odd car ride or bed, and to ignore this one's taste for drugs, and that one's taste for morons, and to stuff the more malnourished babies with what was at hand, and to keep abreast of each tragically unavoidable court date, until the afternoon came when she saw her husband exorcise the drunken swarm of them from his yard, after which they drove up and down the street and shouted threats to kill him, after which he shouted threats to kill them sooner, after which I find it hard to believe that my mother did not reflect upon the likelihood that she had thus far escaped this lot's lot only by grace of the humble sums she still asked for, and received, from her kind if disappointed town parents.

Town for me will forever remain a place where one put a bag of questionable design on one's head for Halloween, and acquired what candy as the bag allowed, and vomited in surprise and fury the next morning on the filthy tile floor outside an aunt's efficiency apartment, wherein slept a beloved infant cousin whose metal-toothed sire was unaccounted for and who would in time (the infant) grow up to burn down his high school and find steady if unsung work as an adjunct to the beef industry. My younger sister's memories of town may be few but surely include the day the worse-off people around the corner, whose sole consolation in life appeared to be the fried-chicken dinner an area philanthropist stood them to once each week, leashed a mutt by means of a frayed electrical cord plugged into an outdoor socket, so that the entire neighborhood might hear the poor creature's shrieks as it caught fire and perished. She has shown a fondness for almost all God's animals since.

Our brother alone seemed to extract some pleasure from town, being older and hence afforded friends and a paper route, and having gained for himself a measure of boyhood fame when in guile he lured the thieves of a treasured lunchbox down into the ravine through which ran the local sewage creek, and there received them cruelly with his friends' fists and his own, not to mention the impressive might of the sewage itself. His was the earliest recognition of, and the only real objection to, the fact that our family was set to quit the company of mankind altogether if it could and plant itself once more in the desolate slough from which it had but recently crawled.

Tarnation

We would have done well to heed the dissenter, for as frail as the rest of us found town to be it was, and always had been, the one conceivable bulwark against an annihilation that has hunted every human who dared, or was by circumstance forced, to set his foot upon this treacherous soil. Did the Indian not spread himself over the new land by band and by village? Did the Spaniard or the Frenchman not pause in his slaughter of the Indian to put up his forts against the bear and the water and the wind? Did the Englishman not hurriedly arrange, in his attempt to destroy the Spaniard and the Frenchman (and, of course, the Indian), the huts of his vanished Roanoke, and did he not raise up his Jamestown and his Plymouth all the faster? Did the Dutchman not hoodwink the Indian so that he might secure his New Amsterdam, and did he not war with the Englishman over that slight and others, and in the end swap the whole of the operation for some sugar stalks down in Suriname? I ask you: Did the plantation not arise and have its run, however truncated, because it was, in effect, less a farm than it was a township populated and maintained by slaves? Did the pioneer and the prospector not normally die at once, and can it be said that the lonely homesteader who survived was anything but miserable in his barren and pitiless surrounds?

I suppose that my parents, who were not innocent of history, might have given the evidence against seclusion in the

American brush its due, and seen fit to discount their own hard time of it among humans, had town here not decomposed by the 1970s to the point where one could expect no more than the same polluted rill or "river" oozing through its heart or along one rib, and the same cluster of mediocre chain stores with a shared and weed-broken parking lot, and the same Democratic or Republican electoral machine, and the same contagious Kiwanis- or Rotary-club swimming pool just west of the trailer park, and the same sclerosed gauntlet of schools whose far end was a football team with no better shot at state than it had the year before, and the same bars and whores in imitation of bars and whores in larger towns, and the same summer visit from the stringy-haired druggists and statutory rapists who ran rides at the local fair, and the same debate about which street signs had by their presence or absence caused which oddly relished traffic fatalities, and the same brand-new brick pokey full of drunks and whores and high-school footballers and destitute neighbors and blood relatives as one could no doubt find in the next town over.

Yet can town's letdown alone account for the keenness with which my mother and father envisioned the ruin of each of their children in turn by coach or cousin or carny rapist? Can it explain the ease with which they came to believe that town's alternative was not a bug-bit hell but rather a tit-cuddled arcadia? Can it excuse the swiftness with which these people determined to hurl themselves, and their children, headlong into the national briar patch, there to itch and to bleed?

I deny it.

I deny that town is the root of all harm to these United States. I deny that our blighted communities owe nothing to the land upon which they were made. I deny that this continent, unlike all the others, wishes to graze cattle and grow foodstuffs for the benefit of its invaders. I deny that tarnation has a grip only on those Americans who lay claim to more than one neighbor, and who direct no great suspicion at the universities, and who refuse to believe that the Revised Standard Version of the Bible was written (and then presumably revised) by the Baby Jesus, and who have yet to purchase, out of imagined or actual need, either a pickup truck or a Soviet-issued machine gun. To my mind, he who turns his back on town is as prone as anyone to become evil's eager and ignorant sponge.

For the sake of the republic

I wish for the sake of the republic that I could call our decision to flee town's omens a mere reaction to them, but as gamely as town worked to push us away another force, of a much higher order, and with the potential to devastate all that humanity has raised up in defense of itself, tugged at us all the while, and muddled our thoughts, and drew us out into the trees to glare at omens more powerful than any we had seen with their pants off down on Main Street. The very least of what awaited us, perhaps by way of reproach, were drunks with a better reason to imbibe than in town and a good deal farther to drive, and carnies whose rickety rides were less well cared for than in the populated areas but who nonetheless represented all the glamour a fourteen-year-old country girl was liable to encounter in her lifetime, and whores who were older and less toothsome renditions of that selfsame fourteen-year-old girl, and furious high-school football players whose Baptist prayers had never won them so much as a break-even season, and neighbors of such paltry means that they generally lacked the amperage required to electrocute a dog and so were left to use a firearm on it or on any other animal they happened across during the course of an otherwise empty day.

No more than ten at the time of our departure from civilization, if what we treaded in for so bleak a stretch can be said to warrant the term, I did not know, nor would I have approved,

of our subscription to the very lie that had, some seven generations previous on my father's side, and a competitive number
on my mother's, orchestrated the grand farce by which I first
entered the American hoedown in the first place. That I
emerged and took air in an Illinois hospital and not a cornfield
I count as something of a miracle, given that my forebears were
suckered out into the region not by a promise of suitable communities there, which anyway did not exist then and arguably
do not exist now, but by a promise of land, countless acres of it,
advertised to be rich and bountiful and blessed, if not actually
occupied, by God Himself. It seems hardly to have occurred to
my ancestors, or to my own parents, that this same God had for
centuries shown a marked preference for town, and a tendency
to yield the whole of the wild expanses to Satan, and had inspired (at least in His New England penitents) a fear and a
hatred of the natural world intense enough that anyone who
expressed an admiration for the woods, or a curiosity about the
high grass beyond the village, was likely to be dubbed a witch
and set directly on fire.

How exactly God was persuaded to leave town I do not
know, but I assume He was removed by the same men, now
rotted, who long ago condemned my bloodline to oblivion on
behalf of the enormous real-estate hustle that today comprises
the worthless plains adjacent to the Mississippi, and the obviously infertile desert beyond those plains, and the murderous
mountains beyond that desert, and the perfectly alien far coast
those mountains traitorously guard. He may have made a go of
it on the steppe, or up in the hills, and He may eventually have
come to take a stubborn pride in His predicament, as country
people are wont to do, or He may have gathered Himself up
and vacated the continent entirely, provided the soil had not
sucked away His power to do even that. At any rate He ap-
pears to have become separated from His American flock, and
He has since provided little real, as opposed to claimed, com-

fort to those millions of His presumed neighbors who once parted with dependable town money to work and inhabit, if never in truth to possess, an unkind land they had been told was proximate to Glory.

As an accomplice to this scheme, and perhaps a principal in it, Thomas Jefferson seems to me to have sinned cardinally, with his comfortable slaver's dream of an agrarian wonderland and his criminal transfer of public funds to the Napoleonic war effort so as to avail us of the hectares needed to prove that dream a nightmare. I also hold accountable Daniel Boone, first realtor through the Cumberland Gap; and Fenimore Cooper, whose salesmanship of the prairie and the waterways as a playground for white boys continues to plague us with foreign-exchange students and unwatchable Hollywood films; and Mr. Greeley, who encouraged the young to believe that a westward trek would not, in fact, kill a number of them outright and deliver the rest into penury; and Mr. Audubon, whose still lifes do little to indicate that actual birds flap around overly much and tend to spread influenzas; and Messrs. Alcott and Lane and Emerson and Thoreau, who were not satisfied that the land should be thought benevolent and wise but sought also to equate these ludicrous properties with the American soul; and Senator Calhoun, who damned the nation to Armageddon (though he would not live to enjoy the scene) with his fantasy that somewhere between the smug agribusiness of the plantation and the observable grief of the tenant farm was to be found a "way of life" whose protection was worth the risk (and, as it turned out, the reality) of death and dismemberment and subjugation.

I would add to this list Mr. Whitman, who approached the senator's war with no more insight than that both the bramble and the self should be celebrated, and came out of it with no better improvement to his art than that putrefaction and "de-

mocracy" deserved some say as well. I would also include here the worshipful Mr. Muir, and every pupil of the Hudson School, and every man named Benton who lifted voice or pen or paintbrush in the naturalist cause, and every Joel Chandler Harris who saw fit to attach pretty morals to an ugly rural past, and every Nashville Agrarian who failed, in this same facile nostalgia, to recognize Jefferson and Calhoun as madmen or liars. Special mention is due E. B. White, who prompted the rich to believe that a weekend retreat in the country qualified them for the position of calm rustic sage, and every back-to-the-land hippie who managed to further this absurd idea with his inheritance-funded commune, only to suggest something truer with his California killing spree.

Whether we were swayed by these particular boosters of the simple life or by others is for my parents to say, not me, though I do think it germane that we found ourselves banished to a desolate Virginia county at the foot of the Piedmont Plateau, to the east of Jefferson's labor camp on Monticello, and to the west of the Confederate capital Calhoun's rhetoric made inevitable, and to the south of the wounds Whitman peeled and scraped clean on account of the agricultural lie's most spirited attempt yet to defend itself. Could chance alone have fetched us to such a nexus? Was it wholly arbitrary that we landed within a wind-aided scream of the very spot where the effort to farm the interior of this continent began?

I thank God, if He has not by now entirely acquiesced to the rural cause, that we ventured east and not west, as Mr. Greeley would have liked it, because I doubt I would be here to complain had the opposite occurred. That we chose to head south, though, is a blow no God who retained even the smallest affection for His American subjects would have dealt us, and that we settled in so useless a stretch of the kudzu is a masterstroke no combination of Jeffersons could feasibly have arranged. I must therefore conclude, as I was moved at least to suspect during my long years of exile from town, that the land itself, and especially the land of the Virginia Piedmont, wooded and weed-choked and encased in hard red clay where we had been led to expect some semblance of topsoil, was actively, and perhaps even knowingly, involved in our doom.

More pessimistic circles

Since those days when England's rubbishes wagered all they had for the wisdom that they would shortly be dead in the Virginia brush, if not by native axe or flesh scoop then by the bloody flux or some other microscopic remedy to man, it has been the American's destiny, or else simply his style, to head off into perdition unburdened with the price of a ticket home. Apparently the cost of a single rented U-Haul, as well as the gasoline required to traverse Kentucky's failed imitation of industry (and then to negotiate the food-stampy hollers and tax-kept scenic viewpoints of the Appalachian range), sufficed to include us in this ritual of diminishment and despair. Even before they had seen for themselves the depletion along the once ballyhooed and now rightfully ignored James River, my parents were tapped out and frightened enough to make for the comparative oasis of Richmond, where a couple of weeks left to amuse ourselves in the parking lot of a waffle house near the motel, while our father looked for construction work and our mother searched in ever more pessimistic circles for an address within our means, made it clear that Richmond cared no more for us than had the decomposing forts back in Southern Illinois. We knew that within a month or two we would need to seek shelter elsewhere, most likely in one of those sad and vacant James-bound counties we had driven through on the way out and already agreed to detest.

My brother, in what I take to be a stab at kindness, has claimed that our parents could not possibly have intended for their children to come of age so removed from the basic comforts, and so divested of human decency, and were bent for the nearest Kentucky town when, somewhere between Richmond and Charlottesville, the gas money gave out. Against such a theory I would offer our sister's insistence that throughout this dark time she was continually promised a horse, which would indicate (a) that our parents nurtured a bucolic goal all along and (b) that they meant to have some money left over once their goal had been achieved, which would further indicate (c) that they were in no way impelled but actually chose to raise us in our subsequent isolation and misery. On the other hand, since my sister never received anything like a horse in the Virginia hills, despite the fact that a pony or a half-dead mule could be had out there for as little as fifty dollars, her claims about when the promise was first made, and how often it was repeated, might be considered tainted by a former *Black Beauty* enthusiast's understandable thirst for revenge.

I myself do not care what plans my parents made or unmade or altered or adhered to: no blame can attach to those caught fast in a pit of excrement who flail around for something by which they might pull themselves to safety, or who opt instead to remain immobile so as not to be sucked under any sooner. I do not care whether Richmond was, in fact, the sturdy overhead branch we required at the time. Richmond was, and still is, suited primarily to wealthy people able to tolerate the boredom and tastelessness and humidity that account for most of the culture there. Nor do I care if my parents neglected to make an honest grab for that branch: the countryside to the west of Richmond was clearly the better match for us, being suited primarily to poorer people who could tolerate their own measure of boredom and tastelessness and humidity, or who had no choice but to try. I can find fault with my parents only for their failure to hammer out the terms of our surrender with more finesse, and to recognize that the place one's children hail from is a tattoo ever afterward, and to steer us with what strength they could still summon into a county with a more agreeable name than the one we would all come to loathe and deny.

Ugliness

That my siblings and I hail now and forever from Goochland, Virginia, and not from Powhatan, or Chesterfield, or Hanover, or Louisa, or Fluvanna, or Appomattox, or any number of decently named counties within a bankrupt gas tank's reach of Richmond, is indeed a heavy log to bear, but even here I see evidence of a cause larger than my parents' inability to consult a map properly and think ahead. For into this same county, which in 1743 encompassed a wider swath of uselessness than it does today, was born Thomas Jefferson himself, and it was within its present bounds that he wasted his childhood among the tobacco plants which prior to our arrival had relieved the soil of what simple nutrients it once possessed. Cornwallis passed through on his way to Yorktown, and later Sheridan on his way to Petersburg, and before him a detachment of soon-to-be-dead Union fools who believed that a tiny band of horsemen could penetrate Richmond's western defenses and canter away with the Confederate president as a prize, but the county holds real historical worth only insofar as it witnessed the birth and early schooling of that rash ginger prophet who would, through his words and deeds and acolytes, convince millions of Americans to martyr themselves on the altar of an agrarian delusion. No more is wanted: if great holiness can be claimed for Bethlehem and Mecca because of the careers launched there, then surely I am justified in my own claim that a certain unholy ugliness emanated from within the bounds of Goochland County, and commanded our attention, and beckoned us out into those pine shadows and those unremitting fields.

Richmond has since been generous to the eastern part of Goochland, having long ago saturated the intermediate county, Henrico, with the customary gifts of townhouses and strip malls and golf courses and industrial parks, and I hear the Goochland teens are now taught in a modern facility that does not ask them either to confront or to ignore the reality that they attend the white high school, as opposed to the black, which after integration had become their impoverished junior high. Well-paved roads now obtain throughout the county, where dirt and gravel were once the norm, and one may detect a species of progress in the satellite dishes so prevalent on roofs and in yards as to imply that all of Goochland is host to some grand project to contact the aliens, which would interest but hardly surprise me, as I often enough prayed to be abducted myself by spacemen during our time out there.

Yet I do not think that Richmond's largesse has much affected the westernmost part of the county. The farmhouses there, although approached now and then by more modern dwellings, and surely aware of the subdivisions in bloom just a few miles to the east, seem no less jury-rigged, and no less austere, than they did when we infested a particularly poor example of one thirty years ago. The tar-paper shacks have neither vanished nor abandoned their tradition of yards swept clean of all grass and dwellers swept clean of all hope. The churches seem no less fatigued for the fact that their congregations have lately managed to bankroll a fresh coat of paint, or a course of aluminum siding, or a rather-too-obvious brick façade. The fields offer no indication that they will ever support anything more ambitious than the next shy crop of feed corn or hay, or the next silly ostrich farm, or the next state-sanctioned facility for juvenile offenders, or the next overpopulated boneyard.

In the untamed patches between the fields and the farm-houses, and the shacks and the boys' homes, and the ostriches and the graves, it is still possible to glimpse something akin to what must have greeted Europa's petards as they made their way up the American bowel (with a brief stop at the spot where Richmond herself would metastasize), and it is still possible to imagine the conditions under which these people, or their children, or their children's children, succumbed to and incubated and spread the pastoral fever that would cheat them of any real chance at happiness, and would in essence enslave them, and would grant increase only to those with the will and the where-withal to enslave others instead. Such crimes startle but do not concern me. I care only that this fever so boiled the brains of my people that they were disposed, after more than 250 years spent sampling the agricultural brutalities on offer in Maryland and Pennsylvania and Ohio and Illinois and Oklahoma and Illinois again, to prostrate themselves, in Virginia, before the very source of their already rampant infection.

Illinois bull

My father, perhaps heedful of the fact that his great-grandpa
had been gored to death by an Illinois bull who did not
fancy servitude, and having been touched by the poverty that
results from such a miscalculation, did not involve us directly
with cows, and for that I am grateful. Nor did he purchase a
tractor so that it might pin and crush himself, or me, under its
weight, as had befallen his mother, who had survived it, and a
boyhood neighbor or two, who had not. Then again, he could
not afford one. A combine, such as the enormous instrument
that gnawed the legs off at least one of his former schoolmates,
and for "hours" held the rest of its meal suspended by shoulder
strength alone, lest the entrée follow the appetizer, was, thank-
fully, even further beyond his means. What animals we accou-
tred ourselves with did not bellow and bawl but only woofed
and clucked, and what machines we got hold of, most of them
workaday tools lent out by or stolen from Richmond-area construction sites, or else purchased with great reluctance from the
Southern States cooperative at the county's sad center, were
employed not so much to farm as to create the impression of a
farm that had long ago been destroyed.

We were aided in that pursuit by the house itself, which was
put up, badly, in the middle of the nineteenth century and
looked about ready to fall over, which in truth it was. My father
was obliged in time to shove pneumatic jacks under its southerly

side (the structure, longingly, faced west) so that it would not collapse entirely and kill us all in our beds. Otherwise his attentions implied that a partial disintegration would be acceptable and even preferred. The tin roof, where it was not covered by a dull green paint that must have been designed to blister in the sun, was rusted through to an extent that suggested replacement even to a child, but my father made no move to hinder its corrosion and seemed almost pleased with the gothic sentiment it related to the road below. The front porch, which within a few seasons of our introduction to it had chosen to commit suicide, my brother and I tore away from the house completely, and left the detritus to blanch in a pile in the yard. Yet our father neither ordered nor himself began the erection of a new approach there, and so the front door, which without its preface floated a formidable two feet off the wormy ground, was never afterward used. Even company, rare, could see to go around back.

My mother, the town girl, screamed and on occasion effected some small augmentation to, say, the indoor bathroom, which was probably tacked on in the 1950s and, although retiled, could not be made to smell much better than the old outhouse did, or to the kitchen, also tacked on, which because of the distance to the nearest town grocery store (we could not afford the country prices) came to host a freezer the size and shape of two stacked coffins, in which slept quaint venison stews and pig meat got locally, yes, but mostly the frozen pizzas and loaves of processed bread that would become our lifeblood. She also held forth on the house's airflow, or lack thereof, which my father's installation of a huge electric fan in the attic did little to revise, unless, like the now greatly agitated black widows and brown recluses, one happened to live in the attic. Apart from these half-answered fits, she adopted a pose not unusual among Americans who have made a dire mistake they cannot pay to unmake: she pretended that our plainly lessened state was somehow a step up from town life, and she insisted, with no real success, that her children back her in this ancient and wearisome falsehood.

Her face, when not wet and distorted with panic and re-crimination, set itself in a smile that managed both to convey and to subvert the notion "Isn't this fun?" while my father, ensnared in his own attempt to sustain what level of denial was necessary to his pride, worked to erase any hint that the stead was, or ever had been, able to sustain human life. We all allowed, outwardly or inwardly, that our position was sore and liable to worsen, but my father could not be sure that the farm's inherent limitations would cleanse him entirely of guilt in the tragedy to come. And so he practiced to enhance them for the benefit of anyone who drove or wandered by. That a man would choose to be the direct cause of his decline rather than its mere victim is, after a fashion, admirable, yet this was not the sole, nor even the primary, impulse behind his campaign. An anger at himself, and at his situation, and at the weight of his dependents, caught hold of him too, and where he could not direct that anger at us he moved directly against the property, and brought his wrath to bear especially on its outlying elements, and did not stop to consider how this program of ruin might impact the family's chances to lay in even a modest store of dignity and hope.

Sunder

I recall several days spent in the effort to sunder an ancient gray shed, formerly an icehouse, that had surely done harm to no one, and had probably been of enormous benefit to the beings around it, and did not give over its wood and tin and nails with an ease that implied a welcome end to a worthy term of use. This shed fought us with an obstinacy unlike what would present in the old outhouse, or the remains of the front porch, or the strangely elaborate system of deserted bee boxes near the deserted chicken coop, or the uninsulated walls of what was supposed to have been our living room, and groaned considerably in the struggle, I now believe, to shield us from what lay beneath its cracked and rotted floor. When we had yanked up enough of its boards to enable us to stare down into the chasm below, and to contemplate what might be exposed once we had ripped away the whole of that lid, I told my father we had better let the building be. In my attempt to make out the bottom, I had sensed, and smelled, something of what awaited us among the roots. I was also pretty sure I had seen something move down there.

Because he was not spurred by vanity and rage alone; and because an attitude of forfeit (which soothed the vanity and excused the rage) was his birthright as a child of the American wilderness, and was his only recourse now that he was trapped out in it again; and because that attitude had already begun to decay into a simple indolence; and because that indolence would cause him to look upon any structure, including the main body of the house, as ready firewood for when the weather turned against us; and because this lunacy would persist until his sons were of sufficient size to serve as his proxies in the drudgery that would see them carry or push or drag chunks of felled tree from forest to field to yard, there to cleave these burdens with axe and agony into pieces small enough to be consumed by the house's wood stove (which would, despite its gluttony, heat no more than the room it was in and would actually attack and dissipate, by means of convection and black magic, what few pockets of warmth could be found in any of the others); because of these and other inebriants, my father resolved to wave off my counsel and to apply his crowbar, borrowed or stolen, to what was left of the shed's floor, as well as to what was left of our claim on self-preservation.

He pried, then, while we pulled, careful not to offer our palms to the spiders that frequented the underside of just about every piece of wood in Virginia, and what planks we did not clumsily or spitefully send down into the space below we raised up and spirited to the yard's green hillock, there to await the frost and the axe and the stove's pitiless glow. When it was finished, and nothing remained that could be pointed at any longer and called a shed, we could see clearly that what had thrown me was not, at least spatially, a chasm at all but only a foundational hollow of about three feet or so, whose walls of orange and red clay gave a fine indication of the land's hostility toward us and toward the discarded generations that had come before. I was, and remain, amazed that even a fescue could grow out of that stuff, let alone the more complicated weeds that filled the middle distance.

I suspect that my father considered those walls for some time, and basked in their ability to announce his blamelessness to the world, if also his lack of judgment. For my part I considered mostly the heap of additional boards my brother and I would now have to haul out of that hole and stack among the other scraps bound for the stove. Yet when we stepped down into the wreckage, my eye (I cannot speak for my brother's) was drawn not to the wood itself, nor to the useless clay that cupped it, nor to the relentless explosion in the sky above, but to the high grass that crested the foundation's far side. There, in apparent flight from our onslaught, slid a snake so black and shiny that it simultaneously absorbed and repelled what sunlight was not engaged just then in an attempt to burn its way through my skin. I could not make out the head, and so I could not discern the level of the creature's ire, but I knew at once that we had demolished either its home or its vacation spot, and I knew that the insult would not be allowed to stand.

A great sorcery

I did not fully comprehend then that a great sorcery was at work all around us, and intended to inspire in the mesmerized a suicidal result, and had found satisfaction many times over in those addled enough to think the land a precious asset rather than a sadistic foe. We were in no danger on the precious-asset count, as we could see as well as anyone that our particular sliver of earth was worth far less than the meager sum we had proffered to gain it, but to my mind that accrued against the purchaser and not the purchase, as did the generational mortgage by which we had made of the land a debtors' prison when my parents were unable to pay even the meager sum up front. They might have rented, and for as little as $150 a month provided me with a better home than the sweatbox-cum-windsock in which I would be forced to eat and sleep and feign sanity, mine and theirs, for the remainder of my childhood, but rental would have constituted an impossible admission on their part that they had erred not only in their decision to surround us with spiritual revivals and animal crap but in their shared assumption, with so much of America, that ownership of the land was a natural right handed down from heaven, as opposed to a shameful ruse perpetuated by the banks.

My parents had, it must be said, briefly rented a farmhouse upon our arrival in that accursed county, and in their defense the episode had played out poorly. Although greatly superior to the compromised lean-to we would later inhabit, this house continuously gave off, from the orifices of its sinks and tub, an odor of excrement, and I have yet to meet its better in the art of drawing flies. One afternoon there I encountered a wall so thick with these black and green demons that my attempts to slaughter them left hand-shaped impressions among their number, and the quickness with which these spaces then filled led me to flee the building in horror and disgust. I would not be surprised to hear that a corpse, or several, had been discovered behind that wall, and I am grateful that my own will most likely be allowed to rot elsewhere.

Our landlord, who had grown up in this very house and afterward refused to enter it, owned and operated a pointless gas station, back from which sat the house, and was involved with his brother in a feud that had either resulted in or been set off by the brother's construction of another pointless gas station across the road from the first. The negligible traffic thus divided, our landlord tried, not without success, to appear at least busier than his unprosperous brother by the regular cremation of dead tires behind his bleak concern, the thick black smoke from which reached us daily and was a welcome distraction from the usual smells. When not at such aromatic theater, this man found time to collect the rent, and to ignore the loss of what firewood my siblings and I were sent out nightly to steal from him, and to explain to my midwestern mother that it might be all right to have "coloreds" around back for a glass of water now and then, but one did not invite them inside. None of which, apparently, was sufficient to shoo my parents not just from this house but from the whole of that Godforsaken land.

So it was that they promised and purchased, and stuck us to our lot, and ensured that we would not escape it until we had found another victim to assume our arrears, as well as our sadness and our terror and whatever additional insults came gratis with the dirt. So it was that whereas we were led to believe we had acquired the land, when in fact the land had acquired us; and whereas the land was, in my estimation, perfectly happy with this arrangement, though in a remarkably short time we were not; and whereas the law in no way met its onus to correct, or at a minimum to address, this injustice as it might any other; therefore my father's war on the property, and its war on us, could in no way be considered actionable, which left as his only incentive to sue for peace the psychological welfare of his family, which he seemed to regard, if that word even applies here, as no more than an annoyance. So it was that we came to suffer under, if never quite to accept, my father's intention to use the land not to feed and further us but instead to express several borrowed ideas without practical use save the one to which I am able to put them here. So it was that we stumbled into the country life like an infant who takes his first astonished steps and then, as his frightened grin dissolves, reaches out to catch himself against the side of a red-hot wood stove.

Affront

We pretended as best we could that our father meant no more than a vain plea of innocence, but the evidence was against us. He left untouched a charming little slave shack, done up in the same abused white and nauseated green as the farmhouse, which we took to be a perfectly reasonable announcement that no one could be expected to wrest subsistence from this mud without captive labor (I am frankly surprised that I was not immediately installed in that shack), but his decision to spare the old outhouse, if only till a lust for its few stinky planks could overcome him, fairly shouted to all the world that we were not yet sold on the notion of indoor facilities, which could not help but connote a harder sort of pride.

The first sort implied only that my siblings and I would be enlisted now and then to inflict new damage on our position, whereas the second ensured that we would be made to endure the existential threat of a chicken society, and the less abstract menace of a yard mined with dog feces, and the hokum of a pickup truck whose bed we would have cause but no permission to use, and the self-consciously rustic affront of cars being "worked on" next to or in front of the house, and at one point the shock of an entire engine block hung by a chain from a tree, and a record player now enamored of Flatt and Scruggs's banjo travesties, and too often the indecency of a television set that still fancied *M*A*S*H*, yes, but came increasingly to favor episodes of *Grand Ole Opry* and *Hee Haw*.

He also began to whip us for our sins, committed or not, with switches cut by our own hand, which was the country way and I hope still is. That was a tough lesson, because central Virginia is shaded mostly by scrub pine, and no one with a lick of sense wants his legs torn into by a conifer. Something pulled from a conventional bush might suffice, or from a sassafras, though this might be returned for lack of firepower. Most saplings provided an acceptable bite, or a mutant shoot pulled off a full-grown tree. Birch was what was wanted by our father; balsa was what the condemned always sought, though that effect was to be found only in older trees that had died and decayed: I never saw it in anything green enough to pass for a switch. Young maple would do, and walnut of course. I would like to have tried baby oak, out of curiosity, but the earth right around us seemed unfriendly if not openly hostile to acorns. Plum was unthinkable, and cherry, and all the fruit-bearing trees: the sweetness in them promised too much. Magnolias and the like were a gamble: one might come up lucky with a flimsy specimen, but even the smaller armlets could prove deceptively sound. Dogwood held its own special thrill: it was the state tree! Locust was to be avoided, given its thorny bough, and no sane parent would misuse a child with a switch taken from that plant, just as no sane child would retrieve such a thing, unless he had it in mind to euthanize his own backside by seeing it whipped away for good.

Pride exacts its price, but this was collaboration, and as such we greeted it with the same resistance we had learned to employ on visits to my grandparents' small farm back in Southern Illinois, when for a weekend my father would become feral again and treat us all like stolen mules so that his people would not get the idea that education, and town, had softened him any. I took to pulling on every pair of underpants I could find on those days when I thought myself likely to be laid into, which was often enough, and one of the reasons I still bother to call my father a good man is that when, on a humid spring day in Virginia, this ruse was finally uncovered, and everyone anticipated my screams and my humiliation with that rarefied variety of glee known only within families, he thought to let me be. It is a strange thing to esteem a man for his decision not to raise welts on the skin of a defenseless child, but there it is. I would probably seek to deify him if I did not suspect that what had saved me was only that the indolence in him had temporarily outclassed the rage.

I might blame rage for his decision to whip us, and indolence for those times he did not; and I might blame a blend of these and other elements (pride, an urge to self-destruct) for his decision to store his books out in the chicken coop, and thereby feed his former sense of himself to the rats and the termites and the silverfish and even, in time, the chickens; and I might blame a similar blend for his decision to have his sons tear up patches of an acreage he should never have bought in search of a topsoil he hoped never to find; but a worse ailment surely underlies the style at work here. In my recollection, no banjos accompanied the howls of a child being tortured in our house, yet I do not think a father's pride or rage or indolence or death wish can fully account for the presence of such insults, musical or otherwise, elsewhere in our lives. Something more is asked to explain why a man would not stomach a grocer between his mouth and an egg, or a mechanic between himself and any motor that came near, or an abattoir between himself and his meat, or an ordinary household item between his arm and my ass.

Call it fear

C all it fear, because fear surely lurks somewhere beneath all matters of style. Call it fear because fear surely engendered, if it did not merely masquerade as, the pride and the rage and all the rest of my father's afflictions. Call it fear because I do not care to imagine that a man's taste and intelligence and morality can be sucked out of him so quickly by something entirely external, as opposed to being chased out of him by an internal and possibly even sane response to that external something.

The public-broadcasting set never tires of the conceit that one can look out over America's hills, and through her swamps and forests, and across her valleys and plains and deserts, and sense in those features a presence far greater than one's own. I do not deny it: there is definitely something out there. I doubt, though, that these people would be so dug in about the supposed goodness of that presence, and would so easily claim a "profound respect for," or even a "love of," an entity concerned primarily with their destruction, and would roam so far afield as to speculate that this entity might be "God," could they be prevailed upon to spend more than a long weekend or two away from the uterine comforts of town each year. Nor am I impressed with their ability to identify and implicate those rural folk whose brains have been sufficiently cooked by the sun's radiation, or by the waves of their own fear, so as to leave them happy to testify to the truth of this or any other fairy tale. Despite all protestations to the contrary, God does not wait for us out in those trees.

Fear made my father believe, or pretend to believe, that we needed a basketball court; I am sure of it. He may also have realized that his devaluation of the property required in recompense some small improvement to it, or that his devaluation of the children required some small improvement to them, or he may simply have come to understand that we would require a better distraction than the switch if we were not to shy on him one day when told to break more wood and hack more weeds and till more soil and sow more corn. For all I know, he may have fled for more obscure reasons toward a half-remembered and wholly midwestern idea that "real" American farms have a basketball hoop on them somewhere, but it was certainly not from a position of courage that he informed us one morning of his intention to devote our strength to the manufacture of a facility we had neither the talent to make use of nor the inclination to enjoy.

Our assumption was that he meant to have us drive a pole with a rim on it down into the former shed's foundation, and that he had some method worked out by which we would then flatten the pit's bottom and so avoid the ruin of our ankles as we ran around down there, and that he planned to circumscribe the whole business with a fence meant to catch the inevitable loose balls as we tried and failed to master this game he thought so highly of, but again our hopes betrayed us. He sent us out instead with shovel and hoe to chop away at the ground just east of where we had murdered the shed, behind it in relation to the road and beside it from the vantage of the house, where by the time we had carved out even a few cubic feet of that hateful clay we were forced to sit and soak our hands and wait for the blisters there to form the calluses he was probably after from the outset. His affection for basketball, and his concern for the property, and his desire to see us find some pleasure in that hellscape, were all shown to run no deeper than the shallow grave's worth of Virginia we had displaced before finally being allowed to abandon the job altogether. We nailed the rim to a big maple out front and rarely afterward went near it.

I know from what followed that our father had conspired with his fear, and in this case with the institution of basketball, to toughen us against what he saw as a formidable opponent, and I will not challenge that call. In the first place it is nice to have been thought of, and in the second the environment would prove itself a threat to his children soon enough: it would extract their blood by stinger and thorn, and would unsettle their innards with parasites, and would puff them up with plant and bug venom, and would cause them to claw at their limbs and to vomit, and would roast their little skulls until they saw dots and more complicated ghosts in the fields, and would leave them in no state to question their father's wisdom that the proper attitude toward nature was to prepare for her inevitable assault and be watchful. Why he could not have reacquainted himself with this simple truth before his line was marooned out in the hinterland again is beyond me, but he is surely due credit for an eventual grip on the fact that we were in no way wanted as caretakers of the American muck and may even have been intended as hapless sacrifices to it.

What was to be gained by this sacrifice, aside from the enrichment of those with the effrontery to hype and sell a worthless land that did not anyway belong to them, I cannot say. Perhaps a compact was struck in the olden days to ensure that the bears and the alligators and the snakes and the floodwater would avoid the better settlements, and that lightning and tornadoes would not target them from above, and that earthquakes and sinkholes would not come at them from below, and that ants and termites would not amble in and carry off all that was edible in the meantime, so long as undesirables were sent out into the desolate places to be drained of their wits, and then of the will to proceed, and finally of life itself. I do not know. Every child, I imagine, would like to believe that it has been thrown away for a higher purpose, as opposed to just thrown away.

Trash pit

I had seen from the car window where the rural man's husk went when there was no more work to be had from it: to a sad little churchyard cemetery if he was lucky, or to a smaller and still sadder cemetery in the tall grass behind a farmhouse if he was not, there to explore eternity alongside a wife he could no longer touch, and a mother he could no longer do for, and a father he could no longer hope to impress, and in-laws he could no longer hope to avoid, and siblings he could no longer laugh with, and an uncle or two the drink had taken, and the odd aunt no man would marry, and of course all those infants who might have lived longer had they only been born in town. A bleak country churchyard waited patiently for us all back in Southern Illinois, ripe with the remains of my cousins and ancestors, but I worried that my father might turn that invitation down and send his children out to scare up something more expedient in the Virginia weeds. I planned to argue, if he had such a thought, that we should dig our graves in the hole where the shed had been, as the work there was already half done.

Neither graveyard nor basketball court would occupy that space, though, nor would this depression manage to transform itself, despite any machinations of mine, into a swimming pool. It would morph instead into something poor and strange: an emblem of my father's imbalance during those regrettable years, a testament to the family's continued tradition of inelegance and despair, hard evidence of our failure to live any more decently in the country than we had back in town, a catalogue of all we had consumed there in order to survive. It would prove a fester on my childhood unequaled by any other, and an embarrassment not even the stripes on my legs could outshine. It would become, from the moment we first asked what to do with that refuse we could not burn off illegally in the rusty old oil drum just beyond the aborted basketball court, and our underwear-clad father looked up from his umpteenth cigarette and answered with a finger thrust in the direction of the by-now overly familiar crater that abutted the twin ruts we had consented to call a driveway, that darkest of all country landmarks: it would become, though I would not have imagined such a thing possible, even in that county, an enormous open-air trash pit.

We threw a world down there, or so it seemed to me: every store-bought can scraped clean of its predictable treasure, every glass or dish dropped in numbness or hurled out of anger, every tin tray ruined in the attempt to warm a meal of Banquet fried chicken or off-brand fish sticks, every jar not commandeered to hold the inedible pickles my mother made to show us what a hoot it was to be self-sufficient, every supermarket bottle or foil-lined box of wine she then emptied to demonstrate otherwise, every window fan that had perished in the effort to push a few lungfuls of air through the house, every stretch of mesh pulled away from the back porch or the chicken coop by the wind or the gravity, every load of coals and ash our miserly stove had vomited up into its pail, every tool my father could not salvage with oaths and blows and electrical tape, every car battery he could intimidate no more work out of, every oil can sucked dry by a parched and damned engine, every air filter choked to death by the dust from the roads and the driveway, every cinder block too broken to support its share of a car's dead weight, every armful of plaster hauled away from my father's attempt to "remodel" the house's two front rooms (and so silence at least one of his wife's complaints), every sheet of tin roofing the shed or the front porch or the outhouse had donated to our embarrassment, every nail or hinge that had managed to loose itself from the pile of boards in the yard, every chunk of cement that had broken free from the mushroom cap over the well and somehow not plummeted down into it, those faucets that had formerly filled the bathroom sink and tub, the sink itself, the tub itself, an old commode, three cheap town bicycles the Virginia dew had corroded and the Virginia hills had anyway rendered useless, a plastic radio or two, a television set, and I seem to recall at least some part of a refrigerator, though a lingering disgust may mislead me there.

I will not pretend that a trash pit in the yard held no attraction for a young boy who now had cause and opportunity, after all, to discover what happened when a glass jug met a toilet bowl at considerable velocity, or to see how deeply a car battery could be made to penetrate a television screen, and who now had something to shoot at with his BB gun besides birds and siblings, just as the latter now had something to shoot at besides him. We took to the hole with air rifles and hammers and even the axe whenever my father was gone, glad to be free of the need to convince him every ten minutes or so of our attention to whatever senseless labor he had assigned us that day, and we aimed every trip to turn the garbage down there into an undifferentiated gravel by means of our violence and our joy.

I trust that our violence would have been adequate to the task, but we were shorted on the joy. We soon enough saw that a country trash pit contained fewer friends than had the underground pipes back in town, and that the promise of a slow death by septicemia was no replacement for the glamour of a quick one by sewer gas. We saw as well that the passerby's eye sought out signs of humanity in the countryside, rather than the advertised delights of a flora and fauna that in truth only annoyed and oppressed him. Each honk heard from the road below, even when there was no derision in it, reminded us that our debasement in this place was far more public than it ever had been in town. We had supposed ourselves hidden in the wilderness, but we, like those cruel walls we felt thicken each summer and then thin when winter came on, like the cars and the weeds and the wreckage that surrounded our tin-hatted treachery, like the pit in which we cavorted with our waste, were undeniably a spectacle, gawked at like any other. Ridiculed by the ignorant, pitied by the less so, we occasionally met with a certain mortified and honkless recognition.

A judgment

In town we had lived next door to a man who once crashed a stock car so hard that both eyes flew out of the bucket seats in his head and dangled helplessly aware against the stick shift of his nose until a doctor, or else a mechanic, was able to reinstall them, but aside from an intense attention paid those eyes on the few occasions they floated near we never, in my recollection, gave a thought to this man, though our houses shared an oily garage and had yards mere feet apart. In the country there was but one house we could even catch sight of, a small brick sarcophagus up and across the road, wherein a brace of grandparents quietly awaited oblivion, yet no lack of activity there could discourage my interest in their plot, and I knew that unless these people were students only of the trees, and the insects, my wonder over their slow consumption was bound to be returned.

Every dish goes down its own way, I suppose, its wriggles or its stoic stillness being the extent to which the devourer's throat will allow it one last representative gesture. We wriggled; they did not; and unless this was because they were dead already, or close enough to it to preclude further movement, they might now and then have looked out from their living-room window (the larger on the face of their walleyed home) to behold the trash-filled snarl of our pit, and the tasteless mustache of nail-ridden boards in the yard just beyond, and the noseless upper countenance of our obviously insane clapboard tormentor. And if they chanced to see, as I did one morning, a dog of ours with a leg lifted against what had formerly been part of the well cap but was now an open-mouthed absence of concrete, and if they deduced, as I did, that our drinking water had likely been flavored by this animal's urine since the day the hole was created, then I hope their destruction in that awful little rancher was eased at least by one last belly laugh.

There were others nearby I could not normally see, and who could not normally see me, but I felt a judgment from them all the same, and I sensed that this attitude was but a mask for their own desperation, or at least a useful distraction from it. A more active pair of decrepits farther up the road, future employers of mine who kept a few cows and took an unhealthy interest in the manufacture and storage of hay, limited their social engagement with my family to the odd wave from the field, and the even odder lecture on the dangers of a liberal education, and seemed at all times drunk on a private and unknowable sadness. Across the road from these two sat a sparsely stocked country store that doubled as a post office hardly anyone used but whose lonely proprietors, yet another ancient couple, had discovered that the federal government fixed a postmaster's salary by the number of boxes at his disposal, whether or not those boxes would ever be filled. To the best of my knowledge, these people, who were polite but embarrassed for us children whenever we visited their wooden fib to buy candy, or else to steal it, retired rich, if no more comfortable, and then died.

The younger couple who had sold us our trees and our clay now occupied a newer, sounder home across the southern pasture and back in the woods somewhat, though they would be delayed no longer by the second trap than they had by the first and would, before their vanishing, provide no particulars as to what wickedness had befallen them, or the idiots who came before, at "our" place. Because of this, and because in the war between persistence and departure they sided with departure and we did not, and because in the gerrymander that forever cleaved our land from theirs they had kept possession of what was our barn in every sense but the legal, and so had saved this structure from the rapacity of our stove and from an afterlife as proof to passersby that we had not even a barn to aid and protect us, my father held these people and their barn to be an insult and a remonstrance, and he gave off an unusual amount of pride, I remember, on the day a dog of ours pranced before us with a dead cat of theirs in its maw.

I have no idea whether these people harbored a remorse at our being the means of their escape, or an anger over the cat (a kitten, really: Boots was its name), but before they fled that land forever I recorded in their stares a note of astonishment at our obvious and immediate washout at squiredom, which must have struck them as willful and even aggressive when measured against their own. The stiff neighborliness extended us whenever they came by (as a confidence man will follow up on his mark to determine if the scheme has been discovered and the authorities called down) hid no better a mix of trepidation, relief, curiosity, and ordinary human concern, which trepidation I scoff at, and which relief I stipulate, and which concern I return unused. Only the curiosity pertains.

These people made no direct mention of the devastation in their former yard, nor did they acknowledge the depressed heap of garbage that was the property's single recent improvement, but they were aware of our pit and our shame as surely as we were aware of their barn, and our muteness on the barn, and their muteness on the shame, made for what I recall as an almost boisterous conversation. Their side of the silence seemed to convey an amused understanding that our business with the sticks was not about disappearance at all but rather was about a perfectly common wish to be noticed, the fulfillment of which did not normally require an open trash pit in the wisher's front yard. On our end, if I translate correctly, it was mostly curse words.

O Goochland

O Goochland, O county of blood and pus, O breaker of families, O bed of agriculture's deceit; older creature than the nation you betrayed; promiser of plenty, provider of naught; stalker of happiness, thief of hope; butcher of nerves, baker of brains; proud home of the skill-less, luckless Bulldogs; site of my elementary- through high-school education:

I should have guessed, when first we crossed your bounds, that my father would opt for a performance of his anguish rather than a deliverance from it. I should have seen that your houses did not shun one another but only watched and waved, and struck signal fires, and huddled together in an attempt to form hamlets that by your witchcraft would not take. I should have noticed that your necropoli met no hindrance at all in their efforts to congeal and expand. I should have gathered that your paper-thin infrastructure (a backwater school system, a sparse and unselective police force, a farmer's bank, a "community" college, an overmatched clinic near the pompous little courthouse, a bloom of schismatic churches, an enthusiasm of volunteer fire and rescue squads, both a men's and a women's "state farm") constituted an equally instinctive, and equally failed, ploy to cover the whole of your population (less than twenty thousand souls, all told, in a space the size of Greater Los Angeles) with a single municipal exoskeleton, so that we suckers, we pilgrims to iniquity, might know what it was like to exchange a settlement at least of sufficient density to keep the pests at bay for one so rudimentary and diffuse that it did not understand this to be town's purpose.

Could not the same be said of the nation's farmland at large? Do the kit houses and improvised huts in our clearings not reach out to one another in desperate bids to create and defend communities whose inhabitants insist are unnecessary to their unreal and unearned Edens? Are we to imagine that the pride these people have since shown in their technically townless lot is not a reflex natural to anyone confronted with the terror that accompanies assured defeat but not yet (and here again I must employ the word "technically") dead? Is this pride not so bitter and so powerful that it has long infected even parts of town with the desire to go without what humble refinements are available there (a superficial proximity to education and the arts, a cinema-learned facsimile of reflection) in order to indulge instead a fancy for mud, pickup trucks, cowboy hats, retribution in Jesus's name, and the legion twangs and whines of American ignorance?

I honestly do not care. One may strike like a fool at the sprigs of this wrong or one may set at the root, and Goochland County, in whose dirt our national evil was gestated, and out of whose grass it sprung, and on whose stock it immediately fed, and through whose dummies it first worked its cruel ventriloquy, and within whose tomahawk outline can still be found a peopled wilderness more ruinous than just about any other, is where I judge that root to be. I will not stunt my rage with reference to what this prideful and cowardly blight has done to the uppermost boughs of our republic: the reader is free to lift his chin, and expose his neck, and see for himself how pride and cowardice alone are now represented up there. My own aim is the root itself, and my whetstone is the memory of how casually, how mechanically, this entity sent forth its spores to destroy what might have been a perfectly acceptable childhood.

That I have only this mean alignment of words for an edge, and that I can control my axe no better than to bring it down upon those who are of my own blood, and so are due not an accidental violence from me but rather a purposeful love, is a shame we have always with us. Still, I make no apology for the fact that I have raised up and swung. My object is, and only has been, that unclean and hideous root.

Blackberries

I abhor blackberries. I would surely eradicate them if brought to power. My brother might say bees, given all those attacks on him through our screenless windows by what looked to be a mutation of the species, neither bug nor bird but fully three inches long, the boy probably dreaming in his bed of the last time he was stung into surreal and agonized consciousness by one of these winged freaks, which our father called "king hornets" and I at least held to be the result of some experiment gone horribly awry in those abandoned bee boxes in the yard. My sister, sustained if not comforted by her *Black Beauty* books and her Laura Ingalls Wilder, might say horses, given how she was led on always by that promise our parents had made her, and teasingly saw our pasture used to winter nags from a cheap and imitation riding camp nearby, and knew that this one was "Chief Joe," and that one "Prince Smoke," and that one "Granny," but had neither the clearance nor the ability to saddle and ride any of these creatures, let alone call one her own and call herself its, until sent at last by a fugitive kindness to this same cheap and imitation riding camp nearby, where her affection for these animals could not overcome the cheap and imitative quality of the instruction there, or her late introduction to the art, or the degree to which the treacherous land had spooked every animal that walked or ran upon it, and so could not prevent her being thrown one afternoon, and dragged by her pretty heel, and very nearly killed, after which she went in for an altogether different kind of book.

For me, though, it is blackberries. I would cite their dull sourness when not perfectly formed (milk and sugar were invariably required to make up the difference), or their metallic sweetness when for a day or two they finally agreed to ripen, or their melodramatic tendency to fall apart and bleed to death if not applauded at once, but in truth my claim against these berries is no more than a tangent to my anger at having been forced to pick them in the first place. From afar a hokey charm attaches to the image of a rosy-cheeked lad sent out to fill his pail with the fruit of a bush whose sole ambition on earth is to serve him as a free and wholesome candy store; up close, a darker scene presents:

This same boy, the red on his cheeks a primer for some future melanoma, holds this candy inferior to what he can steal from the store up the road, and he resents that these distant green bushes have so punctuated themselves with black as to engage the attention of his parents, who surely do not appreciate the cloyingly stupid taste of such nodules any more than he does but are committed to the myth that their sort of person delights in nature's treats just as it accepts her hardships, which pose will harden the boy in winter, and will make of him a baked and mushy cobbler by blackberry season, and will in fact be so thorough as to qualify less as an acceptance of hardship than a surrender to it, and will never be extended to any hardship inherent in the boy, who were it not for the threat of physical retribution would forgo the sacrifice of his Saturday to the retrieval of a foodstuff he knows no one in the family honestly wants to eat.

Encased in his sweat, a uric bath at most times and a gelatinous bodysuit whenever a cloud stops to sun its back for a moment above his head, he plucks at these berries until he can no longer tell the juice on his fingers from the blood the briars have extracted in payment for their supposedly free baubles. The wind that animates the piney wood to the north reaches out now and then to give the leaves before him a good shake, but it takes pains not to cool the spot where he himself stands, and he begins to wonder whether the salt in his eyes, or the start of a heatstroke, is not responsible for some perceived instability in the bush. After a particularly violent bustle, which sees the hairs on his arm raised a great deal and the pine needles not at all, he thinks finally to inspect the bush itself. He parts the briars and looks back into them, there to discover the stem of his fear: a long black serpent, unmistakably the old ratter he had seen slide away from the wreckage of that shed not long ago, twisted up in the innermost branches, already in the act of disentanglement and pursuit, its head reared in umbrage, a-hiss.

The boy drops his pail and runs for the house, across a field in which nothing but weeds and snakes and blackberries will ever grow, over ruts that lead back to a tepid and muddy pond where he will learn to seek an impoverished amusement, up a hill adorned with patches where a crude attempt at cultivation is evident, over an orange gouge where a basketball court was once attempted, past a garbage-filled crater that even now is able to holler at him with its shame, and into an unkempt yard where his progress is at last arrested by an impossibly deep bite to the right foot. His horror at this turn is met by a sudden and unwilled admiration for the snake, whose hatred he had not imagined could produce such a speed, yet when he looks down he sees not the snake at all but only a broken gray board, formerly a rib or metacarpal of that doomed old shed, stuck to his sole like an indigent ski.

Afraid to go forward (lest the board's rusty tooth push its way upward through his tongue), afraid to sit down in the unchopped grass and work the nail out (lest the snake catch up to a more valuable part of him there), the boy remains upright and frozen, loud but unheard, pinned to this withered ground, this enemy of humanity, this magnet of despond, all because his parents have agreed to pretend, with hippie and hick alike, that the countryside is an antidote to town and not a poor imitation of it; that town is not anyway a wall thrown up in obvious panic against the wilderness; that a child removed from the protection of that wall is bound to grow stronger by the throb of the nail, and the sting of the switch, and the constant companionship of his own filth; that lies and blood and terror and trash, as well as the eternal war against reality that might erupt in anyone exposed at length to such elements, are therefore a fair exchange for blackberries.

BOOK TWO

Partial birth
Rattle
Balloons
A fictional magic
National color wheel
Bloodless composition
Brief window
The confluence of
    long roads
(Gestation)
The second sort of suicide
Names
Rifle
Pistol
Shotgun
Sanctuary

Partial birth

I could see the yellow beast coming for me a long ways off, as no impediment of trees obtained to the north, only an eerie undulation of pasture that seemed almost in cahoots with the road against it, and when the weather was hot, and the windows were open, the creature's groan could be heard so far prior to its appearance that I was able to wash and dress and even swallow something before the time came to descend the driveway and be swallowed up myself. When it was cold out, and thin panes obscured the sound but got nowhere with the frost, and shiver fits throughout the night had anyway abolished my dreams, I was often enough still in my bed when I heard the muffled bleat from the road below, and I knew then that I would need to run or else be left behind. Neither snack nor toilet would be mine on those occasions, but I at least had the advantage of being fully clothed and shod inside my sleeping bag, without which foresight I do not think I could have been convinced, or would have been able, to rise at all.

I wonder: When the great root below us inspired in Thomas Jefferson his idyllic hallucinations, and began to grow its system westward under the Appalachian range (toward the Mississippi snake oil it would require in order to reach and pervert California), did it bestow upon him a vision of the roving metal stomach that would, a century and change after his presidency, gobble up the nation's schoolchildren by law each morning and vomit them into a freshly graveled parking lot? Did he understand that whereas this process would inflict upon the town child no more than a momentary and perhaps even a healthy terror, it would prove for the rural child a journey so drawn out and confined with the personality flaws of his peers as to allow for the partial birth of those communities his shacks and his farmhouses had tried and failed to form? Was the architect of the American dirt clod aware that these mobile townships would exhibit none of the grace and wholesomeness he had predicted for his agricultural societies, and would in fact be predicated on a hatred of self and surrounds, and would be policed no better than the shacks and the farmhouses themselves? (Which, after all, stayed in one place, or appeared to.) Did he know, or care, that the introduction of such a predator into the Virginia hills would ensure that I received my first nonfamilial Virginia whipping, and enough thereafter to make me question my assumption that Virginia homes were to be got away from whenever possible, long before a Virginia schoolhouse had even come into view?

Almost as soon as I sat down on a Goochland schoolbus I was beaten into tears and rage by a teenage boy who with wide worried eyes yelled, "This ain't slavery days no more! This ain't slavery days no more!" which refrain I recall as clearly as I do my confusion about what the statement meant and what action of mine could possibly have prompted either the rhetoric or the volley of blows. Less violent passengers, saints to my mind, pulled me free of those fists, and up off the dull green vinyl where I had uselessly sought shelter, and shoved me aft, toward the equally amused faces of the children who more closely resembled me. I would make a clever reference to Rosa Parks here, but that would find me guilty of a great anachronism: in 1977, enrolled in what the Virginia Commonwealth loosely called the sixth grade, I had no idea who that woman was, nor could I discern much difference between the bow and stern of a vehicle that seemed to me an insult to everyone on it. I found a place in back near my brother, whose size and potential for violence might have protected me had the shock of life in the countryside not rendered him impassive and largely mute until puberty, at that point still as foreign to him as were the ominous firs he watched file past, from left to right, through the dirty windows of what he had instinctively understood to be no better than a cattle car.

When later I pressed my father for some clues about what had befallen me on the bus, he told me patiently of how the darker people in America had once been slaves to the lighter; of how a great conflagration had been set to free them; of how this effort had been doctrinally successful but not practically so; of how more than a hundred years later the slaves' descendants remained in social and economic bondage; of how countless men and women had struggled all the while to change this; of how these people had made such a slow progress in their art that as recently as a generation ago, in this part of the country and many others, it was still possible that a brown boy who said hello to a pink girl, or in any way challenged the illegal and immoral order of things, might be set upon by a band of pink boys who would beat him senseless and maybe even to death; of how this notion of justice never seemed to apply to a pink boy who said hello, or did worse, to a brown girl; of how even a secondhand knowledge of that not wholly bygone era was bound to engender a certain resentment in children whose parents and aunts and uncles had themselves been so victimized; and of how none of this was any excuse for a boy of his to lose a fistfight on the bus.

I had a follow-up question (*Why did we move here?*), but it went unanswered and probably unheard. Within a day or two my brother and I found ourselves in front of the house with cheap padded gloves on our hands, our father keen to train us up so that we would not be made fools of in what he apparently mistook for the landscape of his own childhood. I remember that I began to cry, mostly out of anticipation, and set upon my brother with swings of the overhand type, which he casually countered with swings of the underhand type, which shortly left me aware of a great sky before me, and the earth against my back, and an intense nausea centered at the base of my skull. To my right, on the perpendicular, my father jutted out, shocked by one son and no doubt ashamed of the other. At my feet, my brother, whom I knew to be upright but who seemed just then to be lying back against the nothingness behind him, stared out, as he often did, at the nothingness above us all.

Rattle

He had lately become host to prophetic dreams, this brother, and for a time his relation of those dreams was our only real conversation. *A rattler,* he might say, and sit up in his bed, and point at the woods, and although we were far enough east and north to make rattlesnakes a rarity I would nonetheless hear, when I dared approach the patch he had indicated, the distinctive sound all those hopelessness-themed westerns my father watched had taught me to fear. *Blackie will vanish,* would come his next glimpse, the finger aimed this time at another patch of woods, and although I took comfort in the thought that the nearly human mutt we had brought with us from Illinois would not be killed by a rattler, that evening there would indeed be no bark and run and wiggle when we called the little dog's name. My sister may have understood that there was a locust or a cicada in these parts whose sound (from a certain distance, and enhanced by the echo chamber of the trees) was very much like a snake's rattle, and she may have concluded that the dog's absence was easily explained by his previous attempts to desert us and return to town, or at least to locate a family less obviously doomed than our own, but for my part I put great store in my brother's weirdness, and I believed that even awake he was especially attuned to the future being urged and constructed in that awful place.

If his features froze up while we were at play in the trash pit, then I knew a car would soon pass by and see us, or just had, and I knew the family's already loud reputation was again on the rise. If his eyes sounded anger, with grace notes of resentment and enervation, then I knew we were about to be, or just had been, called upon to perform yet another dirt-intensive labor that would diminish rather than augment our situation. If his eyes read guilt, with descants of panic and rage, then I knew he was about to be whipped, or just had been. If he avoided my presence all day long, and did not simply stand beside and ignore me as he did at most other times, then I was probably about to be whipped myself. If, from field or yard, he looked to the house with pursed lips and narrowed lids, or stared hawkeyed and open-mouthed at same, or stayed fixed on his chore, or went slack in the shoulders, or went suddenly rigid, or considered the middle distance, or threw his implement down and wandered off into that middle distance, then I knew our mother was due for, or had just begun, or had just completed, her next hysterical aria in the opera buffa that had resulted when her folk-guitar fantasy of a country life collided with her husband's more powerful Jew's harp.

And if my brother did not show his usual relief when the recitative set in, and if he rocked back and forth on his bed after dinner, and listened through our window to the softer but no less horrible hum of yard and pit and weed and forest, and if he seemed particularly attentive to the silent scream that rose up off the obliging little road in the background of this étude for washboard and moonshine, then our weekend, I knew, was over, and I understood that when I awoke, and perhaps even before, the beast would be here to summon us again with its own despicable music.

Balloons

I was more prepared for my second fistfight on the bus but still lost it. A high-school girl who had had a bad day lit into me when some boys in back asked me to get her attention; I did. She had an overhand style that was hell on my ears and the top of my head, and although I caught her here and there on the breasts I was soon overwhelmed and started to bawl, which seemed only to inspire her: the blows came faster and with greater force than they had at the outset, and by the time they tapered off I could not say with any certainty where I was. This girl beat me with such an exuberance that I thereafter conceived of human beings in her part of the world as no more than hatred-filled balloons in search of a rent by which to empty themselves on me. Once delivered of their gasses, these balloons could be reasonable and even kind (such as when this girl phoned our home to apologize for her assault on what was, after all, a blameless boy still in elementary school), but I learned that circumstance soon patched and reinflated them, and caused them to wear again a bloated and uncomfortable look, and ensured that they would be ready to vent themselves on whatever fool was unlucky or unwise enough to nick their rubber the next time around.

That was my first taste of rural intimacy, and no similar encounter has since outdone it. All the elements were there: the unforeseen approach, the unwilled brutality, the ebb of awareness, the inchoate shame, the fear that abides. Even the apology will not strike the initiate as uncommon and may actually spur in him, as it does in me, a nostalgia for that lull after the passion when, the bruises still fresh on his face and his arms, he reviews the event and searches vainly for a victory in it, and considers what program of defense might at least have eased the defeat, and wonders whether a sudden diplomacy might not have avoided the insult altogether, and asks whether the phoned-in apology was not in itself a variety of insult, and so considers a hopeless revenge (balloons), and so considers a hopeless truancy (balloons at home), and finally ponders the worth of a soothsaying brother who could not be bothered to sit up in his bed and point at the road and say, simply, *A high-school girl will beat the shit out of you on the bus.*

While this brother denied me useful intelligence, and for the most part kept to the cocoon our predicament had caused him to spin, and while our sister endured her own haunted hayrides to and from an even smaller brick building in which little was taught and less learned, I became the regular chump in short but violent bouts whose only purse was my all but guaranteed humiliation. No offense on my part was necessary: the schoolday or the night before would see to that, would so swell these creatures, and so fray their fabric, that only the slimmest pretext was ever required for the inevitable breach to be directed at me. I was set upon for being "white" (I was pink), for being "racist" (I feared all the hues I saw equally), for being a "honky" (which word amused me), for "laughing" (I admit to it), for being "funny looking" (fair to say), for being "buck-toothed" (I was never), for having "freckles" (I concede the point), and finally I was called out by a fat boy roughly my own age on the charge of being "skinny."

Due to what pressures had built up inside of me, and due to what bus-and-blacktop combat techniques I had picked up from my recent string of defeats, and due also to some weight-bred slowness in the fat boy, I came out the surprise victor in this one, and so began my parents' sad introduction to our Jeffersonian community, such as it pretended and failed to be. Apparently all was right when I was the victim in these beatings, but as soon as I gained a foothold, and caused a bully to bleed and sob (I am told that toward the end I made a serious bid to break the fat boy's arm), I was judged a nascent sociopath, the clear instigator of a number of previous disturbances, and there was some talk of my not being allowed to ride the bus at all.

Because my mother had recently found work at a juvenile-delinquent home nearby, in a forgivable attempt to locate what few town-like elements could survive out there (and in the certain knowledge that we would otherwise all starve); and because this job availed her of a strange new lexicon that considered any child who pled his own innocence to be a potential "incorrigible" who was "putting up a front" in the hopes that he would not be "held down" and made to confront either his "authority issues" or his "homosexuality"; and because my father, although pleased with this sudden brutality in his son, was not fool enough, or man enough (perhaps it is the same thing), to oppose both his wife's new science and her eternal belief that there was something "off" about her second child; my guilt in the matter was assumed and agreed to, and I found myself treated thereafter as a special case.

An ad hoc committee of driver and principal and parents decreed that I should sit in the frontmost seat of the bus, on the right, just above the door, and beside me at all times should sit the innocent fat boy. The idea here, I knew (and the fat boy must have), was to force an intimacy between us and thereby a friendship, despite the fact that an intimacy already existed and a friendship never would. He caught me unawares and won our second fight by means of a quick move that saw me pinned beneath his fat; I went for his eyes that afternoon and was able to take the rematch. The fourth or fifth encounter ended with an uppercut to my privates; the fifth or sixth, to his; and so on. Even my brother began to show some alarm at the brute predictability of these bouts, if not also an anticipation of them. As for me, I remember most clearly the long rides afterward, the fat boy and I both in tears as we swore additional violence but mainly stared out in silence at the scrub pine and scrub pasture that were our common yet undeclared enemy.

A fictional magic

There were other foes the fat boy and I could not share. The degreed hippie types who worked at the delinquent home, amongst whom my mother believed for a time that she had found an air pocket of sophistication in the gob of tobacco spit that had become her existence and ours; these "group workers" and "group leaders" and so forth who thought that thermal underwear and down vests bought at a Richmond mall, as well as jugs of corn liquor bought off the odd local, put them well in touch with the rural experience but in no way compromised their superiority to it (given the sort of progressiveness that would enable them, for instance, to consider the purchase of a sexually explicit educational film their criminal charges did not require and would not anyway be allowed to see, *as it happened to feature one of the degreed hippies*); these bearded mediocrities who approached every being they met or engendered as a broken wing they might nobly fail to repair, whose minds were but marginally less dented by drug and drink than were those of the teenagers they cowed and annoyed; who with these marginally better minds perceived only a benevolent and therefore a fictional magic in the earth below, and in the pine needles above, and so were flabbergasted each time yet another boy bolted in yet another frantic attempt to achieve town; these denim-butted frauds who led my mother, and eventually my father (*my father!*), to half believe all over again that nature could be a palliative to human despair and not merely its origin, which idea would inflict upon us the redundant horror of camping and canoe trips we could not afford to take but for equipment borrowed from the boys' home and idiocy borrowed from the same; these damp-eyed sensitives; these hypocritical bear-huggers; these vicious pacifists; these martyrs to self-involved frankness somehow convinced my mother that her son's "anti-social" behavior might predicate a well-meant but legally disas-trous physical intervention by the delinquents who, because their keepers were too "understaffed" to school them privately, and because the law demanded (and I believe still does) that criminal children be granted the same poor chance at education as any other American, found themselves shipped daily into the county high school on the very scow that collected me.

I cannot adequately describe the shock with which I greeted the news that juvenile delinquents rode my bus, but I might do all right with my worry over the fact that I was to be held per-sonally accountable for any damage they caused or caught be-tween their confinement and the high school. Which particular riders these young addicts and stabbers were eluded me for some time, either because they had gone to some effort to disguise themselves or because they were so comfortable with what level of violence presented on the bus that they saw no need to raise it, but I did identify them finally by their utter disregard of me. Destined to disprove the ludicrous theory that delinquents will rise to a runt's defense, and apparently unaware that they could now beat me themselves without fear that anyone but their vic-tim would be blamed, these T- and flannel-shirted boys, who fancied the same chokers and hickeys as everyone else, and in whose hair could be read the same struggle between the Vir-ginia humidity and the Virginia dirt, gave themselves over to the depressed topography our bus studied twice each weekday and, I imagine, paid particular attention to those spots where a teenage hitchhiker might not seem too great a threat, or a temptation, to a driver whose desperate passenger had no idea in which direction town actually lay.

What escapes this flytrap of a county allowed those boys I cannot say, nor do I recall which one of them was later executed by better-prepared criminals in a Richmond warehouse once the degreed hippies had either cured him or inspired him to run away. Certainly no delinquent of my acquaintance chose to settle in Goochland afterward, though that may have resulted less from a hatred of the degreed hippies than from a fear of the weedy and wooded tick nursery in which troubled teens, and troubled midwesterners, were meant to be reborn. At any rate the place tended to breed its own delinquents and had no need to adopt. It tended also to grow its own hippies, albeit of a sort who romanticized non-nonviolence, and owned guns not to hunt but because there was "a government conspiracy against pot," and made use of their freedom from society's "hangups" (and of their jobs at town sewage-treatment plants) to buy great heaps of cocaine and pornography and automotive equipment that almost demanded resale, and who considered bluegrass "too classical" (and the blues itself "nigger music," where not interpreted by Lynyrd Skynyrd or the Allman Brothers Band) and were ever eager to "fight for" what they believed in, though I noticed that they kept no muscle and trusted more in mandalas and spirits than in soap and simple medicine to ward off the "bad energy" they and their college-pressed counterparts alike believed to radiate solely from town.

The county produced its own cops too. I am told that the fat boy with whom I fought on the bus became one.

National color wheel

Only a dull allegiance to fashionable notions of the truth could convince me to argue that these hippies and delinquents and fat future cops and sad future relatives were somehow responsible for what befell me on my long ride through that excuseless desert. Excuseless because the sun had never managed, for all its effort, to turn the soil there entirely to ash, and so had never managed to impoverish Goochland's impoverished to the degree one might ignore in, say, Ethiopia or the Sudan. Excuseless because the storms drawn there did not pinpoint and obliterate trailer homes as one might laugh at in, say, Missouri or Kansas or Oklahoma. Excuseless because the River James, although it made an effort to flood whenever the air warmed and a sun shower came near, displaced mostly cows and not people, and kept at all times a Richmondly course, and despite a full complement of deadly potions did not sicken and destroy the county's residents, or deform their children, with enough enthusiasm to rival a Bhopal or a Love Canal.

At a certain point the Goochlander comes to accept that no great drama is likely to arise and give form to the evil he perceives all around him, not because such a drama is impossible but because it has been staged already, so immense and unfinished that the eye is unable to see it for a breach or a flood or a storm or a sun. Grateful for the fact that the mosquitoes there impart nothing worse than sluggishness, and that local snakes and spiders rarely kill, and that something like water can usually be sucked up out of the gault, he seldom looks up from his toil, or from his trip to the gas station or the convenience store or the clinic or the courthouse, to consider that although this maelstrom has long since wandered off, across hills and plains and oceans and decades to claim its countless, nameless victims, the conditions under which it was whipped up in the first place still apply, and find him in the fields, and work themselves upon him as they did upon those who gave succor to this hypnotizing force in its infancy, and preached that it would be a boon to our world and not a burden on it, long before anyone thought to call it the United States of America.

I hardly mean to imply here a regret over the foreign lives ruined by my native arms and industry, for I understand that a brown belly distended by hunger abroad allows a pink one at home to be swollen by gluttony. I understand that a piece of shrapnel through the brain of a sand dweller's child allows a subdivision dweller's child to acquire a piece of parchment it has not earned and probably cannot read. I understand that for every outlander tortured to death in a faraway jail cell an American retains the freedom to announce that he has taken Jesus into his heart and will not release Him until all the homosexual abortionists have been killed. My purpose is not to belittle these gains: I aim instead to shriek and point at what made them possible, to show that they are not the product of a notion one group says has been wisely expressed and another says has been utterly betrayed but were in fact spawned by something older, and hideous, and considerably more real.

I side with those of my fellow citizens who hold that a great being, rather than a mere idea, created our nation, and inspired every principle by which it was then codified and rendered explicit, and tinted every aspect of its rampancy thereafter, from the beiges and greens of its squared georgic cells to the tars and grays of roadways made to circulate the bumper crop of idiocy grown out there; from the rainbow varices of urban centers where that idiocy is then repackaged as American pride to the domed white skull in Washington where our elected minds think no better than to turn that pride into law; from the bright red stumps of the once proud and now foreshortened soldiers formerly charged with the enforcement of said law to the duller red bricks of the country high schools where so many of these victims are recruited, and the slicker red (or orange, or black, or blue) of the paint jobs on the pickup trucks these children bankrupt themselves to buy at sixteen, and the rusted green or silver beneath which they pray at night but neglect to make a go at their homework, and the stained-glass wonders behind which they are dependably led to believe that what set the national color wheel in motion was not their own delicate pride but rather the divinity of a preacher just as prideful, and just as delicate, two millennia previous on the far side of the Mediterranean.

Of all this wheel's tinctures, I say that there is none so bleak, and so powerful, as the vitamin-rich urine backing the black symbology on those enormous metal bees that continue (despite, or in possible collusion with, the pickup trucks) to ferry our sacrificial nonvirgins from home to high-school parking lot, and from high-school parking lot to patriotic field trip, and from patriotic field trip to high-school parking lot, and from high-school parking lot to pregame prayer circle, and from postgame prayer circle to hamburger joint, and from hamburger joint to high-school parking lot, and from high-school parking lot to Bible retreat (is this legal?), and from Bible retreat to hamburger joint, and from hamburger joint to high-school parking lot, and from high-school parking lot to military base (has this honestly never happened?), so that the flower of our native ignorance might be pollinated and multiplied, and its rancid dust might forever rain down upon the world.

Bloodless composition

D o I go too far? Is it wrong for a grown man, no longer a boy, to argue that the American schoolbus has been cruel to humanity when in fact it has not been wholly cruel to him, and regularly got him away from a panic-stricken home, and drove him on occasion to a teacher of some worth, and once even showed him an uncalled-for mercy that altered and perhaps even bettered the course of his life? What consideration is then owed this vehicle, and this situation, by one who to this day blames the vehicle, and the situation, for the very peril from which it eventually delivered him? What praise should he bestow upon an entity he knows full well to be a destroyer, by proxy if not by nature, when he finds that he himself has not been destroyed?

Marijuana first entered this boy when he was thirteen years old, and for that I might in good conscience blame the schoolbus, or at any rate its back-road emanation. I might upbraid it as well for the fact that the boy began to attack girls a year or so after the plant's first attack on him. A familiarity with alcohol followed the onset of the girls (or, from their perspective, the onset of the boy), and this too I lay at the beast's accordion door. Were it not for the constant watchfulness required of him between home and school, on top of what vigil he was forced to maintain at either destination, he might have adjusted to his lot with less grief and more grace. He might have understood that in the country, and possibly even in town, alcohol was meant to *precede* relations between the sexes (and certainly relations between the same) and that anyone who did not know this had failed to approach either hobby soon enough. He might have understood that such a child was bound to be left out when better-prepared students snuck off to drink in the woods that surrounded the elementary school and just about everything else in that insipid county, or when older girls, the ones who had flunked, grabbed boys of his acquaintance and forced them to simulate (or, rumor had it, actually to perform) intercourse on the multihued yet drab bathroom floors. He might have understood sooner that a natural life, such as the naturalists promote and fail to comprehend, has little to do with a moral life, such as the moralists promote and fail to comprehend. He might have understood that ten or eleven, and not a hopelessly retarded thirteen, is in fact the proper age of introduction to dope.

I did not meet the hydroponic kind but rather what bored country children will cultivate in a clearing out back: small and pathetic plants, without sister or brother, that seemed well acclimated to the dew and the mist but surely found the sky's unregulated heat lamp a hindrance to maturity, as did we all, and were anyway slaughtered well before they amounted to much, yanked from the earth to be dried and chopped up and fired and inhaled by higher beings whose boredom and desperation could not be undone by so spindly a remedy and could only (the boredom) be enhanced by what lethargy as the plant had to offer, or (the desperation) by what whiff of paranoia had crept up into the twigs and seeds from the awful clay below. Later encounters with industrial improvements to this weed would impress upon me the value of basic environmental controls and would secure in me the notion that I might not have troubled with the outdoor stuff at all.

I saw no natural prototype, though, beyond the berry or the nugget of gold, for the pills these children passed among them-

selves, and bragged about, and fought over, and built great rep-
utational fortunes upon, and eventually gummed and swallowed,
just as I could see no rustic model, beyond the leather saddle-
bag or the tin bucket, for the plastic containers in which these
psychotropic treats were kept. Identified from without as aspi-
rin or Tylenol, and from within as dosages lifted from a parent's
understandable attempt to overcome the realities of the simple
life by an appeal to what complicated illusions could be manu-
factured in town, these pills, and their counterfeit drugstore
coffins, rode to school in the pockets of Levi's jeans and the
folds of Bermuda-bag purses and the anklets of Frye boots or
Chuck Taylor sneakers, the idea here being not subterfuge of
the usual type but rather a coyly conspicuous display such as
Mr. Veblen might have appreciated, had Mr. Veblen been
forced to spend two to three hours out of every day trapped
with his subjects on a country schoolbus.

Proud of their bounty, and beholden to the relief it promised from the tedium of the day, larger than I was but not cor-
respondingly so stupid as to assume that their shoes and their
purses and their jeans would be free from investigation by
weary and pissed-off administrators once we got to school,
these children were forever on me to act as their surrogate and
their stooge. Although a refusal to smuggle their bottles risked
further bodily insult, and although a pill or two gone missing
would have been considered no more than fair payment for a
morning's servitude, I turned those offers down, and for that I
am almost sorry. With little effort I might have cornered the
pharmaceutical traffic in that sad little county, and branched
out into more fetching goods, and arranged things with the
idiot fat boys who were even then expanding into idiot cops,
and made a place for myself in the hormonally overburdened
high school, and married and impregnated (in either order) the
captain of the cheerleaders, or else her best friend, and bought
up one of the nice plantation houses out there, and joined a

political party or both, and subsidized new uniforms for the football team every five or six years, and shaken hands at the homecoming games, and made increasing reference to the importance of Jesus Christ in my life, and paid for the upkeep on several pink churches and the biggest brown one, and so achieved a sufficient majesty, elected or appointed or stolen outright, as to allow my wrath to encompass the whole of that abominable county, the better to tax and incinerate it.

As it was, I chose a course that won me not useful employment but only continued humiliation, and gained me no reputation except that of a naïve and unhelpful coward, and did not recommend me either to future cops or to cheerleaders, and ensured that at the football games I would be in a marching-band uniform if present at all, and that later I would be unable to attend even one of these predictable routs with a reasonable assurance that hands would be offered mine in friendship and not swung at my nut in contempt. In the end I was robbed of what spiritual consolation I might have taken from the practice of politics and real estate, and afforded no better revenge on that county, or on the people who had so willingly surrendered themselves to it, than this frail and too bloodless composition.

Brief window

Then again, my decision to shun those pills did delay a personal dependence on them by nearly a decade, and it would be evil of me to pretend otherwise, or to ignore how grateful I am for that brief window in which I saw more clearly than afterward and was not always a complete bitch to everyone around me. Said window was small, yes, and painted shut, and itself dependent on what class of pill could be got hold of each day, but that it presented at twenty-three or so, when I could thoroughly enjoy its blessings, and not at thirteen or fourteen, before my pallial palate had fully formed, was a stroke I cannot help but ascribe to the American schoolbus, and all that it threatened me with, and all that it led me to attempt.

How, then, to continue along the path I have thus far hacked out of memory's bramble? How dare I apply today's half-remembered hatred to an object that long ago, and without apparent motive, thought to exempt me from its own? By what right do I persist in my claim that this vehicle was, and remains, worthy of a violent and selfish attack?

The confluence of long roads

Let us praise, then, or sing, or at any rate take a wider view of, the great American schoolbus: 450,000 of these behemoths gone out twice each weekday with no more than three or four children slaughtered on or by them in a good year. That is a remarkable record: three or four out of a possible score of 25 million. It is a testament to the restraint of schoolbus and driver alike, especially when we consider that most of these deaths are not fiery, as the rare if dramatic schoolbus explosion would have us believe, but are due either to a child's being crushed by the wheels of the bus, or to the fact that many of these containers hurtle down the road, in the rural areas at least, at speeds of up to forty miles an hour (fifty on a decent downgrade) without the handicap of seatbelts.

I say again: this is a remarkable record.

We might ask what link could be drawn between the conditions on these moveable villages and those deaths that occur later, in homes (such as the one I was stunted in) where no more than an unlocked closet door ever stands between a child and a rifle or a shotgun or both; or in schools where these guns, which apparently do not kill people themselves, arrive now and then armed with deadly children; or in bars where the prison-like atmosphere of the bus still prevails; or in prisons where the bus-like atmosphere of the bar still prevails; or in cars and trucks whose occupants have just left the bar, or the prison, and know far more about the confluence of long roads and alcohol than they ever will about the confluence of human beings and seatbelts; but we cannot establish beyond a reasonable doubt that our scholastic transport has made any deliberate effort to erase us from this Earth, or that it has been directly responsible for anything more than its own fair share of preventable murders.

That is why I must now raise my voice in approbation of the American schoolbus. That and the luck that I was not killed on or beneath it myself, nor did I die later in a bar or a prison, or on one of those gray asphalt arteries that seem almost designed to connect these sad termini. My death was more spectacular and, as of this writing, has yet to conclude. The cause was self-abuse, and although I learned a good deal about that subject on the schoolbus I am forced to acknowledge that I might not have survived as long as I did, and might already be confined to a hole in Goochland, or in one of its numerous imitators across this dim continent, were it not for the tutelage I received as we rumbled past those sullen pines and along those irate dirt roads.

Do I regret that my education was not of the sort to be had from books but was more in line with the "common sense" half the nation now believes to be of greater value than the ability to read? Let me answer that I was thankful to have gained any wisdom at all out there, seeing as how little was being offered through the schools. Do I count myself a weaker student of the cornpone philosophy because, by the grace of ruined yet thoughtful parents, I came not to fear and avoid the written word but to fear and approach it? From what I saw, the country child fared no better with the land's lesson than he did with the book's. True, he tended to announce a mastery over the former when it was clear that he would fail at the latter, but he napped in nature's classroom as he did in any other, and sought to get by on good attendance alone, and put the whole of his faith in a glib native cleverness he wrongly assumed was not also available to those possessed of a library card and a paid-up residence in town.

I myself blew nearly every test the weeds administered, but out of horror I did remain awake in that place, and worked through the problem sets as best I could, and spent considerable time on the experiments, and just as I will not recognize as my superior in the field the jean-shirted fool who has removed himself from town for moral or aesthetic reasons (which are anyway the same thing) and now pens tone-deaf encomiums to the dirt, I will not bow down before the baseball-capped, goateed man-child who attaches himself by vacuum seal to the government tit yet insists that the nation's wealth flows like a river from its pristine source (himself) to condescending town, and who will cast his vote in fury for whichever candidate most convincingly implies that Jesus hates all the tax-exempt town fags too.

He had the same schooling as I did, this patriot, and the same long sentence within that mobile metal hull, and the same chance to observe for himself the limits of a life defined by the conviction that town is the source of all hurt known to man, and that Jesus is not the peaceful town Jew we encounter in the New Testament but rather a vengeful country Christian who attends all the gun shows, and that town dwellers would take their punishment right here on Earth (so that heaven-bound country folk could enjoy it too) were it not for a school-bred habit of liberal terrorism against God's American law. Some part of science is always Satanism, insists this citizen. Wrestling tickets are a thoughtful anniversary present. A ring around the moon means snow.

Except for the ring around the moon, and that part about science, only the notion of an angry country Christ makes any real sense to me now. Had I been dragged from the comfort of town by lesser beings so as to profit a real-estate scam that would never in turn profit me, and would forever cause town people to assume that I hailed from the weeds by personal choice and not by someone else's criminal action, I might be inclined toward a vengeful attitude myself. I might raise up an army of ignorant orcs to go against those who had so shamelessly enriched themselves by my removal and then shunned me for my provenance, or I might recognize in the orc's plight something of my own, and so come to pity him in his victimhood, and so come to despise him for his weakness, and so come to torture him by means of an extended and then suddenly withdrawn favor. Energy permitting, I might also do my best to curse, and to salt with humanity's tears, the land beneath town and country alike, provided I could find a spot that had not already been cursed and salted eons before by another creature of vast and unspeakable consequence, whose motives I could guess at but never quite discern.

The schoolbus was, I have no doubt, a servant of that creature, and oftentimes I took it for, or beheld in its dun and green innards, a physical manifestation of the creature's great animosity toward me. It ought to count for something, though, that at one point or another I suspected every vehicle and building and plant and person in Goochland of the same, which opinion time has not softened any (and time in town has only ossified), and that none of these entities ever educated me so thoroughly as my schoolbus did, nor showed me so intense a concern, nor suffered from me so grave an insult. I know full well that I owe this benefactor a debt whose principal I will never be able to touch. By my gestures here I hope only to pay down the interest.

(Gestation)

Here, then, is what I learned on, or because of, the American schoolbus:

(I should make it clear that what follows is but a sample of the ore I struck there. The lode itself stretched back for acres behind the self-pleased grins of the tormentors on the bus, and for fathoms below the excuses they or their playground counterparts gave on the rare occasion when one was solicited ("We was just playing" or, if there was blood, "He told lies on my momma"), and for light-years beyond the calm with which these overused lies were then accepted by the adults who settled such matters with what at first appeared to be an uncommon laziness of mind and morality but eventually showed itself to be a perfectly common inability on their part to free themselves from the contexts of their own childhoods, which were likely as rude and odiferous as the ones they now failed properly to police.

(Few moments can compare with the realization that one's state-salaried protector, who stands before one in physical maturity, with children at home, and perhaps another in gestation at eye level, is in fact a huge and brutal child herself, with humiliations to avenge or to reenact so that her bitterness might be alleviated or heightened. In particular I recall an elementary-school teacher who refused to see my mother at a parent-teacher conference because I was "in jail," by which she meant that I had been suspended from school as a result of my having been stalked, before her rheumy and delighted eyes, by an ambitious classmate who assumed that an initial victory in a playground scuffle entitled him to score additional points on me by insults to my panicked yet conference-attending mother until (it was actually scheduled, this fight) bloody snot issued forth from our nostrils, and saline from our eyes (or was it the other way around?), and we were both of us "jailed" not for our crimes but in order to end the entertainment on a note that promised, to an irresponsible and nostalgic audience of grownups, the best chance of a recidivism.

(Among these spectators was a gym-teacher-cum-recess-monitor whose vanity was such that the sound of his own voice, and even the smallest indication that it could still intimidate children of eleven or twelve, was enough to distract him from the severity of our mayhem as he pimped across the blacktop and took account of who took account of him. Now and then, to his credit, he did realize that a football game had been arranged on the field below between a team of brown students and a team of pink, at which point he would stop and yell, "Mix it up down there," though as soon as the brown team sent over its worst player, and we sent over ours, he seemed satisfied that his authority had been recognized, and he never troubled us again. To my disappointment, and eternal shame, I hoped always that he would look down and record the fact that I had not myself been traded, as this was an occurrence rare enough to invoke in me a pride almost as blind as his own.

(This fraudulent adult was complemented by a math teacher who struck me as a sane and serious gentleman disinclined to notice what ugly plot lines we children wove all around him but who reputedly (I did not see it myself) took a boy out into the hall one day and beat him without mercy, the boy having reputedly (I did not see it myself, nor, I am sure, did the math teacher) raped a young girl. Across the hall from where this alleged beating took place, over an expanse of waxed tile where many others certainly did, there taught, or pretended to teach, a woman whose enormous flaps were supported by stems so thin I thought the whole of her flower sure to collapse one day and crush me in my chair. Her subject was history, or geography, or some apt American amalgam of the two, and her method was another apt American amalgam: of outright violence and the delusion that she was somehow a star. She was forever throwing erasers and chalk at us, lest our attention wander briefly to our studies and we forget to study her. When that approach failed she would bellow out, "I'm a go blerk!" which promised the physical deployment of her bulk against one or more of the children in her care, a situation much feared but of course out of boredom encouraged. ("Blerk" may have been a rural bastardization of "berserk"; that is certainly how it behaved.)

(I remember too, a few years later, a biology teacher who answered someone's inane or mischievous question with an impromptu lecture on the subject of circumcision, which in her telling involved the removal of a layer of epidermis from the penis and scrotum, so that the entire apparatus was essentially skinned. At first I took this to be a brilliant joke on her part but soon came to realize that it was an actual tenet of her belief system. When I then challenged her interpretation of the procedure, and asked how a person could become a certified teacher of biology in the Commonwealth of Virginia when she could not answer so basic a question about the human anatomy, she explained that she was a married woman and should know. I countered that I was a circumcised man and should know better. (I was not: I was a circumcised boy, the son of an uncircumcised man who could not be bothered to cover, as he stumbled down the stairs toward the stinky little bathroom in which we were all of us forced to empty ourselves at night, an enormous piss erection we would certainly have seen less of in town.) When I went further, and suggested that her husband might have been mutilated in a farm accident he was too ashamed to recount with any accuracy, I found myself in the principal's office, seated across from a man who for all I knew had forfeited the whole of his genitalia, as he could not be convinced to dismiss this teacher and so spare us the damage of her continued instruction.

(Worse even than these failed chaperones, yet somehow more glorious, was the preacher's wife who operated, and acted as if she owned, and by any practical measure did indeed possess, our schoolbus. Held in this woman's compacted frame, and apparent in the herniated vessels of her eyes, was all the western Goochlander's disappointment and suspicion and rage, concentrated by troubled years out there into a single beam of arbitrary judgment upon everything she thought she saw. When that beam found me in the elongated mirror just above her worried brow, and swept across my face, and probed me for signs of earthly misconduct and spiritual stain, I did my best to remain still, whether I had sinned recently or not, though I could never quite quiet my eyes, which focused alternately on her stare in the glass and that from the trees along the road just beyond. Ultimately this vegetation would show me less kindness than did the woman, but in the moment it could be counted on at least to provide a constancy in its belligerence, whereas the woman seemed almost to flirt with my future, and to play the demiurge with my destruction or survival, and to amuse herself with the question of whether, by her petty rewards and institutional punishments, I would come to recognize her dominion over me and every other terrified creature on the bus. I will allow that I did.

(I will also allow that no one's anticipation exceeded mine when she pulled her vehicle to the side of the road because of some fight between the older boys, and rose up in her might and her housedress, and indicated by smirk and by beam which combatant she would hold accountable and which one she would likely forgive, though she could not have known any better than we did what had sparked the dispute in the first place, and had caused all those disappointingly muffled impacts of bone-backed flesh upon bone-backed flesh. Hence the mystery of which boy she would finger took on an import, and promised a thrill, that the fight itself could not possibly match. How exciting, I agree, to see a carless twelfth grader beaten into subconsciousness by another carless twelfth grader over some imagined or inflated slight; how much *more* exciting to know that the dazed teen might then find his world wrecked for good because he had, a day or a week or a month earlier, looked the wrong way at, or dared entirely to ignore, his driver.

(Good on this woman, and good on every country person who does not consult the facts before dispensing justice but insists upon resources more readily at hand. Though those resources be amputated from reason they might still provide, in the interstice between what the land has done to her and what the land has done to her passenger, the possibility that an actual criminal, a true sinner, might be shown a random mercy the courts no longer care to provide. I am that criminal; I am that sinner; and as such I am one who looks back with some fondness on a witch who drafted and applied a personal law to her personal hell, and whose stranglehold on her riders tightened wisely once we had left the theme of the main road and turned off onto those dirt-road digressions that sent pebbles to ping against window and wall, and dust to settle in the folds of our clothes and our memories, and a melody of tortured rubber to harmonize with the basso continuo of an overtaxed engine and, sempre toward the end of our westerly route, the high ostinato of children weeping.

(This woman either heard none of it or was unmoved, seeing as how it was inferior to the music produced by her own son, a particularly gifted soloist, when the sickled cells within his pipes caught and clogged and he sent forth a cadenza, loud and low, which could not help but impress. I do remember that on at least one such occasion, prompted by a private hurt the boy might have understood but the rest of us did not, she answered his groans with a melody of her own. For miles and minutes, as the gravel shot up, and the soil crept in, and the seats jostled, and the engine bucked and pulled, this woman threw her head back and screamed, for anyone who had ears to hear it, "People do they devilment in the dark! People do they devilment in the dark!" Good on her, and good on every country person who insists upon resources more readily at hand.)

The second sort of suicide

A mosquito has just now managed to kill itself in my drink. Am I to conclude from this that the creature was overly attracted to sweetness and so doomed to die sooner or later in someone's pool of poison? Or am I to conclude that this bug thought itself more clever than the usual bug and so deserved to be shown that it was not? Was this action, in other words, a display of hillbilly derring-do, or was the mosquito being uppity? Is the second sort of suicide to be judged less ignorant than the first, and is it therefore to be called more sinful? Does the soul contained in the first mosquito repair to heaven, where its death is applauded for a lack of pretense (even if that lack was plainly contrived), while the second goes directly to hell? Will the first return as something better than a mosquito? Will either be among the next wave of tiny winged demons that stab and sicken and annoy me? Perhaps I should simply pour out the contents of my glass and begin again.

Some years had passed before I was able to understand that the odd adult who pestered me was not my teacher per se but was more properly a lesson to be learned. I did, now and then, come to think of one full-grown Goochlander or another as an angel sent to deliver me, but even the angels out there could be sobering examples of what a country boy might turn into, and so I tended to study them rather than give myself over to their care. My true schoolmaster, and I imagine everyone else's, was that fungal entity beneath our feet, that foul root whose works now surpass those of the hopeful republic which once sprang up in opposition to it (and not, as fools have commonly supposed, in communion with its opposite) and then began to wilt. My classroom was everything this entity had managed in the meantime to touch and taint: farm and family, field and tree, stillborn neighborhood and ubiquitous church, playground and parking lot, road and rut, bike and car and truck and bus. My schoolmarm was that child who sat beside me and chided, or a few seats before me and wept, or anywhere near and threw fists down upon me, or across the aisle with her back against the hull, her jaw engaged with gum or cud, her eyes in search of a vessel into which she might pour what helpful knowledge she had gained in that place but never found cause to employ.

Long before I knew what the continuation of the species entailed I was privy to its utter debasement (both the species' and the continuation's) by my supposedly wholesome young instructors, each of whom was, and probably still is, a fine advertisement for why humanity might just as well be allowed to peter out. I was grabbed by an older boy and asked, or told really, "You play with it, don't you? You rub it till it feels good," and not released until I had answered in the confused affirmative. Another boy taught me (I had asked him nothing) that there were "two holes, and you put it in the top one," which even then struck me as unimaginative. A girl of fourteen or so informed me that her "titties" now drooped (I could not make out either one) because she had allowed too many boys to suck on them, *according to her mother*. And here is a taste of what country children had by my day accomplished with the Socratic method, which blessed me with a number of practical insights: "Why did the farmer trade his wife in for an outhouse?" "What is transparent and lies in a ditch?" The answer to the first question was, apparently, "Because the hole was tighter and it smelled better." The answer to the second was "A

nigger with the shit beat out of him" or, for extra credit, "A nigger with the shit fucked out of her."

I do not mean to propose that a town education at the time
would have been any classier, only that it might have lacked the
particular nuance we enjoyed out in the country. The town
child was not, I imagine, presented each day with the theory
that brown people are lazy and stupid and so worthy either of
pity (from the pink person whose heart is open) or ridicule
(from the pink person whose mind is closed). (Or was it the
heart that was closed and the mind that was open? And did the
heart not then go in for the ridicule, and the mind the pity?)
The town child was not likely to hear menstruation referred to
as a "nursing period" with no lack of comprehension on anyone's part, or to learn that a high-school girl's pelvis had been
"shattered" the night before in the backseat of a car parked on
a dirt road near one's home, or to hear a father say to his son
outside a rural grocery store, "I wouldn't fuck her with your
dick," and to know personally the twelve- or thirteen-year-old
girl under discussion. The town child was presumably spared
the indignity of involvement in a half-hour-long debate about
whether "the man" or "the woman" does "the humping," with
only some of the participants familiar with the gerund and the
rest somewhat too familiar. The town child was not eventually
confronted, as I was on a schoolbus in the early 1980s, with the
metaethical horror of the following exchange:

He: You got AIDS.
She: Well, you got the *her*-pess.

(Understood, the latter, by all who heard it, and held to be a
great victory over the original statement.)

I doubt the town child normally smelled marijuana smoke
as it infused a junior-high classroom in which the great-
grandmotherly teacher was too blind and too daft to regulate, or

even to locate, the smokers, though obviously they were situated in back, as where else would they be? I doubt the town child ever turned around in such a situation to behold a teenager who already lacked teeth he had but recently grown, his pale lips in league with the rotted or punched-out dentition to form a grin of great contentment, his shirt open, his shoes removed, the waistband of his jeans, at which he pointed helpfully with the hand not involved with the joint (or with the hand that was: I do not recall), breached by the tip of a full-on erection.

This young man deserves, I know, and may even expect, to be spared my derision, as he was likely the product of a true poverty, as opposed to the simple poorness my own family had caught, but what was the place in all this of the erection? What was its purpose? Why did it demand my attention, that ordinary barb attached to an ordinary child? Why do I pay it any now, thirty-some years after our initial acquaintance? Why must I remember that it followed me out into the hallway when class was over, and might have pinned me against the wall had its host not been forced to ferry it off to a remedial lesson elsewhere? Why must I suspect that its object was, by force of will, or by divine intervention, to join with me there, or with some notion of what I might become, and thus fail, not for the first time, and certainly not for the last, to crawl up out of what generational ignorance hole had prompted it to peer out over the top of its jeans in the first place?

Names

Because these words could refer to an actual boy, with an actual penis, which at one point reared up at me during my actual childhood, I might be expected to name the boy, or else his penis, but I think that neither necessary nor wise. "Boy" and "barb" and "teen" and "penis" will suffice here, being names enough to identify what animated our rural societies then and mostly animates them now; names enough for what the land regularly charms and deploys against invaders old and new; names enough for what put those deep bruises on a bus-mate's face after her father discovered that a brown boy had caused her pink belly to swell (the issue here being not the swelling so much as the brownness that had gone into her and would eventually have to come back out); names enough for what prompted a newly nonvirginal idiot I knew, by birth and inclination a suburbanite, to crow like a perverted farmhand after only a few short months in that place, "You ain't never had none o' that stuff, han ya boy?" We called him Han Ya Boy for the next two years.

His name alliterated comically, this proud initiate to the Park and Ride, but I remember him best by how perfectly ashamed I felt for all of humanity on account of what he had said. The pregnant girl had a name too, so apt to her sweetness and her situation that it would be a pleasure to render it here, though in truth I remember her less by her tag than by the fact that she quietly confided in me, of the boy who had climbed through her window that night, "He *mmped* me. He *mmped* me good." She actually said the "*mmped*." What is a name compared with that?

What is a name compared with *I have the fear of Jesus in me* or *They had to use the jaws of death*? Why are writers so easily enamored of the stupid technique by which "John" is made to convey a certain blandness, or at most the notion "herald," while "Jane" calls out with her own sort of blandness, even if the clumsy intention is to reference Lady Grey, say, or Ms. Mansfield, or any number of other Janes (or Jaynes) who by their boldness lost a plain or pretty head? Whether I am beyond such tricks or they are beyond me is beside the point. I will permit myself neither the luxury of names that have no claim on my memory nor the laziness of them that have plenty. "Ronnie" means more to me than every "Romeo" and "Charles" in the world put together, more than any flighty and bothersome "Jay," yet its employment here would rent me only a word-doll we might dress up poorly between us, powerless (it or we) to render what the land led actual Ronnies to say and do out there, always to my chagrin. Could any doomed "Juliet" or "Emma" or "Daisy" possibly compete with my doomed "Jennifer" or "Cindy" or "Sera"? Surely not, though even the most talented reader might gather from the latter three no more than queen (the first) and ashes (the second) and angel (the last), in which case all is lost, despite the fact that those particular interpretations, in that particular order, do draw an eerily accurate map of the tractor path down which American country girlhood is usually forced to sashay.

The one character I am tempted to name at all in this narrative, if only as a form of copyright protection for his descendants, is a boy whose name I do not even remember, though he produced what is easily the best line from my childhood, if not from my entire life. I say "boy," but in actuality he had failed so often that I guessed him to be in his early twenties by the time he caught hold of me in the back of a junior-high classroom, and hypnotized me with eyes no less horrified than my own, and yelled, by way of boast or introduction, "My dick don't get hard till it *sees* the pussy!" Later on I heard he was killed in a car wreck, along with some others, but that line of his is immortal, or ought to be. In walking, waking life there was a name for him, but not for that. Some actions, some utterances, deserve to be their own name.

Rifle

I t was a rifle, not a shotgun. "Shotgun" might sound better here, and might make for a flashier tale, but it was a rifle nonetheless, and I did not load it, and I did not intend to fire. That is, I had a fair idea of how to load a rifle, and I knew where the ammunition was bound to be kept (conveniently near the firearms, praise Jesus, in my house as in any other), and I was a good enough student even then to match the numerals on the box with the caliber requirements of the gun. Still, I did no such thing. I merely retrieved the rifle from the closet under the stairs and carried it down with me to the road below, thinking not of the violence it could do but only that it seemed, of the possibilities before me, the closest to what I imagined a Hatfield or a McCoy might have on him, or a sun-bloated corpse from the War Between the States: a dark brown stock devoid of any style, a long steel barrel devoid of any accuracy: a gun that looked able to kill, and was purposed for that, but seemed wholly unconcerned with where its hole was finally punched. I confess that my father owned such a gun, and that I fetched it out of the closet one bright afternoon and took it down into the road, thinking not to bring destruction along with me but surely a kind of terror.

I do not remember if before or after this incident my brother and I attended a party for young people at the volunteer firehouse a mile or so south, astonished that we had been asked to go and even more astonished that we had been allowed to; I do not know, therefore, whether to count said party as yet another rejected excuse for my behavior or as a desperate vindication of it. Neither is worth much, but the excuse has at least the charm of being refused.

We walked to this party on newly paved road, and not on the old stuff, which might be a clue that the party happened after my indiscretion, except that I remember the road being paved well enough, and not made mostly of cracks and gravel, when I stepped out into it with my father's gun in my arms. The formal approach to the firehouse, which jutted off Richmondward from our road, comprised the same twin tire ruts we knew from our driveway, and from God knows how many other such byways pumping that sad little county's animus around, and so offered less of a surprise than that the firehouse's cheap aluminum walls hid from the elements an excellent wooden floor, suitable for dancing.

That floor may not have been made of wood, of course, and those walls may have been made of something fancier than aluminum, and the approach may not have been the ruts I recall but rather a truck-shat gravel, which would surely have eased the fire trucks' way out onto the road, unless they were not fire trucks at all but only area pickups and secondhand town ambulances bought with too many miles on them, in which case this was not a fire station in the first place but rather a "volunteer rescue squad" outfit, though I cannot say as I care. It is within my ability to do an all right job with the facts, I suppose, and were the facts any match for the truth, which I swear formed me more than I formed it, I would probably do so. But a fact can lie as dependably as can anyone's truth, and is often enough only what most people will agree to out of their own personal stashes of error, or else what was once said or written down long ago by someone no more diligent, and far less tasteful, than I. Americans will, I have noticed, stomach a great deal of mendacity, and spread it around, and rally to it even when they know it to be mendacity, so long as they can be assured that in doing so they have acted "professionally." Yet I need not stomach and spread such mendacity myself. I need not exchange a flaw I know to be true, because it is at least mine, for what is likely no better than a pilfered guess.

It was a rifle, not a shotgun, and I did not load it, and I did not intend to fire.

This party, whether I remember it badly or well, or whether I remember it well but render it unprofessionally, stands out with such insistence in my mind that I am tempted to think it an analogy for my art and way in this world. There were no adults around, that I could see, and I wondered how an unattended child, our presumed host, could possibly have secured such a space, at once new and strangely disappointing, all on his own. I wondered how he could have gathered us to him as he had, and placed a can of genuine Budweiser beer in every hand (when he was in a legal position to obtain none), and maintained on his face that generous country smile, and ignored the signs of obvious and impending disaster all around him. I wondered where the stereo had come from, and why that redhaired boy, the rumored swain of the girl who had complained about her titties on the bus, kept putting his head between the speakers like he did. I wondered what the hell we were supposed to do if a fire broke out tonight.

The beer helped with that, the concern over parents and charred country remains and so forth, as did a particular girl. She was from the center of the county, older than I was and with hair the color of dark, oiled wood, and she gave no hint that she either despised or pitied me for the numerous times I had probably been beaten before her large and curious eyes. In fairness I cannot say for certain whether she was physically present at any of my humiliations, only that she would have known about them, though it would be nice to be wrong about that too. As I stood beside her, already altered by the beer, and stuck on what to say, a boy came into the firehouse and demanded that the music be turned down, whereupon he announced that two of our number were "doing it out in the ditch."

What I have related thus far is not necessarily what I meant by that audacious "analogy for my art and way in this world" above. Nor is the phrase explained by the fact that upon hearing of the goings-on in the ditch I began to laugh and (in imitation of television's imitation of vaudeville) spit my latest mouthful of genuine Budweiser beer directly into the pretty girl's hair. I remember that she glared at me, bedraggled, with either a new or else a renewed scorn (I will never know), and was quickly taken off by her friends to wash the incriminating odor out of her hair. I myself was taken off by my brother to witness the fornication, which act we had heard tell of but never ourselves observed, let alone performed, in a ditch or otherwise. We were bound to be disappointed. All the ditches we came upon were empty of people, if not of sin, and the grass around these gouges admitted of no rustle, except where we yelled "Copperhead!" and kicked the next boy's legs out from under him, sure in our inebriation that he would not land ass-down on an actual snake. By the time we returned to the firehouse, and the too-bright bustle within, the girls had rinsed out my victim's tresses and were indicating by means of folded arms and theatrical huffs that a formal apology was expected. We decided that I should probably go ahead and offer one, as that was bound to be funny, whereas a refusal to do so would not necessarily be.

I found my lady with a comb in her still-wet hair, and as I opened my mouth to speak she took my hand in hers and led me away from the others. She walked me to a spot in the front room where we could be alone, if not unseen, and I made no objection to that. She sat herself calmly on a wooden chair there, and pulled me down beside her, and held my eyes for what seemed like a minute or two but was probably only a systole. She then asked if I was sorry for what I had done, and I said I was, which was true but also, by that point, a thoroughgoing lie. She smiled at this, the lie I think, and leaned in close enough that I could smell the soap and mall-bought eau de toilette in her hair. Her eyes met mine at a distance of two or three inches and allowed me to focus on what I hoped or even believed might be her intention. This accomplished, she reached back and pulled the hair off her neck and whispered, in a voice too womanly for either one of us, "Then blow it dry."

Pistol

That was my second erotic experience in the rural parts, that I know of, and the only reason I do not count it superior to the first is that it involved no direct dealings with pain and so can hardly be considered representative. I felt little beyond a sudden rush of warmth, and a dizziness that increased the more I stared into those eyes, and blew into that hair, and asked myself whether I would vomit before or after I had kissed that self-satisfied pout. I harbored some further concern that a vomit might propel a further round of alcohol into her hair, and so undo not just the pout but also what delicate ministrations had lately been done in the bathroom, yet I cannot locate any real guilt in the thought. My attention was applied, as it has been ever since, to the aesthetics of the problem: even then I understood that a vomit might rob the scene of its crystalline charm, or else overdo it, and so I resolved to attempt the kiss prior to any discharge, rather than after, which to this day I contend was the proper approach. Sadly, I was unable to test out the theory: word began to go around that a young man, "bullshit" over some perceived slight by a girl on the premises, or possibly out in the ditch, had squired a pistol to the party and was wholly prepared to use it.

This is what I meant, mostly, by the "analogy" business above.

Said development prompted nearly everyone present to make for the relative safety of home, yet a few stayed behind, out of curiosity, or gamesmanship, or because they felt safer in the fire-house than they did in the dark of the countryside, all of which I can understand. Later I heard, though the tale may be apocryphal, that these stragglers found themselves obliged to listen while the young man waved his gun around and sang forth his complaint, and that by the time the police arrived he had convinced them all of his need for immediate incarceration, yes, but also of the undeniable righteousness at work, somewhere, *somewhere*, in his decision to come to the party with a gun.

I do not claim to have any such righteousness at work on my behalf, only that I wish to be heard, and that I will take such measures as are necessary to secure myself a pulpit. I am unable, of course, to track down and shoot any member of my congregation who attempts to run off, but this should not be taken to mean that the runner will be safe, for ignorance and loss will attend such a creature always, and cowardice will be its constant shadow, and disdain will be its eternal reward from those who have made no retreat into that demimonde wherein a page or two glanced over is sufficient basis for the lie that the whole has endured. Were I not word but true flesh I would hunt these carpetbaggers to the ends of the earth, and show them what mercy as they have thought to show me, and water all the dried-up creek beds of my childhood with their blood, and fertilize all the half-starved crops with their innards, and winterproof every farmhouse window with their skin, and make hippie dreamcatchers out of their bones and sinew, and throw those chunks of them without obvious use (their brains) into the nearest ditch not occupied just then by a pair of country lovers unable to afford, or by their supposed common sense to locate, a simple town mattress.

Shotgun

Enough! Enough with asides and pale echoes of my shame! Enough with the fantasy that my past, or rather this wordy imitation of it, can be made to expectorate a worthwhile excuse for my crime! Enough with the conceit that a weeviled memory could possibly meet even the most basic requirements of this work! My brother has lately told me, and my father has since confirmed, that I took a shotgun down with me into the road that day, an old .410, as opposed to the rifle I remember with such vividness and such idiot pride. I have no doubt that their powers of recall far outclass my own, and so I hereby stipulate and declare:

It was a shotgun, not a rifle, and I may have loaded it, and I may have intended to fire.

Enough, anyway, with the claim that an excuse has the power to absolve. Enough with theories about whether Jesus was or was not my bosom neighbor out there, and where He might have been (in town? abroad? tending His pot crop out back?) when I needed His hand to stay or steady mine. Enough with attempts to portray intemperance and incontinence as a subsidiary of sin, which arises not from us but from the land we walk and lie upon, I am sure of it. Enough with the notion that the schoolbus was anything more than a vehicle in that hideous place, and that its fermentation of an intemperate society within its walls did not constitute a form of resistance, or else a variety of prayer, even if the prayer went unanswered and the resistance was no more than a snare laid by, and to the benefit of, Goochland County, Virginia.

Enough with my clumsy dance around the matter of skin: I did, in fact, notice that my schoolbus driver was not colorless but brown, and I did notice that the teacher who misconstrued the act of circumcision was not colorless but pink, and I did notice that the principal who refused to rid us of this woman's inanity was also pink, and I did notice that the teacher who continually threatened to "go blerk" on her students was brown, and I did notice that the math teacher who had supposedly beaten the boy in the hallway (I was not there) was brown, and I did notice that the supposedly beaten boy who had supposedly raped the girl (again, I was not there) was pink, and I did notice that the gym teacher who yelled "Mix it up down there" was brown, and I did notice that the boy I did harm to because he had insulted my mother was pink, and I did notice that the teacher who then refused to see my mother on account of my being "in jail" was brown, and I did notice that the pill smugglers who tried to make a mule out of me were in every case pink, and I did notice that the young man who passed me my first marijuana cigarette (I thank him, I curse him) was pink, and I did notice that the fat boy with whom I battled on the bus was brown, and I did notice that each day in that place was a loud reminder that I was under threat by either and each of these shades.

Enough with the pretense that a bouncing back and forth between "brown" and "pink" will suffice here. The boy who brought his pistol to the party was the color of a ghost, or so I was told. The girl whose hair I did my best to aerate was a delicious sort of red-tinged yellow, though I would not think to call her orange. The gentleman who explained what his penis needed to see before it would consent to inflate was the color of well-steeped tea, with milk, and cinnamon freckles. The damsels whose names I reluctantly invoked a few pages back were, in order, shyly tanned cow leather, supermarket honey, and a white rose petal bruised by the sun to absolute perfection. The Ronnies I knew were, respectively, mahogany and young pine.

Enough with this new little game, which allows me to pretend I saw so many tints out there that in the end I saw none at all, so freethinking was I at twelve or thirteen. Enough with the implication that I paid no mind when these people constantly referred to themselves, and to one another, as "black," or "white," or to some dignity-starved variant thereof, and that I made no use of this simple accounting system myself when recording the state of my pregnant friend (white, frightened, beaten), or of the boy who had achieved the impregnation (black, frightened, gone), or of the father who had lashed out at this circumstance with his fists (white, frightened, stupid), or of the suburbanite who had allowed a single taste of intercourse to transform him into a straw-chewing braggart (white, frightened, stupid), or of the boy whose penis had peeked out over the top of his trousers in an attempt to make my acquaintance (white, frightened, not necessarily stupid), or of all those children who believed that AIDS was less to be feared than "the *her*-pess," and that despite these diseases the sine qua non of adulthood was always going to be "humping," and whatever harm went along with that (black, white, most of them stupid, all of them doomed).

Enough with the implication that in my urge to assimilate and survive in that place I had never succumbed, for a week or two (or a month, or a year), to that style of thought which combines the mysteries of menstruation and lactation into a single, willful act of iniquity (apparently by way of the humping), and considers it a kindness to think the blacks no better off, really, than when they were slaves *and did not have to do for themselves,* and takes as gospel truth a moron's worry that her daughter's titties will droop if sucked on too much, and is somehow able to work the algebra by which a young boy's masturbatory adventures are worth far more to an older boy who demands to hear about them than they could possibly be to the masturbator himself.

Enough! Imagine a child in that bind, as often I do, and then saddle him with what idea of success a pair of unsuccessful parents have carried with them out of town, where good grades attract scorn, yes, but tend also to pay off in the long run and are not always taken for signs of arrogance or homosexuality. Give this child to understand that any deviation from his goal of good grades will be met at home with penalties he would gladly trade in for an everyday whipping, and by this method cause him to think his schoolbooks great and impossible charms. In the meantime, sit him on a schoolbus and make him wait.

Make him wait while the policemen who have followed his bus in anticipation of a scheduled fight there pull up behind its idling hull, and find their unhurried way around to its door, and lumber up its steps, and sidle among the children as if cops were the protagonists here, not the boys who have been fighting, nor the driver who will likely finger the bullied victim as the culprit, nor the former town child who had hoped that this brief cessation of movement might allow him a moment to study a suddenly readable page. Make him wait while the new girl starts to cry as the bus nears the field-bound loneliness of a home in every way superior to his own, and let him glance at the page while she refuses, as usual, to disembark. Make him wait, unable to think at all of the page, while that obese boy in back finds his mournful way up toward the exit, the dark stain at his crotch proof that the rutty roads have yet again bested his kidneys, his head hung low while he passes, as if to say, "I know, I know."

Now:

Steal this waiting child's books one afternoon under the cover of "play" (the game being never to give them back, though he begs and explains that he has a test the next morning), and push him off the bus and into his driveway with the driver's full collusion (she will, in fact, fold the bus's doors on him as he tries to reboard and fight for his property), and leave him standing in a storm of red dust and derision while his future recedes. Allow him more patience than he has heretofore shown, and grant him the knowledge that his schoolbus will disappear down a nearby road for fifteen minutes or so, then return with no intention to stop, only to show him through the windows a familiar tension in the driver's pursed lips and raised eyebrows, and a mockery of faces fanned out behind her, and a book or two held up in display of what has been lost.

Now:

Permit this child access to his father's shotguns and ask what you think he might do.

Sanctuary

My aim here is not merely to describe how at the age of thirteen or so a frightened and pissed-off white boy held up his mostly black schoolbus with a shotgun, though he did surely do such a thing; nor is it to overstate the worth of those stolen books, for they were of appallingly poor quality either as didactic tools or as objets d'art; nor do I have anything more than a sporting interest, really, in the argument that a child should be held blameless for his sins simply because he has been beaten on the bus, and beaten at school, and beaten at home, and has finally decided to set a few boundaries.

The crime itself is almost too plain to recount. I stood at the end of the driveway, where the dirt ended, or rather jumped out along the road toward Richmond. (Evidence, I suppose, that since losing town we had been trying always to regain it.) My brother, half hoping to see me kill someone, stood off to the right and behind me, his muteness relieved now and then by bursts of laughter. I took a step forward as the bus neared, the gun not fixed on anyone but only pointed downward, its long eye cradled in the nook of my arm. The wheels stopped shy of where I had expected them to, and a tenth or eleventh grader was sent out, probably by lot, to lay the books on the asphalt (or was it the gravel?), after which he walked backward, slowly, his arms raised, until he reached the door and scrambled up those stairs to what he might have believed was sanctuary.

At the time I considered those arms a tad dramatic (I had neither lifted the gun nor flirted with the trigger as I planned to), but once I had collected my books, and the bus had sped off, and the afternoon light had dimmed just enough to allow me to reflect on the fact that my parents would soon be home, and I would then have to explain what I had done, that unmeant mimesis of surrender came to represent everything wrong with the place, and with me, and with how I would likely respond when made by our father to pay for my vengeance. Yet my ass was strangely spared that night. Unable to reckon how a boy's decision to meet his schoolbus with a shotgun could be explained away by either Bob Dylan or Minnie Pearl, my parents entered into a fugue state in which physical exertion was impossible and the rhetoric of my mother's job at the boys' home seemed the mind's only refuge.

I remember how she worked the phone as the sun went down, sure that she could not get me out of this and in truth not wholly invested in the idea, because even more than she wanted to protect her child (which certainly on some level she did), and even more than she wanted her husband to whip the child (which on some level she always did), and even more than she wanted to reverse an injustice that could legally be charged against her, my mother wanted to be proved right in her fearwish that an action by one of her children, and not by her man, would ultimately be blamed for the family's destruction. She seemed almost to look forward to the day when the courts would take her second son away, and would subject him to counseling sessions and restraint holds and whatever other tortures the degreed hippies had devised for their little Jonestowns, and would release him only after his voice had changed and he had completed the steps in some or other "program" designed to crush any trace of his soul's dissent.

Would not such an outcome imply, to anyone who looked into the matter, that this "special" boy had been so rotten as to explain, in an ethical sense, his parents' previous workhorsing of him, and all those mishandlings he had dared to resent, and the constant belittlement that was his apparent reward for having intruded upon their lives in the first place? The question, happily, was moot. RSVP no, delinquent homes of Goochland County. Regrets, military school (discussed that evening as a "best-case scenario"). Apologies, of course, to my mother, whom I do love, and whose good works are legend, and whose desire to be vindicated at any cost I surely share. Apologies as well to my father, who may secretly have preferred that a son of his gun down an entire busload of children, black or white, rather than allow a few textbooks to be stolen. Apologies to both these fine Americans if today they credit themselves, and a few frantic phone calls, and a borrowed hippie logic, and a half-dead bourgeois courage, with my subsequent freedom, for they would be wrong. It had already been decided, ages before, by the land itself, how a violence such as mine should be treated: delicately, lest in time a greater violence be lost. My mother, the pretty town girl, could not possibly have known this; my farmboy father could not possibly have missed it. Despite what obfuscations town and college had thrown up against him, he knew full well that the greater violence in him was likely to be me.

That is the truth of the matter, and that is all I mean to relate. There was even less call for my mother's panic than there was for my belief that a young man's raised arms in the road that day had been anything more than a halfway decent attempt at comedy. Fifteen hours after the incident I boarded the schoolbus and told the driver I was sorry for what I had done and would never trouble her again, after which she said, "Well, you see that you don't." So evidently normal was my behavior the previous afternoon that she seemed almost annoyed by my apology for it. We proceeded with the usual gossip and drug negotiations to school, where I repeated my speech to a mostly amused principal, did perfectly well on my test, and was neither robbed nor challenged all day long. Later on, the bus dropped me off in the usual spot and pulled away leisurely while I stood affixed to the end of our driveway in something like grace. I listened for the engine's groan to dissipate, and for the crunch of my brother's footfalls on the gravel to cease once he had reached the softness of the yard, and for the dogs to quiet once he had entered the house, and then I could hear only the wind through the tops of the trees, and the pants and paws coming back at me over the clay, and I knew that something entirely inhuman had worked to secure my pardon out there, and I was overcome by faith and by fear.

BOOK THREE

I feared the corn
American expressions
My mother's ankle
On Sundays
As to God
Faggotry
Patterson
Fraudulence
I was not sickened
In my room
Harbingers all
A box thrown between us
This notion of snobbery
Flower

I feared the corn

The child who holds up his schoolbus with a shotgun and does not forthwith find himself confined to a juvenile facility or a mental home might be almost expected to take a friendlier line with his environment, but I cannot honestly say every change in my attitude postdated that grim afternoon when I decided to approach mere children as if they were a cavalry regiment sent out to ransack the farm. Long before this incident I had been exposed by my father to that virus which causes man to believe his health and soul contingent upon a commerce with the elements, and by my mother to that equally powerful contagion *Be a good sport,* and already the fever was high in me. I ran through the woods and the fields like any child will, and at times I removed all my clothes and leapt into the waterways, never free from worry about turtles and snakes and intestinal parasites and so on, for I was not stupid, but as quick as anyone to get naked and a vigorous if watchful swimmer. Nor was I game only for what nature awaited me below the surface: even prior to my flirtation with closets and shotguns I had begun a close relationship with the trees, or anyway with the more familiar ones near the house, and would climb up into them whether a switch was wanted or not, and would rest in their arms with no thought for their evil and but a small prejudice, really, for the dirt I had escaped by snuggling their bark and their goo.

I was able to put out of my head what an enemy these plants clearly were (and would prove) by a wish not to see my loved ones undone, and myself further shamed, by the loss implicit in our headlong pursuit of simplicity, but whereas the trees could be construed as a benign infestation of the land, in that they seemed to lack any direct capacity to infest me, other potential violators were not so easily dismissed. In particular I feared the corn. We grew tomatoes too, and snow peas, and carrots, and string beans, and lima beans, and beets, and onions, and radishes, and lettuce, and cabbage, and spinach, and green peppers, and red peppers, and eggplants, and potatoes, and cucumbers, and zucchini, and squash, and pumpkins, and cantaloupes, and watermelons, and strawberries, and asparagus, and God knows what else, never enough to sell, of course, but far too much for us to consume naturally, so that when one of these foods came due, and we were sent out to fill grocery bag after grocery bag with it, we could be sure in the knowledge that the coming month's dinners would force upon and into us so much of this supposed boon that we would eventually gag at the very thought of it.

Still, the corn was more terrible. Beans can take cover in a casserole; peppers will subside in a sauce; lettuce is easily laundered in a salad or a sandwich; any cucumber not bound for the salad can be breaded and fried like a tomato, which will make it either more or less vomitous, depending. Peas and carrots will linger in a stew until you barely notice them. Spinach and squash and cabbage can be boiled down into a harmless mush. Radishes and onions one may politely refuse. Most berries will rot before they can be eaten anyway, and the flies will take care of any melon with its side kicked in. Pumpkins, thank Jesus, are not generally fed to children. Asparagus is prone to mowing accidents. Beets can be avoided altogether if one is prepared to regurgitate them, just once, at the table. No one really minds a potato.

What, though, is to be done with the corn? Unless ground up into a meal it will show itself everywhere: on the cob, where butter and salt cannot hide its babyfood sweetness; on the plate, where it sits hard and wet in an inedible pile; in a stew or a soup, where it represents in such number as to render everything else a mere garnish; in a fruit cocktail, where by rights it does not belong; in a salad, where it seems almost a cancer; in the mouth, where its shell hugs the tooth and slips up under the gum; in the stool, where its constant and undigested presence speaks to how little nutrition is actually to be had from this false and most American of vegetables.

I went out to plant it, though, and to pick and shuck it along with everybody else, none of us possessed of a smile, exactly, for the dumb waxy leaves we would be forced to pull away from each ear, and the little green knobs left behind (which only luck or a very sharp knife could remove), and the thousands of moist silken threads we would yank at and try to rub away but would never be wholly rid of until at last they entered our gobs, and were chewed free of their surrounds, and slid tastelessly down the back of our throats, provided they did not lodge up against our tonsils like flotsam, or catch in our teeth like floss, where because we were not overly familiar with the store-bought variety they tended to rot and remain.

I imagine that we all wondered why the bugs and the deer and the weather could not have got at our crop with more aggressiveness this year, and so spared us the need to stomach so much of it, but were we not also, to a one, availed of some small faith in the notion that in time we would be purified by this ordeal? Were we not, in some secret part of ourselves, if not in a perfectly public one, convinced that no family could be expected to endure even our commonplace hardships without being brought closer to the physical truth of existence on this planet, which closeness would imply, if not in fact impart, a wisdom unavailable to those who did not expend a signifi-

cant part of their life force, and their sanity, planting and tending and picking and shucking and cleaning and chewing and
trying to swallow the corn?

That the faith I kept in this enterprise was clearly insuffi-
cient, and likely no match for what was being kept all around
me, does not mean that I was then, or should now be considered, entirely beyond belief.

American expressions

Fashion reaches out through the weeds with at least as much pull as we feel from the magazines and the television set, and has often enough bent these same media to its purpose (human agony), but can it not be refused? Though the mind be weakened by sun and allergen and ennui, does it not remain, on some low and original level, a mechanism of choice? Though the trees wave us ever onward to our doom, do we not yet fan within us some Tinker Bellish spark of will and revival?

I hope so, as I would hate to see them go blameless who hold that pastoral activities alone deserve heaven's favor, and that admission there will be greased by a self-consciously nursed rural accent and a conviction that God smiles down upon all American expressions of cowardice and butchery. I would prefer to see them punished who insist that any vengeance grown here must be a holy vengeance, even as it halves and sets fire to the innocent; and who maintain that homosexuals were placed on this earth by Lucifer to rape what few white babies can be saved from the abortionist's tongs; and who think it the height of nonconformity to hold that many (not all, of course, *but more than one is allowed to say*) black babies are conceived with a welfare check in mind, which premeditated theft should in all fairness be met with penalties more severe than the mere mass incarceration already under way, which program itself is unethical (that is, inefficient) in that it wastes further tax dollars on the care and feeding of prisoners who will never (studies show) be reformed, and are immigrants anyway, or else the burdensome profligation of same (whether they arrived here in shackles is entirely beside the point), and so are in essence the same thing as enemies of the state, and so really (to make the "tough call" here, to protect society as a whole and not merely its privileged minorities) ought to be killed.

I agree that death tends to cut down on the fornication somewhat, but that is about as far as I made it down this particular path, nor did my parents, as thoroughly victimized by the rural myth as anyone else, ever wander off that way. Hence I must conclude that the land does not *of itself* create the bigotry and the bloodlust, does not *of itself* conjure murderous notions and place them in the minds of men, does not ever have to. I believe the land capable of such a magic, and of an opinion to work it should a more awesome display of its power become necessary, but for now the American seems complicit enough in his own destruction that he can usually find on him, in some pocket or other of his blue jeans, the seeds of his pride and resentment, which seeds he will sprinkle after him because that is what is normally done with seeds. The land itself, or rather that beast which today feeds everywhere beneath it, need provide only what it has always provided: annoyance and lack and trepidation. What more is asked for our violence to germinate and grow?

My mother's ankle

No such philosophy engaged me then, while I climbed a
tree, or splashed in a creek, or peed on the corn, or hid in
the trash pit and hoped to be forgotten. Mostly I spent my
energies on my parents' new conception of themselves, and to a
smaller extent their children, as real Americans, which was undertaking enough, and looked to my chores, and mostly completed them, and did my best to stay out of the on-deck circle
for a whipping, where I never stood less than third in line. My
father, enforcer of our common law, had since the incident with
the schoolbus stepped up his operation (or had he stepped it
down?), and my ass and the backs of my thighs knew better
than to deviate from his program of reassimilation into ignorance and want. Although for the life of me I could not see
what was to be had from this stance, I stuck to my work out of
a respect for him, and with an eye toward what pain he might
inflict, and tried not to dwell too much on the intrusions, physical and otherwise, that plainly threatened to thrash us all.

I am past those denials now, thank God or Goochland, and
would like to elucidate just a few of the items I came to pretend
made no real difference to me out there. The first was my
mother's ankle. It was a pretty bone, as those things go, long
and thin and made of sound Scottish and German stock, never
broken to my knowledge, nor tested in the usual manner (with
hard kicks from a parent), but only walked upon (I saw it for

myself) and danced upon (I have reason to hope) and on occasion crossed coyly over its partner, or else folded up under more precious parts on the couch, as women will tend to do. Said ankle had carried my mother through a clean and middle-class town existence in Columbus, Ohio, to parochial schools and ice-cream socials and half-innocent sock hops, down nature-camp pathways and department-store aisles and newly laid sidewalks to meet a boy or two or three, to numerous prom dates fraught with possibility, from the round seats of automobiles to bright urban eateries and back again, and eventually onto trains one still dressed to board, an example of which would transport and append her to an Illinois farmboy upon whom all her sophistication would be charmingly lost, as would all his on her, and whose sophistication or lack thereof would take her by romance and by U-Haul into the pines and hay-fields of south-central Virginia with three hungry children in tow, none of whom knew enough to tell their mother not to work the corn rows wearing only a sundress and sandals.

The ringworm that took up residence on that ankle, just above the hillock of bone, was not technically a worm at all but rather a species of fungus, a cousin no doubt of that vast system below us, which breached the surface here and there to diminish our minds and our spirits, yes, but also, apparently, our ankles. The primary shades of this insult, as realized upon my mother, were purple and green and yellow, made shinier by the application of town ointments meant to dull and destroy them, the awful ring curled around almost to her calf and shin and easily discernable from up in the yard, where we children pretended to make ourselves busy while we wondered whether, or when, the sundress and the sandals would allow for an infection of the opposite leg.

Her husband might have explained that only hippie girls on the communes went out to tend crops with no socks or shoes on, their hips bent painfully like my mother's always were, their feet planted wide so as to draw attention to the Ur-woman authenticity of their labor. He might have mentioned that the hippie girls caught ringworm too, and a hundred other things just as bad as the venereal diseases they famously acquired in town (which were not anyway unknown in the countryside), and that the copperheads would do far worse to that ankle if given half a chance, and that the spiders were not above setting up shop below a tomato. As far as I know he said nothing, or nothing that was heard. Perhaps he did not mind, really, if the dirt branded his woman in this or that ugly way, so long as she learned from her mark that the land could be infectious and cruel, and to expect no further effort out of him.

Yet should my mother, a woman of high intellect and no small worldliness, not have been able to gather all this and more without her husband's harsh instruction? Should she not have ascertained at once the source of the hideousness on her leg and taken steps to see it subdued, for her children's sake if not for her own? Was she a stone, then, this woman, or a saint, or a suicide? What was it that sent her back out into those rows, aware, as we all were, that only continued hurt and scarification awaited her there? Was it some latent wish for martyrdom inherent in the Catholicism she had brought with her to Illinois, and now to Virginia, which her father himself had ignored but in his daughter saw strangely flourish? Was it a collapse toward the preordained doom her ostensibly Catholic but secretly Calvinist mother had assumed for herself and all her issue? Had some proud resistance to the obvious, some habit of contrariness for its own sake, sprung up in her after so short a time in that county, trapped as she was among self-destructive hucksters who talked down town but in their own panicked hearts actually longed for it?

I am no stranger to such motivations myself, yet I suspect that my mother's were simpler still. I believe, or half believe, that she went out into those rows (they could not properly be called fields, nor were they small enough really to be gardens: call them gouges; call them graves) uncovered as she was so as to prove, if only to herself, that any intrusion of the plants into the soil, and any intrusion of the soil into the plants, and any intrusion of the bugs into either, and any intrusion of the bugs or the plants or the soil into her (which, after all, is my ostensible theme here), might eventually be overcome by an intrusion of herself into them. By which I mean only that my mother may at one point have been, despite the preponderance of evidence before her, an optimist.

On Sundays

I suppose a stubborn optimism could have led my mother to seek out God in our new artlessness, as she had in our old one back in town, though a stubborn pessimism seemed just the thing to encourage everybody else out there, and I doubt she got any closer to Him than they did while being forced to bear along the handicap of me. I did, here and there, with a smile toward the pews, and a big show of prayer after Communion, make an effort to aid in her advancement, though while employed at said prayer I might have aped too convincingly the young provincial who feels himself drowned each schoolday and so, on the Sabbath, clutches fast to his waterlogged half plank of faith, asking only that he never be inspired to ferry a shotgun with him to Mass. That I found myself unable to locate the joy in this activity as I did in some others was probably related to the fact that I understood my father to be in no mood, and in no moral position, to whip me for an improper attitude toward the Church, no matter how plaintively his wife cared to prosecute the matter.

This man, our judge and our Zeus, once answered my query about whether he believed in God with a thunderous *Hell no!* and would never consent to accompany us to services, despite the truth that in order to win his town bride he had promised always to do so. Such an arrangement might have bred strife in lesser couples, but between these two it made for a kind of pact, whereby my father would sleep in on Sundays so as to regain what strength he needed to work his children to death upon their noontime parole from the Lord, at which point my mother would partake of the sleep she had surely earned by ratting us out to the Lord in the first place. I cannot imagine what He got out of this, and we were not anywise the richer for it, but the adults seemed almost pleased with the arrangement, and they pressed on with it until I was nearly grown, by which point whatever idea had caused my mother to believe that there was a God to begin with, and had caused my father to insist that there was none, had worked its way far enough into the wood of their lives that it could no longer rot out the fruit of mine.

How my brother's or sister's walk with Jesus was then, or has been ever since, I am unable to say, but my own was not helped along any by my first trip around what our mother had picked, or been forced to settle on, as our new place of worship: a no-frills wood and tin chapel in a failed riverside hamlet in the next county over, Goochland itself being lousy with the descendants of Huguenots and so inhospitable either to Catholic symbology or to Catholic buildings. Catholic people the place did not seem to mind so much, though I suspect this was due less to an understanding of the dispute between the creeds than it was to a thoroughgoing ignorance of it. Certainly no French-named Goochlander I met ever displayed more than a small awareness of what had denied the Catholics a purchase on their land; I myself learned something of it only because I happened to be born on the Feast of Saint Bartholomew, who was relieved of his skin during the first century AD, in Armenia of all places, but whose name would forever be linked with the day in 1572 when the Parisian Huguenots lost their own skins by a refusal to renounce a newer corruption of the spirit in favor of the old.

All this was to the detriment of my mother's plan, for had the American descendants of these people, misled at least as

badly as my own kind were, not been driven by my day to consider all history bunk, and all knowledge of history pretension,
and to offer up this attitude as proof of their patriotism when
in fact it confirmed only their sloth, I might have been availed
of some opportunity to defend my particular Jesus against informed attacks, and to develop an honest affection for what it
was I defended, rather than being left to resent the exile of my
faith as a poorly dressed schoolgirl will resent the fact that she
is not more popular. I might have had means to declaim my
way out of a situation in the fall of 1978, wherein I was removed
from a classroom, to emboldened snickers, by an administrator
who thought herself thoughtful, so that I could watch, by the
miracle of television, and with too much time and space given
over to what mysterious ablutions I might be required to perform, as if I were a Moslem or a Hindoo, the crowning of a
brand-new pope. Mindful of this woman's curiosity, and probable idiocy, I made a deep bow toward the screen, and did a
very large sign of the cross, hoping to satisfy her expectations
and also to poke some fun at them, neither of which seemed to
get through, after which I indicated with a nod that it was now
allowed for me to depart from the television set, and in a condescending silence she walked me back to my classroom, where
I sat thereafter in a state of irrelevance and rage.

Was my Jesus not the same as hers, except older and more
experienced? Could He not have kicked the ass of hers or any
other but for His being settled here late and in chains, a
bitched-out serf of the Protestant pretender? Had His first
visit to this continent not been as an honest gold- and blood-
thirsty tyrant, rather than a slave to the humorless hypocrite
who followed? I ask you: Of these two godheads, which was
the more forthright in His motives? Is my Roman, Spanish
Jesus, earlier arrived and no less cruel, not rightfully to be
thought the sovereign here, or at any rate something better
than a poor Irish parody of a crude English forgery of a dull

German oil? Has He not since been screwed by unfair business practices in the States, which have granted to Protestant
adherents all the decent real-estate money, and all the listened-
to votes in Congress, and all dominion over the means of war,
and all the multiform franchises of usury, until no one but a
moron, or else a town-bred fan of medieval folklore, could
possibly think to back the original?

Yet this is precisely what my mother chose, or was convinced, to do. She sickened herself on a lesser American Jesus,
as I did to the aforementioned degree, and as my brother and
sister did to an unknown extent, and as millions of others have
besides, and I tell you this: that particular Jesus, with no influ-
ence whatsoever in the provinces (and only enough in town,
really, to save for His faithful a seat at the kiddie table in Rome),
might as well have been an Ali or a Vishnu for all the happiness
He won us out there, and for all the help He was with the corn,
and for all the good He did us as we attempted both to grab
and to avoid the notice of smug Protestant neighbors too stupid to understand what ritual gave rise to their own, or whence
sprang their perpetual state of kindly contempt.

As to God

As to God in general, I will assent to the trope that says there must be some mystery to His ways, seeing as no one would possibly lend Him money otherwise, and I will temper this only with the thought that I might therefore do well to inject a little mystery into mine. Like any child engaged in the effort to ignore the birdsign of disaster all around him, and to show himself a good enough egg to be allowed around the shotguns again, I learned early on how to split the difference between a country boy's atheism and a town girl's faith, and although by this formula I earned the approval of no one, and did not help my ass out any in the meantime, I insist that I worked the numbers correctly and that my answer was at least as good as yours.

The God I arrived at was not the inhabited absence my father always held to (for most atheists will not theorize a true lack of God but will instead make a bold gambit in the negative column, so as to balance out better the annoying belief on the positive side), nor did He at all resemble the abundance of goodliness my mother always prayed to (so that she might hope, in the fullness of time, to fail it), nor was He anything so plain as a mere compromise between the two, which would have left me only at the zero sum, too clever by half, that most Americans now unwittingly and unwisely promote.

And Who would that God be? Why, He would be the God we have worshipped all our lives: He would be the omnipresent

God Who has licensed the use of His name to all comers, as if He were the worst sort of whore, but Who, as any Republican or Democrat will tell you, would never consent to a personal appearance down here. He would be the omniscient God Who renounces all knowledge because He has apparently risen above it, as plenty of the hippies will contend (not knowing that they do), or because He has come to see knowledge as a terrible weapon used by college-trained "elites" upon His innocent Christian soldiers, whose attendance at these very same colleges is safely mitigated by the fact that they bravely refuse to learn anything there. He would be the omnipotent God Who was tamed long ago, either by the majesty of our own aesthetic and political achievement, as the artist and the philosopher might have it, or because He was recently invited to waive, out of a fairness that pleases both the neoconservative (still hoping that his rhetoric sways God) and the neocommunist (still hoping that his rhetoric slays God), any further intervention on behalf of any person at any time for any reason. What fun.

As to God in particular, let me say that the above configuration is not my God, nor was He ever, nor will He ever be, unless or until I become so old and infirm that the continent finally overwhelms me, and I am unable to resist the enormous intellectual snooze button that is at once my curse and my birthright. Before the alarm goes off, and the mediocrity sounds, let me try to record some approximation of my position on the matter. My God was not some dull stasis point between the twin poles of belief and denial, of church-taught faith and home-schooled despair, but was rather a violent oscillation between the two, a rapid and continual change of mind so that a kind of frequency was set up: a tone that vibrated within me, and found a natural sympathy there, and hummed each sunset, and grew louder each weekend, and I trust can be heard to this day.

Said tone was liable to change, of course, being subject to

how my parents pulled at and retuned the string, but no matter how the wave may have tensed or slackened over the years I am confident that I can find it still, this peripatetic channel, this pirate whine, over which a great number of things reached out at me in my childhood, none of them in any way, and all of them in every way, related to the Lord our God.

Hark! There it is! There it is!

Faggotry

My father was greatly concerned in those years that I might turn out to be a faggot, though only marginally more so than my mother seemed to be, the two of them sharing, through the auspices of my mother's work with juvenile offenders (and my father's long congress with tool-belted speed freaks), a perfectly common suspicion that the root cause of all deviation from the familial norm, and certainly of all "attention-seeking antisocial behavior," was bound to be drug use and, beneath that, a latent homosexuality. As such he was forever at the entrance to the stuffy, low-ceilinged room where I slept with my brother (innocently) and masturbated (I confess it!) and, yes, sometimes (though only on the rarest of occasions, and then only out of the rarest of boredoms) harbored contraband, to ask, or to demand, really, "What's going on in there?" My stock answer to this humorless and always tardy question was "Nothing." By night he would frown and stare, and weigh this empty if loaded word for a moment, and amble off with an unsatisfied grunt. By day he would order me back outside and to work, which was his usual remedy for anything: a flu, a nail through the foot, a crushing sadness, assumed drug use, and now, apparently, the specter of an unauthorized faggotry.

I was small for my age, and admittedly odd, but then so had he been, and he grew up large enough, and imposing in his way, and sufficiently mean (by which I mean American) that what few friends I caught hold of in that place would not enter the house out of physical fear of him. I have no notion, then, of what led this man to believe I would not grow up the same as he did (was that not his purpose?); and would not outdo him eventually in size, which with work and patience I did; and would not best him one day in physical combat, which crime both shames and sustains me (the sustenance being but a further source of the shame); and would not challenge him moreover in the ancient art of meanness, to which ongoing contest I submit this humble text.

Some others could not see it, but my father was a decent man, whose intellect was at constant war with the violence inside of him (which is only as it should be in anyone worth knowing) and whose heart would likely have received me at once had I but approached him in the pasture, or at the edge of the woods, or by the side of the stove, or on the lip of the trash pit, and said, simply, "I'm a faggot." Such a scene would at least have stayed his hand for a while (one was slightly less eager to beat a daughter out there, though I cannot imagine why) and would have prompted in my parents a more interesting conversation than what I had previously been able to overhear: "He's my child—we've always known that" (silence); "He's like me" (silence); "I know I'm responsible for him" (further silence); until at last my father was compelled to say either "Come on" or "Shut up," I do not remember which.

For my mother's well-being throughout this period, I regret that I was unable to arrange a sexual ingress upon her person. (She was my mother, after all, and although the picture of prettiness she did have that ringworm on her leg.) Such an act would have flattered her, of course, and seen me removed from the list of potential family faggots, though I might rightly have been added to the list of potential schizophrenics, which ailment was a great deal more prevalent on both sides of our tree, due no doubt to the continent's cruel and continued work upon it, than was the far less bothersome moss of homosexuality. As it is I was probably thought a schizophrenic anyway, and possibly still am, and might even have lived up to that diagnosis, with a violent ideation, had my father asked me just one more time about the perfectly harmless goings-on inside my little room.[1]

Oh, to have been a true country queen! To have been able to claim, in all honesty, a difference between myself and rural America large enough to exempt me from the mundane and brutal rites of passage there! To have been free to walk those roads in bare feet, my pantlegs rolled up, a swish in my ass and impertinence on my face and no care for who saw me from bus or truck or field, an advertisement and a dare! To have yearned for attention like anyone else and to have won it in such abundance! To have achieved, without formal effort, an obvious and irreducible celebrity, so that when national stardom failed to pan out one was bound to be less disappointed than so many of the town fags were! To have neutralized the bullies upon puberty with the realization that no points were to be scored upon a target not naturally considered a boy, as well as by the myth that such creatures employed an oriental fighting technique that in a single quick stroke to the genitals might ruin a natural boy's reputation forever, *which myth is real!* To have been so fortunate! To have dropped out of high school, or else shimmied right through, with the understanding that no grade, regardless of how low or how high, could possibly compete with the mark one had already received! To have seen all one's faults and one's foibles, all one's human allotment of pride and viciousness and dissent, boiled down into a single incurable ailment! To have known the advantage of a parent, or two,

[1] Mostly we were only listening to the radio up there, and I insist that we were well within our rights to seek out some idea of music beyond what Flatt and Scruggs had to offer, or the Carter Family, or the New Lost City Ram-

convinced that a miracle vaccine, or a doctrine, or a hobby, might at last be found! To have been studied like a bewitched cow and handled always with kid gloves! To have been hated with more zeal than one's siblings yet somehow better loved! To have been wondered at, and prayed over, and above all feared! My God, but that is the thing: *to have been feared!*

I apologize to my mother, especially, for not having made more of an effort to conform to her wishes out there. Had I but known what a comfort it can be for adults to see just one of their predictions come true in a land that conspires against all prophets, and contrives against all hopes, I might have reconsidered those offers to be fellated in a bathroom stall or buggered in the woods along the cross-country course. I might have done more than simply befriend a few area faggots, and make enemies of certain others, and remain an unknown quantity to most. I might have learned something of what it was like to be a "real" farmboy beyond the fact that at least one of them liked to shove frozen hot dogs up his rectum and then put them back in the freezer for his sister to eat, even as he delivered this same sister from the clutches of a too-insistent football player by taking the offending testicles in hand one locker-room afternoon, and giving both hand and testicles a twist, and saying, softly, "You touch her again and they're coming off." This intelligence (does it not sparkle?) was gifted to me by a young man ignored by his own people on account of an anabaptist predilection, and by others on account of his being black, and by me,

---

blers, one of whose whooping bluegrass numbers actually inspired in me, while we still lived in town, a vivid and not wholly unprophetic nightmare. To be fair, my parents also played Buffy Sainte-Marie on the old town stereo they guarded jealously in their room, so that such phrases as "the love of a good man" and "I'm going to be a country girl again" acquired for the rest of us a hideous connotation. They gave Woody Guthrie a whirl too, and Arlo,

I am sorry to say, for both reasons until at last he came across with those matchless tales.

I have him to thank for any inkling I gained thereafter of who was, and who was not, and who only seemed to be, and of how in the last case I was bound to be disappointed but in the first case I might just be surprised. (Or was it the other way around?) I have him to thank also for my knowledge of how the Goochland fags reached out to one another with their fast hallway doubletalk, and their obvious (to anyone looking) signals at the football games, and their late-night flashes of headlight (not in every case seen or returned) meant to make for themselves, as Mr. Jefferson's heteros all tried and failed to do, a commonality of instinct and vim.

Although I did not shine my own headlights into those woods, and blew no more than the trumpet at football games, and never learned enough of their language to say more than hi in an unlit parking lot, I did gain a respect for these people that was wholly unbegrudged and neither demanded nor proscribed

---

and the young (that is, the rural) Bob Dylan, and Judy Collins (singing rural Bob Dylan), and the interchangeable Ian and Sylvia, and all those unctuous Weavers, and Odetta (who I admit was real fun when we were little), and Josh White (who I bet gives every kid the creeps), and the arthritic and comically slow Lightnin' Hopkins, and later on some John Prine, and Ry Cooder, and Creedence Clearwater Revival, each song bearing with it, somewhere, in lyric or in intonation, an implication that the naturalistic choice was clearly the adult choice here, when in fact it was patently childish; the modest choice, when it seemed to inspire only a great arrogance; the human choice, when in fact it succored animal distrust and, given time, the political prerequisites of an organized death.

So what if Cat Stevens reverberates against the walls of a dilapidated farmhouse now and again? If it is forever the sun-drunk "Morning Has Broby any personal politics of mine. (I had none then and only pretend to have some now.) Nor was my respect for their kind a mere novice respect, such as one might have for those who had ventured into town before one, alone or with like-minded others, to meet strangers at the roller rink, or on rides at the wanting state fair, or to seek a momentary solace at *The Rocky Horror Picture Show*, so that in time I might follow in a carload of my own sort, and grope a punkish tomboy forced by our number to sit too close to me, and be stopped at the Henrico County line by a trooper turned evil by the roads out there, who charged us with having too many in the car, which law we neither knew of nor agreed with but which nonetheless saw us headed back the opposite way, in chastened silence, toward those parched fields and those judgmental stands of pine.

---

ken" and never the more apt and suburban "Father and Son" it cannot count for much; it will hardly drown out the other, more horrible sounds heard there.[1a] What we got from the radio in my room was not exactly an antidote to this bucolic sickness, for Richmond and Charlottesville alike beamed out at us no end of field-and-stream-themed rock, yet for every assault on our souls by Poco or the Little River Band there was at least a palliative in some effort by an odder outfit to agitate and console us.

Should I therefore proceed to list the thirty or so bands that "meant the most" to me during my adolescence, ceding for the duration of that list all music of mine to chance and addled namers? Should I pay special attention to what is claimed now, by bespectacled and aging salarymen, to have been the proper choices then? Should I bend my memories to suggest that an

[1a] From which charge I exempt my mother's Christmas music (Al Hirt, the Kingston Trio, Harry Belafonte, the Columbus Boychoir), as this was in every case excellent and hilarious, though I do wish it had not counted so firmly against my manhood that I cared about, and was occasionally able to pick out, those famous old melodies on the warped and untuned upright downstairs: boredom and dread will ofttimes lead to experimentation.

Better, then, to have been a true country queen, for there were fewer of them, and hence fewer who were likely to be turned back before they could reach town and inseminate, or else be inseminated by, what paltry notions obtained there. Better to have had cause to study the southern laws with more thoroughness than my associates and I ever did, and so forgo a grand waste of expectation and gasoline, and so avoid a surrender to the truth that town welcomes not those who approach it head-on, in desperate and silly numbers, with colored hair and a conceit that they are different, but rather those who

<hr />

ignorant pseudo-farmboy might actually have cared about, and managed somehow to predict, what the conventional wisdom[1b] would be decades beyond his own childhood? Should I bravely claim that the bespectacled salarymen might have been off by a significant band or two, which half-honest stance would only legitimize the remainder of their lies and so work to confirm the slick orthodoxy that has risen up during the course of my lifetime to maximize record sales, which goal has always required the tempting of taste down the American death chute?

Perhaps, because it would seem "counterintuitive" and therefore especially brave, I might champion a band the salarymen have not shunned at all but rather too easily anointed (those sales figures cannot be ignored: they represent a generation listening, and a generation listened to: they are a generation listening to itself[1c]), which the spectacle wearers deprived of salaries (interns in this equation) have all agreed, in open and easy rebellion against their more sold-out peers, to call crap, by which everyone else, from the sala-

<hr />

[1b] One wet Christmas we received, from my mother's wet parents, a gift subscription to three magazines of our own choosing, and my mother arranged for us to take *Newsweek*, *National Geographic*, and *Rolling Stone*. Who can argue now that I am anything more than the predictable result of that decision?

[1c] Does the salaryman not himself hope to appear counterintuitive and brave?

come forward quietly and obliquely, in smaller units, bearing with them an old and unassailable difference, to offer their openings to what suburban monsters await and to what corporations will, out of need and avarice on both ends, eventually agree to grant them employment.

---

ryman to the "hip" listener unable anymore to trust his or her own ear, comes in time to understand is indeed crap.

Why not, then, go against salaryman and intern and listener alike? Why not argue, with one's own money derived from a hardly more subtle form of corporate entertainment (and one's reputation from a peer group only slightly less impressed with, if no less annoyed by, the actual number of units shifted), that everyone is wrong here: the salaryman on account of a shallow cynicism, the intern on account of a shallow skepticism, and the listener on account of a fickle buoyancy in the wake of this silly debate, which cannot help but result in a compromise among the already compromised? Why not simply explain, with a couched concern for what face is thereby risked (which pose one imagines to be "refreshing"[1d]), why this bit of craft with a guitar, or that bit of cleverness with a console, is worth far more, to anyone who with a pure heart hears it, than the backlist sales will ever show or deny? Why not claim that the open state of my hormonal template when I first heard those sounds could not possibly impeach the regard in which I hold them now? Why not confuse subjectivity with sentimentality, as so many have agreed to, and why not apply both idiocies to a commonplace end? Why not assume the mask of earnestness as if it were the same thing as honesty, and why not present this "honesty" as if it were the same thing as truth? That is (and I ask this with the utmost sensitivity, and honesty, and a heartfelt desire to be objective), why not lie?[1e]

[1d] Or can imagine a kind critic calling it such, like a Christmas gift begged and received!

[1e] With ease I might do any and all of these things, except that I would then have to admit that my parents might have been right about me all along.

Patterson

I would like to record that what follows took place at the McDonald's on Patterson (a Richmond street but here extended westward into Henrico County, whence extended still it becomes Route 6, a manmade if feeble stake through the heart of Goochland), as this establishment later caught and enslaved so many I knew from my youthful days: the trumpeter above me in the marching band, who had no musical ability whatsoever yet was, and likely remains, wholly devoted to that martial instrument; the kid who first beat me senseless on a Virginia schoolbus and now took my order with the same stark and pissed-off eyes that had prefaced all his punches; at a certain point my own brother, whom I would watch and wait for in a relaxed position on the hood of a parked pickup, while through the panes he mopped and scraped toward the end of his shift, so that we might at least drive home together, laughing at his lot, and mine no better, under dark skies but remarkably bright stars.

Unfortunately, the scene I intend is properly set a few miles off, at the Hardee's in the Regency Square mall, on my break from a job at the Rite Aid pharmacy there, from which Richmond's West End never seemed to need anything except cigarettes and maxipads. The memoirists, I know, and most of the journalists, would probably go ahead and claim that the incident occurred at the McDonald's on Patterson, given the wealth of further material connected with that site (and, of course, with its parent company), and simply bet against being found out, but that is the way of the coward and the fool. My scene belongs at the Regency Square Hardee's not merely in the dull reporterish sense but also, as a modicum of imagination will show, in the sense of hot isolation from regular goings-on, in the sense of revelation where we may not want or expect it, in the sense of real or suspected country faggots being lent out to work suburban mall jobs at criminally small salaries until they can attract the attention of a sugar daddy, or else a professor, who will make them work a far sight harder for their pay.

As I stood in line at this particular Hardee's, alternately bored and shocked by the custom all around me, I heard a familiar woodland voice say, as its source slid a tray toward a woman up front, "There you go, bitch, and I hope you choke on it. *May I help you please?*" this last directed with fine drag timing at the next horrified diner in line, who then paid a dear amount for the simple Coke he wanted, and so on, until at last I stood before this hanging judge, and was greeted with the expected if unmeant *"May I help you please?"* and then heard, to the certain astonishment of anyone not already frightened off, "Oh hi there! How have you been?" I took his hand across the register and said that I was well, and asked how he and his people were doing, and was told that everyone was either dead or miserable or lying to themselves, after which we got on with the rest of the transaction. I asked for whatever Hardee's had that pretended to be a Big Mac, and some fries, and as he slumped off to fetch my meal I could not help but peek behind the counter to see if he had any shoes on. He did, but I will be forgiven if I choose to remember it otherwise.

God bless and keep our country faggots. One should never discount the amount of faggot in them, nor ever their helping of country.

Fraudulence

What a joy there is in time travel, and what a fraudulence. In just thirteen paragraphs[2] I have brought myself out of that wood-paneled womb where I was forced to take form and have rendered myself an almost viable being set to emerge from the faux-marble cunt of a now obsolete Richmond mall. Only pages prior I was younger still, and had yet to befriend a single homosexual, and had yet to do anything about my hair, and was possessed of no great delusions re God, and held no shotgun in my arms with which I might make a few bus-bound teenagers pretend to cringe and crawl. I am tempted to stick with this new and less indictable self, at a sudden seventeen, with a job in town (and a second at the county bank), and reliable use of a vehicle (if not of a reliable vehicle), and the prospect of imminent release can he but save his town money, and avoid collision with a drunk on some lonesome stretch of road, and dodge the impregnation of whichever country girl has lately caught his eye, and not lose sight of the fact that these last two eventualities would almost certainly amount to the same thing.

That thought is surely unkind to the girl, and possibly also to the drunk, but it does take us, with a considerable savings in pain, to the point where both I and the reader might be done with this trial, and its pretense, and its foolishness, were pain

---

[2] And some liner notes.

and pretense and foolishness not the only themes still available to the honest American writer. Excepting, of course (though it is painful to bring up, and certainly a little foolish, and bound to be called pretentious by someone), honesty itself. I see, for instance, that I have avoided any mention of that distasteful episode wherein I attempted, in a moment of late-onset religiosity (which in human terms covered the better part of three years but here, I promise, will not last out the next paragraph), to convert my gay friend and informant to the one true path, which involved (the attempt, not the path, though I suppose the latter might also be depicted in this way) mornings with him in the high-school parking lot, and my indication of this (male) and that (female) ass, followed by the practical inquiry "Well, which is it?" I highly recommend this method to anyone who hopes to iron out the dimples in a friend's sexuality, but in my case the interview was conducted unfairly, and made it clear that the female ass was what we were after here, which answer he dutifully gave, and which answer I did not believe, and which lie then caused me to question him further, and to judge his constant and exuberant singing of spirituals on bus trips (especially "Just a Closer Walk with Thee," his curtain call) to be a barb and a blasphemy aimed in my personal direction, until at last I took him to see the wisest, most righteous adult I knew, and waited outside for him to emerge from this sit-down with the news that my mother had counseled him not to deny his inner gayness and had remained oddly silent on the question of whether his obvious interest in her second son was likely to bear him any fruit.

Because my theme for the moment is honesty, or else fraudulence (either one), I would like to confess, before I conveniently decide that my self-portrait here will only be damaged by further embellishments to its already broad strokes, that (a) the young man of whom I write was not the same country queen as I later encountered in the Regency Square Hardee's (I allowed the reader to guess that he was, and I did so on purpose, and I am almost sorry for it); that (b) the above ("(a)") is in no way meant to diminish my admiration for the talented Hardee's worker, who was, to be clear, short and white and applaudingly cruel, whereas the friend I mean was tall and black and mostly kind and never, that I saw, went around barefoot (though by this I intend no judgment upon them that did); that (c) I am, or rather my extreme provincialism is, entirely at fault for any lapse in, or discontinuation of, whatever friendships I enjoyed then or have tolerated ever since, including that with this particular friend, who by geographical accident was able to transfer into a high school better able to teach him, and to appreciate his gifts, and perhaps even to accommodate his blackness, than the one he and I had hated together; that (d) nearly twenty years would then pass before I chanced to see him again, in a Richmond parking lot, whereupon I was relieved to learn that he was now living happily with a man, and so had taken my mother's kind advice after all; except that (e) prior to this arrangement he had cohabitated with a woman, and had fathered a child by her, and although he loved the child, and was boastful of it, and would see to its well-being ever after, was fated to find disappointment in the company of the woman, and so was forced to quit it altogether; by which I came to understand that (f) to the debasement of himself, and to numerous others besides, he might just have opted, for a brief but crucial moment in an already delicate development, to prize my wisdom over that of my mother, which idea could not help but sicken me.

I was not sickened

E ven here, though, my fraudulence betrays me, or else my
honesty does, for I was not sickened on account of what
harm I might have done a forgotten friend, nor because those
charming country convictions I held in decades past were by
now so inconsequential to my own experience that I was wholly
unprepared for the impact they may at one point have had on
someone else's. Nor was I thrown, exactly, by the realization
that this rider may have struck out for the false haven of het-
erosexuality regardless of what shove I ever gave him (which
scenario would grant him all agency in the matter, yes, but any-
how fail to absolve me). No, what sickened me was not any one
of these possibilities but rather the overall unknowability of the
problem: I could not be sure that my mother's good counsel
had been either followed or ignored; I could not be sure that
my own had been heard at all; I could not guarantee that this
young man had for one moment sought out his way in any sinner save himself, and, honestly, who would? Ergo, I would
never be able to trust in that faint yet sweet note of triumph
(over my mother? over nature herself?) which sounded within
me one sunburnt parking-lot day. That this is what sickened
me, finally, ought to sicken just about anyone.

One last confession, before I cut short this shortcut across
time's mined macadam: the word "sicken," and any variant of
that marker lately employed to describe how at the moment

of composition I thought and felt about memories of how I once thought and felt when certain other memories (progenitors at best of those above) first put out their feeble roots within me, now strikes me as so melodramatic as to be counted, if only by the calculus of an ever less dependable fraudulence, an ever more dependable lie.

In my room

Back, then, scurrying with shame and regret, to my little room, where at twelve or so I sat in the dark (by which I mean the literal and not the metaphorical dark, or not merely) until my brother moved in, his own room having been surrendered to our sister (and hers to the myth that endless work on an ancient and uninhabitable farmhouse will somehow elicit a charm that had never taken up residence there in the first place), and asked why I sat so in the shadows, and was told that the overhead was done in, whereupon he reached up and brushed it, just once, with his magical palm, and Lo! Light! I was plainly astonished by this twist after a year's worth of evenings spent seated or prone in my doorway, trying to read by the bulb in the hall, which was not a hall so much as it was a four-by-four-foot square of bad wood at the top of a rickety staircase eventually destroyed altogether and replaced by newer steps my father came out of his depression to build, impressively and well, in a single weekend, when we had all of us resigned ourselves to the indefinite use of a ladder.

Whether approached by rung or by step, this platform up top gave onto two other rooms, both of them well lighted and occupied by people unconcerned, or unaware, that one of their number had so little by which to illuminate his homework, which he was expected to do well on despite his numerous privations, which task he accomplished only insofar as the standards of his education allowed for the misreading of a line here and there without too much being taken off for it. I might also point out, in case these efforts will themselves be graded on a curve, that my privations were as nothing compared with those suffered elsewhere in the county, which were as nothing compared with those suffered elsewhere in the world. Yet should my hurts, on account of their relative smallness, be ignored? Should a preventable wound, because it is shallower than the next, be entirely excused and forgotten?

I wish now that my brother had never healed the fixture in my room. By sunlight the faded and peeling pink wallpaper, which of course there was no money to change, caused only a passing fright, but by tungsten its advances were bolder still, and conveyed a sense of old and pungent desperation in that place, of existence clutched at too long or too easily snuffed out, and attached to me an idea, and withal an actual scent, of sweetened rot, such as a poor woman's corpse might bestow upon a grave robber who has not bothered, or yet discovered how, to do his homework.

I would prefer to call my room a friend. I know that sort of thing is popular with the modern reader, who wants always to remember childhood that way, even if an extended program of rape occurred there. (Does this crime not nowadays count double against the assailant, for its being a violation not only of the little one's trust but also of her refuge?) My own tale, alas, is this chestnut in a mirror, for although I went unraped in my room, that I know of, the footage itself never behaved even cordially toward me, nor am I willing to fib now and say that it did. Those walls neither promised nor provided me safe harbor but acted instead very much as they looked: like an ancient bowel unaccustomed to light and intent on a slow (that is to say, an American) digestion of its contents, so as to leave almost nothing behind when those contents finally reached seventeen and were forced out of that farmhouse forever, to negotiate their way through this land's pinched sewers, by which I mostly mean town.

Harbingers all

W e possessed no basement to which I might repair, as the town kids all seemed to, for our house was put up directly onto the soil, and so what sunken living space we implied to the road below was only that part of the foundation time and gravity and the Virginia mud had conspired by then to swallow. Also there was no garage. I might pen a trite little treatise here about why a garage is preferable to a basement from the American teenage perspective, or why a basement is preferable to a garage, but in either case an extended encounter with one or both is required, and so I am bereft. We did, on the other hand, have an attic. By chance or by fate there was, toward the southerly end of my room, a pull-down entrance into the addled brainpan of our jailor, which held only fear for me until my brother moved in, after which it beckoned me up always into its gray rafters, bare in spots but elsewhere laid over with planks enough that a child might easily gather what was needed to suspend a habitat there.

This attic was uncommonly warm in summer, despite or perhaps because of the enormous fan our father had placed in the house's northern aperture, which contraption seemed somehow to pull the hot air toward us rather than fulfill its mission to push the stuff back out, and which, due to the requirements of its oversized motor, produced such a heat on its own account that I sometimes wondered whether it would not catch fire some dry night and burn us all alive. Still, for companionship I ranked this machine above most parents I knew, for there was little chance that one of its blades would come loose of an afternoon and strike me for no good reason, and so raise yet another welt, and so raise yet another resentment, and so raise yet another sentence, and if it turned to arson while I was near I would at least be the first one alight and so, by my screams, might warn all the others. Who knows but by a shrieking, embarrassed death I might have attained a heroism that will forever now elude me in this shrieking, embarrassed life.

A preponderance of wasps and spiders presented up there, but in my desperation I imagined that these could be warded off with pluck and a plan. I was wrong, of course: the spirit of a spider is broken soon enough, and if not one can generally smash her and all her issue with a shoe, but wasps are another matter. Wasps are a resistance movement, and they will fight, to a wasp, to the last. Most town dwellers can probably count, or anyway estimate, the number of times some cute little honeybee has pricked and annoyed them over the course of forty or fifty summers; I could not begin to count even the number of wounds I received, to my neck and arms and fingers (as they waved frantically in front of my face), on the single afternoon when I resolved to evict these assassins, with swats aimed in the general direction of the fan, from what I mistakenly assumed to be not their home but mine.

I bitch now, yes, and with cause, but in the event I made no real complaint. Like most country children, I had come to consider all pain, and all swelling and itch, to be the mere price of admission to this world, and so I wondered no more over what the wasps had done to me than I did over the two-night skin-crawl and inability to breathe properly that had followed my father's installation, with my conscripted help, of the cheap fiberglass insulation he saw fit to staple into our roof's underside with the brown paper backing snug to the wood, and the fluffy pink filaments in and against us, which was surely an error, or else a slow attempt at murder-suicide, though to have voiced such an opinion then would have risked accusations of sabotage and a further suspicion of faggotry.

I shut my mouth too on those occasions when I thought to employ a comb at the pus-speckled bathroom mirror, and felt in my wrist some tension beyond the usual tug and tangle, and reached back to discover a vast tacky wetness there, and a rubberish nubbin attached to my scalp like an aberrant mole, and understood that I had yet again impaled a tick so bloated on what had formerly been my own blood that even a dull plastic tine could pop him. I did not call out for assistance then but simply pulled the wrinkled shell free from its moorings, and tossed it dead or dying into the toilet, and made use of the repatriated sauce to whelm and subdue what strands were closest by, grateful that I would not have to chase after every cowlick this time with ordinary well water and spit. So accustomed had I become to insults of this kind that I went some weeks with a greatly troubled anus and the sight of wriggly white threads in my stool, each seeking hopelessly to regain the warmth it had just now vacated, before I bothered my mother with the news that her second son's lower bowel had become grossly inhabited by pinworms.

Little white pills from the county clinic, as prepared for this contingency as it was for snakebite and the occasional if suspect chainsaw accident, soon routed the little white worms (for a time I feared that my digestion alone would be required to perform this trick), though I would never quite be cured of the impulse to examine what went into or out of me, and I would be cognizant always of where it was I sat, and what it was I had touched to my lips, lest I swallow again the eggs of this worm, if not some worse, or else hatch and invite its babies up into me, where their forebears had already prepared for them a moist and cozy abode.

Up or up into; down or down into: it mattered less to my turned stomach and itchy crack how these demons got in than that they palpably had, and would be back again shortly if encouraged, and had mapped out well their miserable townships within me, and had determined to start new lives there rather than remain any longer in the dirt below my clenched fundament, or in the weeds beyond my loud mouth, and were harbingers all of more terrible intrusions to come.

A box thrown between us

From the raids foreshadowed by the worms in my ass I must in all fairness exclude the rats, as they preceded the worms and, despite multiple measures to the contrary, survived them. These traders in filth, these brokers of disease, who in the popular imagination are denizens only of town and hence enough reason to leave it, were so well represented in Goochland's clearings that I sometimes thought us squatters on their property rather than them on ours. These, and not the heat, and not the constant threat of unsquashed and vengeful spiders, and not the hum and stab of kamikaze wasps, and not the muffled repeat of my father's stolen staple gun against pink fibers let loose to swirl among the fecal motes we normally inhaled, led me to abandon all hope of a retreat any nearer the sky than I already had. For a while I convinced myself that those peripheral flashes of gray in the attic were indicative of squirrels who had mistaken our house for a wide and hollow tree, and so looked to situate their nuts within its reaches, but the illusion would not hold: whilst arranging boards and boxes in my aerie one night I chanced to corner one of these animals, and noticed that it had an oily string in place of the usual bushy tail, and that its face was thinner than what I had come to expect, and that the dots with which it greeted the world betrayed not squirrelishness at all but rather a keen and unbreakable rage, which in a sudden spurt saw the entirety of its body launched against me.

I blocked the rat's assault by means of a box thrown between us, but my evenings in the attic were over, and I rarely
went up there afterward except to fetch some stored and hard-
to-find item, whereupon I announced my arrival with claps and
loud whistles, so as to frighten off, if only for a measure or two,
what sharpened teeth lay in wait for me there. Each subsequent
trip up that yanked-down and unfolded ladder reminded me
that where I had failed two uncles of mine, younger brothers of
my father, had in their teens made for themselves a fine and
rat-free haunt in the eaves of their parents' Illinois farmhouse,
and had music up there, and entertained at least one eventual
wife that I can recall (with fondness: she could really dance:
Hello, Aunt ____!), and a brother or half-brother of hers, and
a girl with him too (whose relation to me is less clear), and had
carved out a space where these and more could congregate, and
laugh together, and play their records, and smoke their dope,
and tease one another, and eventually (if not all at once: who
can say?) couple without fear or foreknowledge of the day when
they would be led, as a matter of simple need, to take work
(after generations wholly aware that their kind could not possibly survive as farmers, even sober and celibate ones) as soldiers and printing-plant workers and long-distance truckers
and attendants at the nearby nursing homes.

My mother (not blood-related to these people but obliged
nonetheless to represent them in what she has always perceived
(rightly) to be their grievance against a social contract both she
and they think (wrongly) was rigged long ago by her sort of
person (being only by small degrees of politesse, and hardly any
more money, removed from their sort of person) for the purpose of holding their sort down (one increment of prosperity
being about as far as the nearsighted American now can or
cares to see, so that the trailer-homed man thinks it perfectly
moral to direct his rage against anyone in a better car, while a
helper like my mother suffers physical guilt over the fact that

her own children are not, or are no longer, on food stamps), when in fact the contract was rigged long ago (yes, that part is correct) by a sort five or six or ten steps above either one of these sorts (or is it a hundred? or is it a thousand? and does it really matter, given that control of this mechanism has scampered up and down the rope with such agility over the eons, in an effort to obscure and protect itself, yet has never sought, and will never seek, asylum among my own particular sort (or sorts)?)) has on the occasion of paragraphs akin to the previous pronounced me a "snob."

I say that if I have any such impulse in me it will show in the paragraph just completed, and not in the gem before that. I say that the truth is, or anyway ought to be, sufficient defense against the charge, and that opposing counsel knows full well where to rank my honesty among humans she has either birthed or ignominiously fled. Do I count myself better than my uncles and aunts and cousins? I know that I was meant to: I know that the primary excuse given by my parents for our removal to the Virginia shitscape was an intention to see my siblings and me reared apart from, and uninformed by, uncles who were soon to lose their small grip on reality, and aunts who were soon to lose their small grip on hope, and cousins who were soon to lose their small grip on cash to what chemical replacements for hope and reality (and cash) could be fashioned in the basements and garages and attics of the middle west.

I intend no objection to this worldview but only cite it here as evidence that I, who am in provable fact blood-related to those fled-from midwesterners, and am no obvious improvement on them, was not by any stretch the first in my circle to grab at a cruel conceit in the pursuit of something higher.

This notion of snobbery

Still, this notion of snobbery does weigh on me, as I bet it weighs on every American who tends to go clownish or stony before what he perceives to be those either better off or worse off than he, lest a word or a gesture (which are anyway the same thing) out of place reveal that he thinks himself better rather than only better off, or worse rather than only worse off, such attitudes being proscribed by his television set yet dependably represented on it, so that in truth he cannot help but think himself better (who would not?), and cannot help but think himself worse (who would not?), and so is forever sent in one direction by his scorn and in another by his bitterness. Were it not for his steadfast avoidance of anyone above or below him in this equation he would probably explode.

For myself, I would like to see the American classes mix more, not because I can foresee a day when my fellow citizen will enter a voting booth or a jury box or a convenience store with some livelier spark in his head than that what matters here is how he feels (not thinks, mind you, because people who think are generally out to make him feel bad for not having thought enough, and he will not be made a fool of, except by himself), nor because I honestly believe the nation would benefit much if its voters and jurists and flip-flopped shoplifters suddenly set aside their feelings, being mostly terror and its satellite states, and adopted the reasoned approach Mr. Jefferson championed publicly (as opposed to the Romantic approach he got wind of privately and, *thinking himself better,* leaned into), which correction might be worth something had this narcotic land, and the sleepy institutions built upon it, and the nightmarish educators those institutions then produced, eroded no more than our habit of thought and not our actual capacity for it.

No, despite all temptations of politeness I can discover no decent way to vouch for the native intellect, nor do I harbor much hope for its betterment elsewhere, since emigration would, I suspect (or fear, or maybe "feel" is the word I want here), only further accelerate the export of New World stupidity to the Old, or to the Older Still, and does that commerce not already redound upon us in towering waves? Do we not daily know our stupidity returned to us in blatant echo, here and there honed and amplified? Will we still maintain that we are alone on this planet, and in our homes, and that this aloneness alone is sufficient defense against the backwash of an ignorant self-assertion, when the next wave sees us all drowned together like attic rats?

Is this eschewal of anyone remotely dissimilar, in case we might be forced to interact at the mall with someone we perceive to perceive himself better, or with someone we perceive to perceive himself worse, really the brave individualism we imagine? Or is it instead a collective and thus extra-cowardly form of suicide? And is that eschewal, or that suicide, since it takes as an article of faith that no one should ever dare think himself better, not strangely evocative of the sad drab grays of Communism? And did that go well, for the Communists? Are we to suffer their same fate: a collapsed ideology and a collapsed economy, a twenty-first-century serfdom to potato-fed bullies with guns? Are we to dwell in a land where (and we have already had a taste of this) the oligarch with the most potato guns at his beck is proclaimed (first by himself, and then by all the television channels) to be our "commander in chief"? Or is this perilous thought, that no one should ever dare think himself better, safely offset by its very American cousin, that no one could possibly be as good?

These are fascinating questions, I agree, but well beyond my purview here. I leave them to the philosopher, of whom this nation will undoubtedly produce, and then exterminate (or ignore, which amounts to the same thing), many fine examples after my time. My own desire to see the American classes mix more must remain as it always has been: a simple, perhaps even a humble, desire to know whether I am right (if not, I have cause to celebrate; if so, I have reason to cheer!) about my countryman's innate potentiality to explode.

Flower

In a field to the north of our house, one spring day when I was in my fifteenth year, I saw a figure walking the opposite way of mine, far enough off at first that I could make out only a yellow on top, and a blue green below, and a purer green in flapping fronds to the sides, and I wondered for a moment whether this was not some enormous species of migratory flower I might tackle and subdue and stake a great scientific reputation upon. As it neared, though, I could see that it was only a young man of about twenty or so, with wild blond hair and the start of a beard, done up below in a too-large green tee beneath denim overalls that if washed once or twice might have staved off forever that ridiculous mirage about the flower.

I took him to be a college student (for how many would have reached the age he was and still dressed that way out here?), but even as he passed and met my sullen nod with a vibrant "Hello" (and even as this all but proved he was not *of* the place, since any local would have known to offer a stranger in a field no better than coiled suspicion) I began to reflect on the fact that there were no colleges to be had for a good fifty or sixty miles all around. Was this an area hippie then, as yet unknown to me and accidentally kind on account of his being "on" something? The clothes only half supported the notion, and anyway such a person, even if (or because) high, would almost certainly have carried a gun. Could this instead have been some new varietal of country homosexual, bred perversely to be sweet to passersby and to show no overt interest in a young country boy come across unplucked in a field? I acknowledge such a circumstance to be possible, but up until then I had encountered no fruit bruised and swollen by the Goochland sun that did not wish to pop annoyingly in my mouth, or to be in some less personal way crushed.

Was I hasty, then, about the college kid? No local son even three or four years removed from those weeds, returned to them unwilling on a break and surely aware that only they, paradoxically, and the surrounding trees, could now provide a haven in which to burn his jay out of sight and smell of his parents, would have been so much as cordial to a passing neighbor boy. But could there not somehow have arisen, out of sight and smell of either one of us, a new strain of student? One liberal enough with his friendship, and conservative enough with his judgment (though most school hippies, I learnt later, went solidly the other way around), that an ostentation of fraternity boys might just, in a brave counterintuition, have adopted him for a mascot, and chanted his name too loudly at parties, and derived a kind of self-affirmation from the very fact of him (and how bad are they, really, who can rally around a creature so obviously unlike themselves?), the hippie having rejected, after all (and is rejection not the mother of courage in America, though more often she behaves like the child?), the mores of his own demographic to pledge?

Perhaps he had not wanted to, had merely hoped to "test expectations" with his happy hello at the open house but was unexpectedly convinced, by the brothers' beer or his personal dope, to explore a bit further what lay behind that half-friendly greeting: ironically, of course, to begin with but afterward with an earnest and unfolding idea, on both sides, of what American brotherhood might actually mean, until the time came at last (it was tradition) for all pledges to be grabbed and blindfolded and loaded at night into the back of a rented U-Haul, thereby to be left with no resources many miles from home (was a time when even their clothes would be taken), whereupon it would be seen who would or would not make it back in any fit condition, and some brother (let us imagine him a new one, a favorite from the group just "jumped in") had proposed, before the truck set out, that it might be funny to abandon at least one of the sub-brothers three times as far out as all the others, which would strand him, by the map here, somewhere in Goochland County ("I mean, *Gooch*land— come on!"), after which the boys in the bay felt the truck lurch out onto the interstate, and heard the brothers in the cab begin to chant "Gooch! Gooch! Gooch!" with no understanding on anyone's part what this word truly meant, or that it had already been decided, ages ago, with no need for a referendum on the matter, which of the cargo would be dropped in a distant hayfield so that he might come across, the following morning, one such as me.

This was fantasy, of course, and must forever remain so, since I received no adequate answer to the question I posed once I had determined that the puzzle in my head would admit of no obvious solution, which saw me stop in my going and trot back the opposite way, there to catch up with the older boy and touch him lightly on the shoulder, which caused him to jerk around almost violently as I asked, "Who are you?" After answering me (a little too quickly, I thought), and then waiting, with folded arms and a forced smile, to enjoy whatever additional language might spring up between us, this hippie set off suddenly, at an impressive clip, for the nearest clump of wood.

Here is how he had answered me (that smile already forming, those arms crossing over his chest in what I initially took

for a sign of haughtiness, until they dropped like petals and
began to pump like pistons for the trees):
"Who's to say? Maybe I'm Jesus Christ."
Here, I swear, is all I had offered in response:
"Then where the fuck have you been?"

BOOK FOUR

Lemonade
Crypt
Arrangement is not
    creation
How those Witnesses
Beckett
No joke
Inner tube/Loon
To wit
Josh
(On a plane)
As we paused in our
    chewing

Lemonade

Of all those creatures who wandered past our yard, or were dragged up dying into it, none unnerved me so much as the Witnesses who arrived one summer afternoon and began to poke around the place with smiles and gentleness and great wonder, as if they had somehow landed on a moon made out of our spiritual weakness. I remember that my brother was engaged at the time, his every young muscle, with the motorized tiller he was yoked to because he was the eldest and hence the strongest, and that he looked up at these interlopers with a face meant to indicate that he had nothing left to offer them: no interest, no wariness, no phony forbearance, since all he possessed of those qualities was engaged just then in the effort to control, with outstretched and vibrating arms, the ugly metal mule they could each of them see a-buck before him. What earth that tiller scooped up and overturned had long since consumed what was human in him, let alone what was bound to be sociable.

Yet this cannot have been the case, can it? For the soil (or what we agreed to call the soil: why? *why?*) was tilled always at the first hint of springtime, so that our father could be sure his firstborn would be sent out to guide that machine, and the rest of us to drag hoes and sticks, through clay that was not merely hard on its own account but had been given no proper time to thaw. Perhaps they came in springtime, then, these three or four pilgrims to our iniquity, or perhaps it was indeed in summer and my brother was not below them at all; perhaps he was back in the woods envisioning suicide, or out in the barn attempting it (who can say?), and my memory of his being tied to the tiller that day is no more than a ghost impression, of which I am admittedly prone to several. Perhaps my sister, whom I recall as being up in her room that afternoon (or was it morning?), lost in one of those books she relied upon to order the reality beyond her walls (and often enough within them) into a narrative with a conclusion more hopeful than what she could possibly have formulated on her own, was actually out in the yard when the proselytizers made landfall, greeting each of them with a how-do-you-do and a ladylike offer of lemonade.

That is absurd, of course. My sister was ladylike enough for such a scene (which aspect of her seemed forever to escape either parent), but we were not a family to have lemonade on hand for company, nor to accept it when we went visiting, except where pressed (only those who thought themselves truly worse stuck to their refusal after a second offer), whereupon we would grip the glass tightly, lest we drop it and prove our unworthiness even of a glass of lemonade, and would not allow ourselves to risk its contents until well after the sugar had sunk to the bottom, which ensured that we rarely made it past the first predictably sour sip. And yet! *And yet!* Were there not occasions when I, emboldened by some illusion of superiority to my host, or too parched after a day's lent-out labor to care who was superior to whom, reached out for and gulped down what paltry drink was offered? Did I care then how the sugar in the glass was apportioned? Did I not sometimes, in my animal thirst, forget to offer even a polite (or was it intended to be a humble?) "Thank you"?

And what would that "Thank you" have meant, exactly? Thank you for the opportunity to jog all day behind the folksy old wagon pulled by the folksy old tractor steered by the folksy old neighbor? Thank you for the opportunity to burn and lacerate my fingers heaving folksy hay bales up onto a folksy old platform baked by the folksy old sun? Thank you for the opportunity to scream myself hoarse in an attempt to be heard over the tractor's folksy engine, so that the folksy driver might turn around just once and acknowledge my folksy arm signals, which in the folksy parlance of the place conveyed quite fluently the notion *Ease it up, coot, or I will climb up onto that tractor and kill you?*

There was no lemon anyway in the Styrofoam jug this decrepit brought out at midmorn for the two of us to share, and no sugar even at the bottom, and no possibility that he would not have touched his papery lips to the spigot before I ever got a go at it, and so deposited his old-man sloughings around the orifice, which convinced me to refuse any interaction with the jug until I had almost begun to hallucinate (and could half envision the tractor tipped over, and the neighbor pulped, and myself happy and explaining to the authorities that it must have been some function of his advanced years, as we certainly had plenty of water), after which, I confess, I did take that thermos up, and sucked like a babe from its crusty hole, only to discover that the water was so warm it could not have been properly cooled to begin with, which discovery, and my alarmed inquiry into the matter, the old man met with a self-satisfied lecture on the need for hot water, not cold, beneath a summer sun, lest a shock to the system occur and accelerate, rather than ward off, your common heatstroke.

Once relieved of this useless lore, and once certain I understood that it was the town people, with their cold water and their lukewarm ideas, who had got it all wrong, he lit up a pipe so as to give me time to drink my fill of his wisdom and his backwash. I remember that he gazed out approvingly over the trees, and helped himself to a puff or two, and then widened his jaw so as to speak again (this time no doubt about how he had learnt that warm-water trick from his father, who had learnt it from his, and so on, until at last I saw how I might one day pass this crappy magic along to some overworked and underwanted son of mine), at which point I threw the jug down and declared him to be an idiot, which outburst he started at, sure, but for the most part pretended not to hear. He simply emptied out the contents of his pipe against what tire was nearest me (the right, as I recall), and got that tractor up and into gear, and for the rest of the day drove it and me so hard across his field that by nightfall I was too tired and too nauseated to care who was the idiot here, or to dwell much more upon murder.

Crypt

These hands, I submit, were not meant for farmers' throats, any more than they were meant for the coarse twin loops that encompassed and defined those bales: too loosely here, too tightly there, so that the knee came up under too early or too late, which then caused a great jolt to the spine, and further tear on the fingers, and a resurrected desire to crush for good the old man's already half-collapsed smokestack. These hands were meant for finer things: for piano keys and pages, for soft cheeks and new hairs, for those parts of people that reward kind pets more than they ever will your numb and calloused scrape. These hands were meant to play, I submit, and one day, God willing, to make something, not to yank up out of the ground something that had long since learned to remake itself, which miracle humans had not caused to happen but only caused to happen here (in this particular field, on this particular patch of grime), so as to aid in a crude vegetation's slaughter by bushwhacker, and its inept mummification by baler, and its removal by pain and by wooden hearse from a field no one saw for a killing floor to a barn no one saw for a crypt.

Arrangement is not creation

Arrangement is not creation. How might sometimes coincide with where, but it will never amount to if. Farmers, or should I say farmers manqué (for how many of us, honestly, take the whole of our living out of the dirt nowadays, or did so even thirty years ago?), are no more the sires of their plants and their cows, or of the milk and meat pulled away from these creatures, than I am of these words I spread around and imagine, for a happy moment, to be mine.

If the thinkers are to be trusted, and supposedly they once were, we are none of us the maker of anything, not even ourselves, but are stardust both in metaphor and in fact, comprising elements far older than the milk or the meat or the words could possibly be. Yet although I see ample reason why this selfless conception of reality might appeal to the Christians infesting what mostly just pretends now to be American farmland, no system by which authorship of the universe is reserved to God alone, and our earthier people receive not even partial credit for what their planet produces (and so no say in who will or will not be going to hell), has ever, to my knowledge, caught on here.

Despite all fashion, then, I will admit to being no maker of reality but only a decorator of its interior, as are all farmers, and certainly all those mall-walking rodeo clowns who are not farmers even in the liberal sense yet stand firm in their belief that by a decision to stand firm in this sort of boot, and to sit pat in that sort of truck, and to cast their vote as if it were a siege weapon against anyone who will not conform to their purchasing patterns, they have sided with the natural folk (whom they greatly outnumber now and have failed even to resemble since at least the 1950s, when it was quickly forgotten that just a generation prior a large number of American farmers professed to be Communists) against the urban, college-boy (and, yes, sometimes Jewish: what of it?) homos who control the media and fail to promote sufficiently the idea that self-congratulatory dirty hands and a penchant for store-bought yellow ribbons wrapped around store-bought flagpoles in support of a tax-bought soldiery whose television-bought purpose and behavior it should by law be considered treasonous to question can be sexy too.

A fly has just now landed on my arm. Why are there still so many flies this far into autumn? Is it only because I am not at a latitude normal to me, nor I suppose at a longitude either, but am down and over and despite myself sweating and remembering, unbidden, the way in which my father's mother kept a swatter always active in her hand during the summer months, and punctuated her talk with a use of it as easy and as coy as that of any great Spanish lady with a fan, so that when her teenage grandson inquired (cleverly, he thought) about the man who had lately been seen taking her square dancing, widowed the same as she was and soon to marry and disappoint her, she told him *swish* that he was a farmer like my grandpa had been and that she did love dancing with him, he really *whap!* knew what he was doing out there, but what most impressed her was that he under*whap!*stood life as being something precious and short, having seen a child of his cut in half by a seatbelt of all *swish swish* things, and before that having served his country in the Korean War (did I know about that? *whap!* that we had a war with Korea?), and having been sitting on a log with a friend of his when a bullet came through and splattered the friend's brains all over the both of them, and why *swish* if you think about it, did the good Lord decide it was the friend's time and not Mr. ____'s? *whap! Whap!*

How is it that in all my adult life I have never thought to purchase a flyswatter? Is it only because I suspected in my youth, and by now am wholly convinced, that the swatter somehow brings the fly? And for whose sake, regardless, have I refused (or forgotten, which is anyway the same thing) to be seen holding even a fly's chance at salvation in my no less mortal hand?

How those Witnesses

How those Witnesses in the yard dealt with life's little nuisances I cannot say. I can describe only the broader differences between us: We were white; they were black. Our hands were dirty; theirs were clean, that I could see. They wore nice suits; we wore clothes not conscionably to be shown at school, since they were likely purchased on the cheap from the dying grocery store near the dead landing on the decomposing river. They offered us heaven; we offered them nothing. They were morons in our eyes, not on account of their skin or their outfits but because they adhered to a faith less popular even than our own yet took such pains to promote it. As to who was poorer, we were probably a draw there, though certainly we possessed nothing like their suits and had never known anything like their joy.

The youngest among them, and to my mind the brightest, was a kid a year or two behind me at school in whose talk and bearing I had detected an insouciance that made it impossible now to accept him as a deliverer of my soul, nor for him to behave as such. He was clearly an old hand at being found out for a missionary, though, and met my awareness of his embarrassment (and delight over it, since it might prevent him from telling tales on my family at school) with a quick nod at me and an interest in something more pressing stage left. While the adults in his party came forward with their handshakes and jabber about Jehovah and so forth, he disappeared coolly around the back of the house.

A short time later, after I had explained to the others that my parents were not home, and that I was not authorized to make large-scale spiritual decisions on behalf of the family, and had seen them safely back to their car (a nice big Buick, as I remember it, though possibly it was a Monte Carlo), my schoolmate emerged with great fanfare into the side yard, engaged in a deadly tussle with Ginger Snap, the violent little half-bred hound we had adopted almost without knowing it and then, to our eternal regret, ignored. He pulled at something while she pulled too, thrilled by the company and of course by the game, which eventually he won, which I thought a bit hard-hearted, and which success seemed almost to propel him toward me, his face made up in its usual mix of boredom and amusement while the dog leapt after him and failed always to reclaim her prize. When he reached me he handed over (with a new look now of dramatic concern, though it was hardly a match for the dog's) one of those wedged-shaped boxes of d-Con rat poison my parents had placed in and under and around the house so as to help along the fiction that rats never fancied and overran country homes, especially those occupied by intelligent and well-meaning white people. This accomplished, he said, as he walked past me toward that big Buick (or Monte Carlo, it might have been), "At least we saved your dog."

Beckett

What threw me about a troupe of Witnesses descending upon us in or around the summer of 1982, I am ashamed to say, was not really that we were seen (or perhaps only I was) in clothes more ludicrous than what we normally put on for school, or that we had failed to offer these visitors so much as an ordinary glass of water, or that our faith both seemed and was a small thing in comparison with theirs, or that the youngest among them had removed from the mouth of our littlest bitch a box of rat poison whose contents she would otherwise have got at and died from, which incident then became the basis of a semicomic routine between the kid and myself at school, wherein when we passed each other in the hall he would call out, "I saved your dog," and I would answer, "You saved my dog," with much laughter on his part, and a lesser amount on mine, until finally, after a six-month run of this inane and almost daily performance, I was taken with a sudden horror at its sameness, and wondered if it did not constitute a hex thrown up between us in order to fill with simulacrum the space where an actual friendship might have formed, whereupon I resolved to break the curse, if it was one, with a threat to kick the boy's ass could he not come up with something better to say to me at school, after which I was greeted always with the mock tremble of *"But . . . but I saved your dog,"* to which I had no choice but to respond, as I did for the remainder of the time we passed and failed to know each other, "But you saved my dog."

That dog, by the way, met a terrible fate. I would discuss it here except that I do not care to see my personal tribulations shown up just yet by what ordinarily befalls dogs out in the American countryside, where they are commonly assumed to enjoy long and happy and touchingly purposeful lives. My own touching purpose was chores. My happiness, where there was to be had any, was derived from those moments when I found myself able to sneak off into the chicken coop with a pinched cigarette, or else my pinched penis, so as to blow smoke or spermatophore out the mesh-covered window in the southernmost wall. The other walls there were to be avoided, at least by my cigarette, as they had boxes up against them full of books our father had not yet consigned to the maw of his insatiable stove. I recall that Joyce and Pound and Eliot and Stein lay stacked in those cardboard coffins, as did Woolf and Dos Passos and Porter and Hemingway and Faulkner and Fitzgerald and Cather and Ellison and Baldwin and Williams (W. C.). Twain was interred out there too, as were Melville and Hawthorne and Emerson and Thoreau, Whitman and Grant and Howells and Du Bois. Welty and O'Connor; Bellow and Roth; Salinger, Kerouac, Kesey, Vonnegut; Pynchon, Barth, Barthelme, Blake; Shakespeare and Defoe; Carlyle and Dickens; Thackeray, Hardy, Huxley, Waugh: all these and more were given over to the termites and the silverfish and whatever else cared to have at them. The Henry James books alone were so crawled over and bit through that I wondered at the time whether Goochland's insects did not harbor a particular taste for his prose.

"Recall," though, is imprecise here and so really the same as dishonest. I ought better to have written "surmise" or some such, since my recollection of which books were in what box, and what condition they were in, could not possibly have predated the day my father abruptly ordered them all removed from their exile in the coop and set up on shelves in the house's front room, which action I would like very much to say heralded his return to sanity but I know now resulted only from the fact that the books were proving a confusion to the chickens we had by then, to my detriment, acquired. The one volume I can remember taking out of its box, prechicken, was a paperback of three novels by Samuel Beckett, and I remember this only because I had recently been bused into Richmond to see, in an educational matinée at the Virginia Museum, a performance of his play *Waiting for Godot* that employed as an actor a live chicken.

We were meant to be impressed by the chicken, even if it did not have one of the speaking parts. In the question-and-answer period that followed the several unasked-for curtain calls, the student actors who had so recently bored us all to death (and besides our meager busload there was only an assortment of pink- and blue-haired old ladies in the rows that day: about an hour or so in we had begun to take bets on which one of their cotton-candy noggins would nod off next) tried to soften up what they apparently mistook for an audience of spellbound suburban teenagers (and recently revived old bid dies) by means of a humorous reference to the chicken. They assumed this would lead on to more serious matters; it did not. Being not suburban in our sensibility (though even then we might have been, if you consider all those vehicles afforded us, and those kept-up state roads, and those town jobs to be had for a mere fifty- or eighty-mile round-trip) but dug-in rural, and so bound to be miserly with our trust, and pissed off about the length of the play, and sure to think any farm animal onstage an intentional jab at us, we asked no question that was not along the lines of "Was that a real chicken?" and "How would that chicken know where to stand?" and "Do you ever have to hit it, or does it remember on its own?" and "Do you use the same chicken each time, or do you eat it after and audition a new one?" In time some telepathy between the adults in the room ascertained that the lesson was best ended here, and we were stood up with apologetic glances from our teachers toward the stage and hustled back onto the bus.

Usually I deplore the attitude that turns us away from language on the grounds that most talk, and all writing, is no better than condescension, but in this case I must admit it was real fun, and I can therefore imagine how it might also be fun, and not the grave and patriotic business our louder scolds make it out to be, to vote in such a way that denies funding to our schools (which do at times place a troublesome emphasis on words), and to the too-literate social programs sustaining an overly talkative poor, not *despite* how this condemns America to ruin but *because* it does, which I agree is the funnier idea; to swallow and pollute as we do not *despite* how this will one day erase our kind from the planet but *because* it will, which, again, is much funnier; to sanction and celebrate, in the meantime, a bacchanal of torture and death not *despite* how this might lower us in the eyes of an omniscient God but *because* it will, if He is anything like our rendition of Him, and so might want us to accomplish more with His gifts of life and word and will, and the science and settlements built upon these things, than the mere obliteration of ourselves and all wordless beings besides, however funny that may one day prove to be.

No joke

My father, with no joke to bring before God beyond his own discovery that humanity is impossible to abide and somewhat harder to escape, and with no share in the popular gibes of the day (see above, and below) than what deceitful politicians were able by his vote to put him in for, and with no real desire (notwithstanding those oiled and death-ready guns in his closet) to down any complex being save himself, was nonetheless availed of a gaiety that we, who were his children, ordinarily sought to avoid. This attitude was not wanting in and of itself, but we had seen too often the hope of it dashed, with disastrous results for the rest of us, to rekindle and fan it without good provocation.

We had seen him crush out his cigarette and spring up from the table, with fire in his stomach, and a coal on his tongue, and who can say what in his heart, to proclaim before visiting angels the news that this was a house held wholly by Satan, or might as well be, for all it would ever have of God. And we had felt firsthand the darkness that swallowed the rest of his day when these apparitions did not engage him on the matter but simply fluttered away. Given his stance and his temperament, we were not about to inform him of the opportunity he had missed, by mere minutes, to set upon Witnesses (not common Word-spreaders, mind you, but Witnesses, like you might get in town!), now that he was surrounded at last by a landscape capable of supporting his claims. We chose to keep our silence, and to live with the fear that he would somehow discover this treachery, and extract a common payment for it, so long as there remained even a small hope that he might hunt for his amusement elsewhere.

Inner tube/Loon

It must have amused our father, on some level, to see his children crawl out a second-story window and hurl themselves
off a rusted tin roof; it certainly did us. He might have proscribed such an activity in town, where we were liable to light
on concrete, but in the country a child met no worse than clay
if he made it past the nail-ridden boards in the yard, and so our
"suicide leaps" were generally tolerated and, by that tolerance,
encouraged. Tree skinning was also a potential pleaser, even if
the skinner had it in mind to throw himself out of the uppermost boughs, provided he went up properly, with arms and legs
wrapped around the trunk, and did not simply reach for the
lower branches and monkey up that way, which was not so ex-
hausting an enterprise and far less funny when the child finally
succumbed to gravity and fell. Our mother, the hydrophobe,
played Ophelia whenever one of us spilt blood from a wound
that would likely scar, but our father kept his grip then, and by
his calm made it clear that he expected and perhaps even
wanted the scars, and on that count we dared not disappoint.

This man wished no serious injury upon his children, I am
sure, and was not so broken himself as to laugh outright at
their hurts, but he did show something beyond the ordinary
schadenfreude when one of us (say, I) felt a thorn driven so
deeply into a knuckle during a "sword fight" that the quack on
call at the local clinic was forced to dig the foreign material out

through the opposite side (though that might have happened back in Illinois, at a cut-rate day camp there), or when one of us (we are safely returned to Virginia now) shinnied up the wrong side of a tree, and so found himself overwhelmed by poison ivy, or oak (I could never tell one from the other), which lotions could not tame and even the slightest scratch would spark, until the whole of the body was subsumed by chancres and all chance of sleep was gone, as was all hope of my thinking that tree or any other a friend. Rubbing alcohol, which I had seen my mother use to cut and evaporate the muck that accumulated on her face in the thick southern air, proved the only means of lessening my skin's whorish welcome to these sores, though I would never quite vanquish them. Almost as soon as they scabbed over there began on my face a new set of eruptions, which heralded the onset of pubescence, a state for which my pornographic rides on the bus had readied me, yes, but had taught me no gentlemanly cure.

I would not be held accountable for my actions during that time, just as I would not see my father held accountable for his, though he did take an unworthy interest in this new set of blemishes on me, and poked much fun at them, and in time pronounced them evidence of his theory that we should each of us bathe less often, lest we relinquish to the creek, or to the sump (where, really, did all that water go?), our "essential oils." Whether this thought resulted from an honest consideration of the evidence before him, or from a madness brought on by the land's constant pestering, I do not know, but I did notice that he seemed never to apply his new science to the pond just behind and to the north of us.

Being on someone else's property, and so not by law afforded him, this pond yet attached itself to my father by another law. Not a law above mankind's, exactly, as the God-fearing folk will always cite, but a law deeper than and far, far below it,

by which not only that forfeited barn across the southern pasture testated to him but also what inheritance had been frit-
tered away all those miles and years to the west. By this law he
decreed that his children should cast themselves upon those
waters whenever the heat oppressed, and at other times besides, and would not retreat from that position even when he
heard gunplay in the woods all around and remembered that
this was an acreage owned, according to man's law, by an inebriation of weekend hunters too daft or too blind to tell a deer
in a field from a child in an inner tube on a pond.

Mr. Thoreau writes with great delicacy about the "sports-
men" who came out to shoot at the loon that now and then
made a pilgrimage to his celebrated hole. He did not take the
loon's part entirely, since that might have shown his self-portrait
to be less country than he intended, but he did construct a fair
impression of joy over the loon's ability to fly the bullets, and he
certainly went on more about the bird than he did about its
executioners. I tell you this: if that loon had set down on our
pond it would have been blown into its constituent fat and
feathers one hundred percent of the time, not on account of any
marksmanship involved but simply because the matrix of
drunken blasts in its direction would have been too impossibly
thick to survive. If I am alive today (and I have no real proof of
that) it is only because my father made a habit of approaching
those idiots in the trees and reminding them that there was
nothing much in season during the summer months, and that
they therefore had no cause to be out here with their guns, after
which he may have threatened to kill them (he usually claimed
later that he did) if ever he caught them on his property again,
which lie, about the property, if not about the proposed murder,
they might have believed for the same reason the rest of us did:
because he so obviously believed it himself.

I am fairly certain that my father never downed any hunters

in those woods, but I saw for myself that he did run a good number of them off: not so many that we were spared the too-close crack of a rifle, or the undulled boom of a shotgun, as we drifted in our tire intestines, one side freshly bloodied from where a sibling had turned the tube spigot side up as we ran and leapt into it, but enough that when dusk came down, and the blasts grew strangely louder, and we scattered like grape-shot for the shore, the cause of our panic was not gunmen losing the light, and so what remained of their sense and sobriety, but simply that the overstocked fish in that place had come up from the bottom to feed, with hard little lips, on our toes and calves and the innocent half-moons of our asses. At such times our father, out in the middle of this pretty but obviously man-made abomination, could be counted on to slap at the water and laugh and laugh and laugh.

To wit

Some part of me wants to applaud this man, and raise his small accomplishments up, and greet him with something better than the blows and disdain with which he too often greeted me. Some part of me wants to excuse him as a clown, if I cannot render him a king, and to argue that his humor might have held in it more fatherly wisdom than ever did his sadness or his fist. That part of me almost seconds his decision to lift a mutt up by the rib cage and fling him like a football out into the middle of the pond, which rise and which stiff-armed plummet were steep enough to make us all grateful when the dog finally regained the surface and paddled his way back to safety, there to shake himself off and be snatched up and tossed out all over again, after which he knew, or I guess remembered, to head for the opposite shore.

Another part of me (specifically that globule of lung I cough up into the sink each morning, and poke at, and squeeze between my thumb and forefinger, and marvel at its awful, perfect brownness before I flick it down toward the drain and start in on yet another round of nearly vomitous hacks, all the while knowing myself to be but a pale imitation of that hacker I hail from, who sold his health with such ease to the weed that had made the Jeffersons so rich, and the rest of us so poor) wants to say that either title, clown or king, might apply to a man who smoked cigarettes as if that were a job, and spent the last two decades of his life sitting in a chair and waiting to die, and even in happier times could not be expected to inform those who asked permission to swim in "his" pond that all recreants there were liable to be mistaken by drunken hunters for a family of ducks taking an afternoon dip and calling out to one another in plain English.

I never heard him say either that his dogs would be back there shortly to bark and snarl at them, since he would not, or could not, control these as he did his own children, who out of sheer embarrassment would clamber after the dogs until they all, dogs and children, stood in rough formation on the southerly bank, the dogs yapping hell at the invariably black bathers on the northerly, who must have thought not just the dogs but also their keepers gravely prejudiced, as we continually yelled "Blackie! Blackie!" in what our guests could not have known was but an attempt to curb the pack's foreman (that same small mutt who knew so well the middle and far side of the pond), whose full name was Blackie O'Reilly and was probably only mad at the water.

Our father had a number of such jests, or kingly lessons, to spring upon us, regardless of whether these would stave off or else hasten on our destruction. To wit: He thought it both instructive and funny to let us discover for ourselves that as soon as we waded into a Virginia pond we were bound to be set upon by inch-long biting horseflies, which normally sought out animal shit, if that tells you anything about the water there, or about us. Beyond this exercise he was able to cheer his children with the knowledge that a quick smack might stun these bugs for a moment, during which we could stick long weeds up their asses and then wait for them to come around and take flight, dying in who knows what agony, until at last we could make out only the wobbling shards of pondgrass against the cornflower blue of that sky.

Josh

By my father's way of thinking, almost everything in that place had a josh or a teaching to it, though the josh was cruel and the teaching past taught. When we became again the sort of family that keeps chickens, and I found myself the warden of those prissy influenzas on feet, I soon discovered that the hens sported open and horrible wounds beneath each wing. My father explained that the rooster, a leghorn, was mounting each one of them too often: the sores were where he "grabbed aholt and rode." He then named this rooster Buttfucker, so that we might never forget (why? *why?*) that the reproductive function of a chicken is contained in its anus, and he lessened (or did he in fact increase?) the chance of any animal being raped to death in our yard by the acquisition of even more hens for me to tend and betray.

Unfortunately (or fortunately, by what I now take to have been his reasoning) these hens, bought or traded for with who knows what, were themselves accompanied by a rooster, a Rhode Island Red, whom Buttfucker quickly separated from the rest of the nighttime delivery and attacked repeatedly until the Red, owing to poor visibility and the strangeness of his new surrounds, balled up and gave way. By the next morning's sunlight, though, that Red made a complete chump out of Buttfucker and would have killed him outright had our father not stepped in and stopped the duel. After which he put the decision to us: one rooster would live on and propagate; the other would be dinner. There could not, he explained, be two. We chose in our panic to save the bird we knew at least by name, though the name was not much and its bearer was clearly the worse loser in the fairer fight, whereupon our father seized the still-strutting Red by the shoulders, and laid him out flat before us, and stood on either end of an axe handle across his neck, and pulled the body free from the astonished head.

As we bit into the Red that evening, we did so in relative silence, and I doubt any person in the room, child or adult, could ignore the tough and sinewy reality of an unfairly got carcass. The joke of a victorious death had bled too easily into the trag-edy of an inedible meal, and we had all of us learned, yet again, that the outside world would not, and perhaps even should not, be stayed by simple human insistence. I cannot say whether the rain came down that night, and beat out its propaganda against the rusted tin crown of our shelter, but if there was any poetry to that place (or justice, which is anyway the same thing) it might have done so, and kept us up thinking, though I half recall the skies just then as suspiciously cloudless and uncaring.

(On a plane)

(I have lately learned that my father is dying. He telephoned to say that the cancer is in an organ with a 95 percent mortality rate, and in another with a 100 percent mortality rate, which, he explained, "means I have a hundred and ninety-five percent chance of dying." I am on a plane now with my brother and sister. When we arrive our mother will pull me aside and say that after I got off the phone she had the following exchange with her husband:

    He: I expected him to be funnier about this.
    She: You just told him that his father is dying.
    He: Maybe he'll be funnier when it actually happens.

(Funny, but this happens, is happening, will have happened, years ago by the time anyone reads this. Funny that it happened in the first place, as we ate and drank and smoked in the next room over, between doses of morphine, while our mother re-taught us all to play bridge. Funny that once, on the night shift, while I prepared his hemlock, my father stirred in his rental bed, and looked over at me, and said, "Josh?" which I took to be a reference to a brother of his he had said I resembled or else to the situation itself. "Yes," I said, either way, and he went back to sleep. (Or was this the same night he had said that his bones felt "all wrong," and could I lift him up, and shake him out, and lay him back down now, and pull the covers over him, he felt cold, never once asking for the medicine I had entirely forgotten to give him ten minutes before?) Funny, but I am unable, after so long a procrastination, to say just when this was, or to feel all that bad about it.)

As we paused in our chewing

Are we to check the date? I do not know it, nor can I pinpoint exactly when it was that we gathered around that table in yet another silence, eating this time out of an orange and greasy casserole dish (the dried-up chicken blood on my "lucky" pants still apparent but eliciting no comment either at home or at school), and noticed that the frill my mother had purchased in her hopeless optimism from Penney's or Sears, and hung with something similar from a dirt-encrusted curtain rod to the north of us, had begun a wild agitation not assignable to what breeze the window normally let in, nor to what eddies were achieved by the cracks around the door. What we saw there, as we paused in our chewing and hastened to look up, is not often believed by those who hear this tale, but it happened nonetheless, and I am therefore bound to repeat it:

The rod itself was soon a-tremble, and the right wing of the curtain dependent began to buck and bulge, as if this mall-bought flap were set to defecate or, in the language of the chickens, to give birth. Those nearest the disturbance (my sister and I) scooted back away from it, while those more removed (my mother and father) scooted forward, so that we were nearly in a pile upon my frozen brother when a dark and coiled lump dropped down out of the cloth and landed with a thud on the old deacon's bench below, and with a softer thud acquired the floor, and we beheld at once a great blacksnake very much like, *if not the same as,* he who had chased me away from those black-berry bushes all those months ago.

My sister stood up and, graciously, opened the door. The rest of us watched, and I at least followed, as the snake slithered out onto the side porch past the dogs, who seemed not angry at the intruder but familiar with and almost fond of him. That they rose and sniffed at this passerby at all, tails a-wag and paws bent playfully to swipe at him, was due more to my sister's presence, and to mine, than it ever was to his, and by the time he rolled down onto the concrete-block step, and out into the yard, they had forgotten even what part of their interest was supposed to have been unfeigned.

Perhaps they understood, being relegated to the out-of-doors themselves, that a meal of house rat, poisoned or no, will attract any number of nature's visitors. Perhaps they understood that this predator would be back again shortly to retry his mission, as would all the others, and that on his way off the property, this time or the next, it might finally occur to him to grab a bite of petrified chicken at the noisy and feathered drive-thru to the side of the house. Had I but understood this then, and realized what inaction might cost me, I would have stomped down harder on the back of that snake, and not just sped him off but rather pinned him to that porch, the better to get at and destroy a shown and constant enemy.

BOOK FIVE

A crueler iteration
I do not refer here to time
By his crooked ledger
Imprimatur
Kindness
Borogoves
"The patterns, incidents,
    and images noted do
    exist"
An excellent theory
There persists a desire
(Forgive me)
Malocchio
Such was not my intention
I had thought to fire him
    sooner
Past performances
A velocity finally sufficient

A crueler iteration

My father has lately achieved his great goal in life, which was a quick and pauperish exit from it, and as you might well imagine I am both happy for the remains and proud. (I make a doomed attempt here, I know, though by my own count only for the second time, to invoke an actual flesh-bound father, as opposed to that word-bound shade I call up elsewhere, out of hazy anecdote and too-garish gripe, or perhaps he is better thought of as an effigy I stuff and sew, so that I might whack at him with the sticks of my sentences (which also, to be fair, did most of the sewing) before I gather these up into neat little fagots and set him spectacularly on fire.) He did not put the stem of a shotgun into his mouth, as our mother had warned us he might do, but rather succumbed to a cancer he had always reached out for, which began to our surprise in the Hamiltonian pancreas and not, as he and we had long predicted, in the fibers of his more Jeffersonian lung. He soured (the man, I mean, though possibly also the metaphor) somewhere toward the offer of lemonade and was ashes before we had paused in our chewing. My mother described him in his obituary as "a builder and a teacher," and I would not think to improve upon that, except to add that he was also an accomplished ass-beater and occasional puncher of his children's smart mouths.

The throng will demand a caesura here, out of respect, or something like it, but I reject that approach as a posture and a falsehood: the question at hand has not to do with decorum but only with personal taste, and by that I am bound, as I ever have been, to his. My own might allow for a leniency on certain points, or even a brief Christian forgiveness, but my father's never would, and in this, again, I feel obliged to follow his lead. It should be known to all the world that this man showed but a passing interest in nature's switches, and before and after that laid into us not with fresh wood but with ancient metal. He started out in town with the twisted grip of a popular make of flyswatter and graduated in the trees to a device he constructed himself, and presumably designed, out of insulated copper wire, which scourge hung with such threat from a nail on the side porch that my brother and I contrived one season to steal and destroy it, only to see a crueler iteration rise up in its stead.

Agriculture has nothing on industry in these matters: a switch will sting and leave its mark, but wire will actually blind for a moment, and will romance blood so near the skin's surface that the whipped will not afterward touch his buttocks, or the back of his thighs, for fear that any pressure on the welts there will initiate a bleed no country remedy can stanch. I have heard it argued that the mind has the ability to forget pain, if never the insult of it, and if so my own might not work quite right, for I recall the bite as clearly as I do the burn, and neither memory has inspired in me what I suppose my torturer intended.

(Then again, it may be the ass, more so than the mind, that does the real remembering here.)

He loved his wife and was in thrall of her, as we all were, and she loved and was in thrall of him, as we all were, which may have accounted for the fact that she made no honest effort to impede him while he misused her children before her pale and pretty eyes, and never fully withheld her approval of this or any other hurt he dealt us, and in the spaces between his strokes seemed almost to accept the righteousness of what was plainly, to all her issue, no better than a bully's hand. In her defense, if

I might believably come to that, she did scream and scream throughout these episodes, though I take it that this was only to provide a suitable soundtrack to them, her children's high squeals and pleas for mercy falling apparently shy of the standard. Should I fault her, then, for a desire, and in truth a fine ability, to cover our novice pipings with a mother's more practiced howl? Should I count it a cynicism (on her part? on mine?) that in my recollection she managed always to stop her madness exactly where he stopped his, so able an accompanist was she? Should she in turn fault me, or else my musicianship, for the fact that my own screams continued on for some time afterward and will not be silenced to this very day?

A thousand words or more I had planned on those expert wails of hers: the soar and wild melisma of them; the head- and face- and chest-clutching gestures with which they were dependably delivered; my initial assumption that these theatrics were but a means to distract her man from his task, and so spare what skin was left on the already thinned-out ass of her son; my later theory, or hope, that they were instead a ploy to distract not him but me, and so allow me a "psychological space" to escape into, wherein the sufferings of one's mother far outweighed one's paltry own and hence were a kind of ballast to the soul (when what was wanted was lift! lift!); my eventual realization that no such space could exist to begin with, in this part of America or any other, so long as there remained even one woman willing to tell tales on her child in exchange for an assurance that the coming week's labor would see no further lip out of him.

Yet death demands, if we stop to consider it, that we speak ill only of the dead (for what harm could come to them beyond what already has?), while to those left above we owe all our half-meant ruth, and all those presumptions of innocence neither asked for nor earned, and all those domestic attentions that might anyway be charged against us one day, simply because we were present at, and therefore associated with, and perhaps even implicated in, the murder itself. And so I say to my mother, who has helped out so many but could never quite help herself: *You are blameless in your man's disintegration. You merely bear some small culpability in mine.*

I do not refer here to time

He despised the trees. He would have charcoaled every one on our acreage had he not been so cheated on an allowance of life. I do not refer here to time, exactly, for he had a fair enough grasp and gander at that. (Two years before he was charcoal himself we shared a Christmas Eve conversation out on my brother's deck, the both of us staring up at the stars with our drinks and our cigarettes and wondering whether mankind would ever break free of its fate, and get far enough gone before this galaxy began to collide with the next one over, which escape might happen only, we posited, given the vast and horrible distances involved, if in the interim we discovered how to harness a propulsive power at least as great as that of our sun, which in all probability would *be* our sun (had it not swelled up and fricasseed the lot of us by then), which after a gulp or two more we concluded, or rather he did, was impossible, since such an undertaking would require the energy of a second sun to pull the first off its axis, and send it spinning out away from the collision with us in tow, and a third to pull the second off its, and a fourth to pull the third off its, and there was not time enough at hand, or nearness, *even if we left right now,* to approach so much as a second sun (or did he call it the last?) in this bright and interminable queue.

(What a venturesome mind he had, this man who had ridden but once on an airplane that I know of, and had sweated his way throughout even that simple hop, sure all the while that the ground would rise up and smite him for the hubris (he was not disposed to think it a sin) of having put himself aloft in the first place, which only by luck (he would never have called it a miracle) the ground did not, nor did it take any immediate action against him once he had stepped down off that plane and onto a tarmac topping just as sown with hatred and decrease as what he had left behind him an hour or so ago, nor did it target him for cancellation in the hotel bed I can see him renting shyly for the night (was this Canada? Chicago? lovers of the saccharine "literature of place" will insist that the answer somehow matters here: I am confident in my ability to imply that it does not), nor was he thrown and killed later by a bump in or under the road along which he then secured for himself a tortuous if unelevated ride home.

(Nor, I might argue, by what powers of reason he partway encouraged in me, did this one useless trek away from and back to an oily, smelly patch just north and east of big rivers whose waters seemed always (but never quite were: by any measure, by any molecule) the same suffice to widen his own banks much. Nor would he subsequently see, this child of Moses, and of wandering Cain, and of every star shifting away as if his planet had by the mere fact of him committed a gross and terrible fart, how easily, how generously, it might have.) Nor would I call him a feckless man, for he worked hard in Virginia, and demanded that his children work hard also, and was still years away from final capitulation to that chair-bound sickness which slackens and slays so many of our American fathers, whose stores of weekend fury cannot possibly keep apace of their weekday earnings of boredom and injury and defeat. Surely he was symptomatic by then, in that his output ceased abruptly once he had chainsawed his latest victim to death, whereupon our own brutal efforts began, but I defy my reader to produce a father who, on his way back up to the house, encased as he normally was in sawdust, stopped to gaze out over the trees, and at the children now apprenticed beneath them, with a more thought-out plan and a more thoroughly vigorous intent.

By his crooked ledger

His Franklin stove, which was the house's sole heat source once our sautéed portion of the planet had finally come to its senses and leaned back away from the sun, he ran like an all-night crematorium (the facility we employed later to dispose of his carcass spelt the first syllable of that word out, to our amused consternation, as "cream"), ayeing it always with an idée that it could and so ought to consume additional plant flesh until its sides glowed their familiar and accusatory orange. Whether we, who were his fetchers of fuel from the dark wet hardness of the yard, stuck fast to our duty or put off his demands while we struggled to complete one last homework assignment, the result was invariably the same: a room off the side porch warmed to an uncomfortable degree while all the jealous rest sucked the life out of any animal who came near, shaking his limbs to stay circulatory and hoping only to acquire his sleeping bag before more rigor was asked or any fresh new mortis set in.

That my father often curled around the claws of this dragon, the better to rouse himself every hour or so and appease it with pine chunks, was to his wife the start of an obsession to be watched and wondered over, and to his children proof of a long-suspected retardation. Had he but known to insulate his walls properly, and to tape plastic over his windows once the temperature had dropped (as the hippies all seemed to), and to purchase a second stove for the shelter's front rooms (if by log alone he intended to preserve us), he might have won more hours abed, and not found himself so rigid when a rumor of daylight arrived and he was forced, by want or routine (which he treated anyway as the same thing), to make his way eastward along the roads toward Richmond, dodging deer by the minute, to hear him tell it, there to wreck an already delicate back lifting beams (which are wood) and stretching wire (which is metal) in service of an abstraction (call it town) he had once so hysterically fled.

I might deem it another joke, or only another sadness, that both wood and wire (if not also abstraction) had conspired in the initial insult to his spine, when he was but twenty or so, and had a college concern cutting staves for the area coopers (how many of these, honestly, could there have been?), and while listening to the car radio had felt, if not actually heard, both legs go out from under him on a patch of Illinois ice, and had felt, if not actually witnessed, the introduction of ass to ice with a log of great concern upon his shoulder, after which for a song cycle or two he could discern no practical feeling below his waist, and so prayed to a God he did not believe in (I refuse to believe he did otherwise) to allow sensation to flow back into him, which after a commercial break or three it finally did, though he may have neglected to ask that no part of said sensation be an undoffable girdle of pain.

I remember how in the evenings, and in the afternoons on weekends, he would kneel like a supplicant before his favorite chair, and would lay his torn torso across its padded seat, and with his head suspended upward and a-drool against what the catalogs still promoted then as a stiff back would try to achieve something like sleep. We pitied him on those occasions, for we were not monsters, or not yet, but of course we rejoiced in the chance to be free of him, and from his arbitrary orders and punishments, and I, for one, being no cynic as he might have been about prayer, asked God any number of times to burden him with what agony could be found at hand, and to cause him to yield his ground-down bone and expanding gut to whatever cushion was nearest by, and to visit him with oblivion especially during the working hours, when we most required our own little inheritance of rest and relief.

Yet our crippled father would not or could not forget, even in his sleep, that for him, and for all those confined to his tragic section of the American cone, working hours took up fully half the clock. He would therefore be damned (or only comically slighted, once we had grown large enough to ignore him) if any child of his had the insolence to board a bus, or to participate in this or that already pilloried after-school activity, so long as there was any "real" work left to be done around the house, which by his crooked ledger there always would be. Neither he nor his helpmeet evinced any hesitation (and, what is stranger, any shame) in their tacit agreement to chastise a child, by withholding permission to engage in whatever function the child had lately been fool enough to admit was most dear to it, for the crime of its having failed to complete a chore that had already, *to their own perfect knowledge,* been completed. Politest appeal of this decision risked seeing the injustice upheld, and the court costs writ in stripes across the defendant's spindly legs, by an impartial length of copper wire.

Imprimatur

Out of fright, then, or only as a collective-bargaining gesture, we signed up for nearly everything the school had to offer, faking his scribble (or hers: harder) where the authentic item would likely be refused (out of dug-in principle: the principle being that any country adult, by virtue of his decision to remain country, or to become country again, had won the right to interpret the law within his own home any way he saw fit, or to banish it altogether), and by our absence from this team practice and that drab spelling bee, or from rehearsals of a play we had won a small role in and then by a truancy lost, and by our failure to line up for a gymnastic exhibition or a 600-yard dash that I estimate bored even its few tiny entrants, or to board yet another yellow scow that might take us with bumps and misgivings to march with cheap student instruments in one more hopelessly crop-themed parade, sought at last to call the authorities down upon our quaintly corrupted household.

Plenty looked, and some even saw, but no one ever came (save Witnesses), and I might make a fuss over that, except that I would then have to explain away all those A's my siblings and I loudly made, and all those kitsch trophies and poorly lettered certificates we fetched home, which were insisted upon, yes, though only insofar as these accrued to our parents in a public sense while privately they represented yet another level on which we refused to do any "real" work. Once accomplished (the unreal work) and once earned (the marks and the trophies and certificates), this great leap forward in our line's empty record of achievement met with no better than indifference from parents unable to accept that a child of theirs could somehow succeed in hopping over humanity's petty obstacles when they themselves had not, or had not bothered to, and no better than outright shock, aped or honest, when it became clear that not one of their children but in fact all three, in open rebellion against a lie we had agreed to *as a family*, actually would.

And did sedition not somewhere inform the truth that these simple ink scratches on a cut of hard paper, when we had not physically made them ourselves, might allow the child to whom they appended (by man's law alone, of course, not nature's) the chance to choose for itself a destiny not in accordance with what its father (out of fear) and its mother (out of fear for the father) had so rashly chosen for it? Was a son of theirs (the first, say, whom they had treated in Virginia like a languageless mule, as I have largely here) rightly allowed by such markings to wish for and obtain, from Jefferson's own university, degrees in both language and the law (the latter being but a paid perversion of the former), after which he would refuse all manner of contact with the countryside and would consent to revisit it only where it might be looked down on from the window of a passing jet? Should their daughter have been availed, by these same poor leavings, of the confidence required to fly her wooden cage at sixteen, once the panties in which her mother dressed by the side of the stove had become too embarrassingly done through with speakeasies for even a sober child to bear, after which she dwelt amid the God-awful racket in Richmond until this mother, in what underwear I cannot say (being by that point flown from those holes myself), sought to reestablish her fiat via an attempt to have this latest escapee committed (by man's law alone, of course, not nature's) to a mental home somewhere along the twisted route between them?

My father was by then a teacher, the builder in him having so gleefully demolished his spine that some years prior he, or my mother, had resolved that he should seek out and win a certificate, of all things, that would enable him to teach English and mathematics to the delinquents at her recent place of employment, thereafter *his*, which decision would condemn us all to a belief on his part that he had mastered not only words and numbers now but also *psychology*, since *psychology* was what presumably caused all those pimply-dicked offenders to grow agitated by the semi-confident drone of his voice (as we all had), and to question his legendarily cornfed but actually television-gorged machismo (as we all had), and to throw their books up into the air (as I did myself on more than one occasion) and try to make it out of his classroom, whereupon they found themselves tackled by his bulk and inherent hatred of them (a legal maneuver, he was forever at pains to point out, since the courts' recognition of his right to employ restraint-type violence against a fed-up JD clearly forgave, and by Benthamesque sliding scale even sanctioned, his more extreme and less rational violence against us), after which these potential "runners" were "held down" and "reasoned with" until a "group meeting" could be called to address the "issues" beneath the "acting out" (never his, mind you, the issues or the acting out), which would (for want of imagination, or for want of language, which is anyway the same thing) be boiled down into an unresolved homosexuality (admittedly an overworked theme here, though only insofar as it was there) or, or *and*, a failure to acknowledge (not merely to recognize but finally to *accept*) an adult's prerogative to dominate a child for whatever reason the adult saw fit to claim. Which is all anyone needs to know about psychology and the law.

This man did not offer up one word to me, that I can retrieve, on the subject of our fugitive poetess, nor had I honestly expected him to do so, since it was really only the boys he knew how to pin down against the earth, or the floorboards, or the nearest flower-patterned chair, until a confession could be publicly extracted, which confession was always given (what choice did we have?) but not once ever meant, so that his wife and daughter and spare son (that one not just recently assaulted) might be availed of the opportunity to watch their man swell with a copper's pride in the time it took him afterward to realize that he had yet again been swindled. Not out of the confession, rest assured, this time any more than the last, nor out of the thrill of natural brutality he imagined himself entitled to by law, but out of that more precious thing he sought: being not nature's imprimatur, which anyone could see was promiscuously granted, nor the law's, every bit as whorishly had, so much as it was our own.

What he wanted we withheld, out of umbrage and by a hard-won personal law. Although any local resistance to his rule could be run out of us in a single session, or half that, we saw how the wider-ranging grievances might forever be detained. We saw how this man, no matter how he felt his neck re-redden when he heard our posthumiliation laughter upstairs, and raged not just at us but at the limits set against him by his status, and his statutes, and his not yet wholly intractable nature, would never permit himself the leniency (or was it really only the industry?) to whip a child of his twice in one day.

Kindness

We cherish the little kindnesses, I suppose, in them that are departed. (My father the teacher might insist upon a "those who" there, and also back in the last paragraph of the eighth part of my third attempt to end all this (not to mention the third paragraph of the eleventh part of my second, nor forgetting the second paragraph of the sixth part of my fifth, or is it now the seventh part of my sixth?), but the builder in him would at least acknowledge that the sentiment is right, and so perhaps also the sound.) I would follow this notion further, except that I think it a hair too late to introduce so fraught a motif as is kindness into what has thus far been an uncomplicated remembrance of the man.

It would not be a lie, exactly, to claim that he showed, concurrent with his spleen, some evidence of remorse after his most recent advances against us, and that he was quick to point out (as I have tried to here) what he thought might be amusing to a captive and terrified audience. It would not be a lie, exactly, to insist that we could eventually discern in his manner a more peaceable curiosity about what we were still refusing to learn in that place, with an emphasis shifted eerily one winter onto our reading, which he seemed almost pleased to know we could do, and which he afterward then encouraged with paperbacks only partially destroyed by the critical termites, and the scholarly silverfish, and those insufferable ABD chickens.

It would not be a lie, exactly, to add that he later then asked what was our opinion of these texts, and did not immediately explode if we conceded that we had avoided them altogether, or had read right over this crucial metaphor or that obvious pun, and could demonstrate no more idea of what went for irony in the 1860s than of what went for decency in our own multifarious decade. It would not be a lie, exactly, in craftsman's terms, to maintain that his words on the original matter (the irony, I mean, not the decency, nor the time, though these are anyway the same thing, or had better be) were years on illuminating, as one might expect of a good teacher, and were in hindsight mostly constructive, as one might expect of a good builder, and were all the more powerful for their being in the moment so annoying.

Yet I do not think those few forced tutorials with a suddenly bookish father ever helped or learned us up so much as did our incessant slave-soldiery in his war against the trees, nor does his death without honor in the fallout from that war justify a perception now that I could see no worth in its waging then, or that I have failed, after years spent in study of this famous defeat, to locate within it some flaw I might in all decency, or in all irony, or perhaps only given the time, call kindness.

Borogoves

We started in early on our thoughts about why a man might have made so outgrabe a persecution of the borogoves, and it is upon this ancient archive of guesswork (I did not know "outgrabe" to be a verb then, past tense, nor "borogove" to denote a fanciful sort of parrot) that I must base my more modern conclusions here, not to mention any subsequent speculation as to why a father might have resolved to deal so harshly with creatures arguably as alive as he once was and inarguably as dead as he is today.

When he had finally regained, by pubescent or literary trial, the human capacity for speech, my brother gave voice to a charming little need-based theory, which held that we would each of us die of frostbite, if not by the wire or worse, did we not line up at the edge of the forest and present ourselves as ready, if not exactly resolved, to shoulder and drag and roll up into the yard, or to kick and curse at and finally (it was inevitable) collapse and weep upon, what hyperbolically large cylinders of wood our father had cut free from his latest self-satisfied kill, so that we might learn by this drudgery how heat is hard, and comfort a ghost, and paternal protection a myth we had best get over right away. My soon to be allegedly insane sister (spared institutionalization (is that the right term here? what I want, more properly, is "the booby hatch," though by such I intend no judgment upon them that have repaired

there) by a brother's half-solemn threat to steal her north to
stay with a half-frozen him) clove to the proposition, or apo-
logia, that our father meant only to make our backs wide and
strong, so that we might not suffer the same as he had, and
would not in time (in irony? indecency?) be compelled to despise our own children as we obviously would ourselves, on
which new way of thinking my brother and I quickly bet (having crapped out previously on the need-based theory) and
stuck to it even when she amended her scheme to include the
possibility that because of Frank's wont to "overdo things," and
owing to his reluctance to "ease off on" any course he believed
to run parallel with (if not in fact to *be*) nature's, our backs
would likely shatter even sooner than had his.

(I have named him, yes. I had not meant to, any more than
he had meant to die, which of course he always had, and I am
ashamed to see that so paltry a trap of diction, met up with
fatigue and a hand-me-down languor, has led me now to do so.
He was not directly of Frankish heritage, that I can trace, nor
was he forthright enough in his motives to deserve that name
otherwise, but was only called such as a compromise, since one
parent had hoped him christened Claude and the other had
said it put him in mind of a clump of dirt, which was nonetheless how the child was then treated, and how he subsequently
came to treat all of us: not as walkers upon this Earth but as
bothersome detachments from it, to be avoided, or tripped
over, or picked up and hurled out of anger and frustration (or
hilarity, which may one day prove the same thing), until at last
we could be ridden over and ground down into something fine
and wet enough to catch hold of his seed, which he had apparently forgotten we already were.)

My own thoughts concerning those trees, and his children's
crusade against them, and what turned soil held these two ruinous concepts fast (three if you count the soil, four if you count
the thoughts), were at first a leaning toward, and then away

from, my brother's confusion, followed by a leaning toward, and then away from, my sister's, until at last I was flung free of this cracked seesaw and alit in a position to decide for myself, by a more objective subjectivity (or was it the other way around?), what plausible explanation of our reality might suffice. None, I came to worry, ever would.

"The patterns, incidents,
and images noted do exist"

I had heard our father say, apropos of what I cannot recall, that he felt himself made "claustrophobic" by the trees in Virginia, and out of that small sliver, and out of a supposition that he meant not only the increased number of leaves and needles along the Eastern Seaboard but also the great earthen breasts that raised them up over us, and bestowed upon mere hairs such a frightful prominence, I formed an idea that he was simply expressing a nostalgia for the flatter, less festooned vistas of his youth back in Southern Illinois, which philosophy saw me through several winters hauling his logs up into that hateful yard, my hands encased in sweatsocks for their protection (he would never consent to see them in perfectly affordable workgloves) and my mind racing over what cold calculations his own might have made when, with me beside him in the cab one sunset, he came upon a hundred acres or so of what was intended for pulpwood (from which is got paper), burnt and obliterated now by what I hoped to have been a can of gasoline and a JD's last roach but was probably only God's latest lucky strike, which vision then caused him to stop, and to extinguish his engine, and to sit in silence before that razed and blackened topography where just the week prior he had known but a daunting sheet of white, shot through with green (lest this sentence run out and convey only part of the pathos I once envisioned for it, I should mention that my father, like so many others before him, half fancied himself an American bard, despite the fact that his production was limited, that I know of, to a single well-premised note on J. D. Salinger, taken finally, when I was already a belt-beaten six, by the journal *Studies in Short Fiction*, volume 9, number 3 (the ending especially I have returned to eagerly and often, wherein my father's pride in having all but completed a "publishable" essay has led him to attempt what he assumes will be recognized, and of course loudly applauded, as a well-earned "poetic" dismount—

> The patterns, incidents, and images noted do exist; and while I might be accused of committing a critical fallacy in supposing that Salinger consciously planned them along the line of my discussion, they do offer themselves to my argument, whatever Buddy Glass, mixing memory and desire, might want to say about it.

—but is actually worth only a collective gasp or two, since following the appalling laziness of the "my discussion"/"my argument" switcheroo he finds no better way to achieve his unstuck landing than to lift, in toto, right there before the regrettable tough-guy cliché, a phrase Salinger had *Seymour* Glass, not Buddy, bum off of T. S. Eliot, who himself got it God knows where, and from whom I would not separate my father now as a fan (of Eliot's, I mean, not God's), except to say that he (my father), this hanged man who made *us* to stir dull roots with spring rain, or without it, and who in winter never kept us warm, and who showed us fear in a handful of wire, would at least practice later to disguise his stealings rather than invite so wide a scrutiny of them, such as when he kept a hand truck off the U-Haul that had so rudely forced us out into the undead land and, in his paranoia (which even as children we laughed at, our arms full of wood, our hair wet with snow in this sylvan scene), painted over its telltale orange (why Poe of a sudden? or is it Burgess?) in order that he might, without worry of a knock upon his door (now I see), roll before us an instrument we were forbidden to employ in any wood- or resentment-gathering activities of our own), followed in his middle fifties by an "unpublishable" novel (why is it that I have set this cruellest mouthful in quotes? is it only because I gave matching barrettes to her better-off cousin, above? am I trying, that is, to be fair? and would that not constitute, in this charred and violent hour, a critical fallacy?) on the theme of Jefferson and his own vainglorious self (my father's, I mean, or mean mostly), once he had squandered off (again, my father), in the near thirty-year interregnum between these disparate efforts (during which he expressed himself primarily through those studied grunts and silences and lashings out), what chance he ever had to grow himself up against the language, and to gain some purchase on it that might have loosened, if not avoided entirely, its kudzu-like purchase on me) where the page before him had rotted with envy and unuse.

Within this dilated moment, as we stared out over the jagged black remains of a hundred-acre wood (poor Pooh! poor Piglet!), and took in that panel of red and gold sky newly visible just beyond it, I swear I could almost smell the synapses firing within my father's brain so as to tug toward his skull what rainbow array of wires our great God-arsonist had laid beneath his cheeks all those fond years prior, which gift and which foresight produced a smile I think anyone would want to call explosive.

An excellent theory

A n excellent theory, and one we might still hear raised by
the surviving members of our party, but I ask you this:
What claustrophobe, really, would have shown such a
calmness as my father did when the snow came down like a
beeless quilt over house and yard and field and tree, and put
an end to any long-term thinking on his part or on ours, and
by the hush that followed drew all near to all? What claustrophobe would not have lumbered away from that hokey
gulag after the first foot had fallen, rather than slump beside
a stove whose fumes (and those of the cigarettes he lit one
after the other with matches scraped across her pouty lower
lip) robbed him breath by breath of the wind required to
order his children out into the yard to gather what scraps of
firewood there could still be construed as dry? What claustrophobe would not have gone naked and expansively mobile
at these times, rather than swaddle himself fashionably in
layers of flannel and denim and down, and tuck himself su-
pine into a dirt-backed snow, and offer his beard to a lower-
ing sky determined by its flakes to cover him completely?
What claustrophobe would then have so stoically scooted,
with atrophied legs, the whole of his torso up under a house
he knew all the while to be sinking down onto him, there to
tarry in that tomb for hours and for eras, melting with a
blowtorch what ice had formed in, and clogged, and threat-

ened as usual to burst (though we had left all the faucets
trickling at night, as he ever commanded we do), a hiero-
glyph of town pipes his floor had neither the aptitude to de-
cipher nor the historical expectation to suspend?

What claustrophobe, I ask you, would have shown so
cramped a mercy as he did when it was finally uncovered that
his sons floated close to their bedding of a frigid night, and
emptied themselves (shyly at first, though later in more ex-
pressive torrents) against what breach had formed, almost
conveniently, between the upper and lower sashes of a chatter-
ing window in their chamber, so as to cause (or by these efforts
contribute to) a frozen yellow seepage that began well within
the confines of the capsule itself and proceeded, seeking gravity and some semblance of atmosphere, down the outer face of
the bottom pane and along a sloping sheet of metal miles
below (or was it inches? we could not tell), at whose far end it
terminated, on your colder orbits anyway, in a stalactite depending from, and drawing special attention to, a stopped if
formerly earthbound gutter?

What claustrophobe, or besides that what agoraphobe
(what flasher, i.e., what slinker? what promoter of his children?
what tucker away of them? what facilitator, by word, of their
passage through this void? what destroyer, by wire, of any hope
they may have had not to fear its wide expanse?), mindful that
our little rock-candy formulation might be spotted easily from
the road below and denounced for the shamelessness of its art-
istry, with perhaps some few points tacked on for the veracity
of the statement being made (or was it the statement that
would call down the censure, on account of a gaucherie, with
some ground given grudgingly on the more delicate matter of
form? one could never be sure), would not then have whaled on
his sons for such an offense, and held them in suspicion ever
after, and laid upon them a penance more severe than the quiet

moonlight removal, by stick and stove-boiled water, of what sculpture their penises had planned out (on the theme of mortality and immediate need), and by a personal warmth carved into, across a rusted stretch of porchtop their father would in time demand rent from his sight and appraisal altogether?

There persists a desire

If he was a claustrophobe, then, I cannot show it to my satisfaction, nor I expect to anyone else's, since the replays here
will tend to confuse. His one recorded text, entitled "The Suicide of Salinger's Seymour Glass," and afforded four whole
pages in the aforementioned *Studies in Short Fiction* (summer
1972; Newberry College; Newberry, South Carolina), strikes me
as a little like that: it counts itself bold where it has been only
careful; it holds itself safe on innovation's bag where it has been
called out paragraphs ago, by contact with any number of
missed opportunities, such as when my father came up short in
this inning yet awarded himself a remarkable run:

> All that is left to explain is the cause of Seymour's suicide,
> and that explanation, I believe, is evident. The nearly con-
> scious desires expressed in his bananafish story and in his
> erotic pretense with the girl are made fully conscious to him
> by Sybil's innocent responses to his story and to the kiss on
> her foot. The only solution for Buddy's saint is suicide.

The first sentence there is a perfunctory swing whose back
half is convinced that it has reached base easily, I suppose on an
error. The next is so steeped in a dead Viennese's weak tea, or
deprived of his cocaine, as to be judged no better than an un-
derstimulated attempt to steal second. (That high-school hop

from "nearly conscious" to "fully conscious," and of course the tossing off of "erotic pretense" and "kiss on her foot," could not help but stay even the swiftest runner.) (So why do I pursue this? Under whose aegis? Chasing what result? My father did not follow, nor that I know of know the first thing about, baseball, and so the fun that it is by far the least claustrophobic of our national sports can earn me next to nothing here, whereas his already established interest in basketball, America's purer pastime and a much more intimate undertaking, might at a minimum allow me to ask how closely he ever observed that game's playing, and how consciously he ever considered its less crickety metaphor to hug our more crickety predicament. Perhaps I should have gone instead, as he surely would have, with a literary analogy, or a theft: Would not the time-honored, or -forged (or is it really only the imitated?), *Odyssey* have gone better in this spot? Better even than the more Iliadic to-and-fro of basketball? Or of that girded and chaotic scrum we call football, which I never once watched him watch? Would it not have smacked the ear sounder, this round and salty sea tale, than ever could the squared-off, corn-syrup argument of baseball?) That last sentence there is your classic bunt: well executed, I agree, but not subtle enough to promote a player already thrown out at first all the way to third, let alone to bring him triumphantly (or was it really only vengefully?) home.

There persists a desire in children, however damaged (the children or the desire), for their parents to be, in some inevitable way, right. I cannot with much probity pooh-pooh that hope, having once been a child myself, nor can I overlook now, out of childish sentiment, the blur in its pus-speckled mirror: that there persists in adults a desire, however damaged (the desire or the adults), for their children to be, in some inevitable way, wrong. My own close shave with American parents has led me to conclude that these images might be interchangeable, insofar as they come up against (if from different angles, and at different times) the same impassable barrier across what still (faint flashes!) exists of my moral-aesthetic continuum. I too find it repulsive to blame a parent in and by our literature for any crime perpetrated against a young and defenseless (or was it really only a memorable?) me, but I find it equally repulsive to pardon a parent in and by that same literature, comprising as it can but impressions of thoughts about memories of thoughts about memories of events I may not have remembered all that well to begin with, or thought about with any great clarity since.

With that baseball foolery, for example (*let's play two!*), I was probably only groping at, or toward, as I completed the loop metaphorically but left metaphysical matters caught in a run-down between second and third, untrustworthy thoughts about untrustworthy remembrances of untrustworthy objects being hurled at my unmetaphorical (at the time) and (at the same time) unmetaphysical head like nature's outré chin music. That is, my father would, on occasion, fell a tree whose chunks were not so easily split as were pine's into pieces small enough for the stove's little strike zone to admit, which decision would see us out swinging exhaustedly in the yard for hours on end, using his maul to drive iron wedges into the petrified wood until it spread open like a schoolgirl beneath the bleachers at the bottom of the seventh ("Which wedge did it? Really? I thought sure you'd put that in the wrong crack"), or else seized up and blew one of these intrusions past our iced and idiot skulls at an audible velocity, in what I took at the time to be a willful attempt by God, or by the log, *but surely not by our own manager,* to brain us.

(Forgive me)

S till, this manager would, I know, could I cool his ash down and interview it (postgame) on the matter, be forced, out of a lingering American parenthoodness, to quibble with me there: not so much on the particulars of my conclusion, which he would get at soon enough, as on its pretense to being, by way of that patently faked desperation, and that hardly-to-be-humored-anymore anger, and that damnable glibness, an innocent string of guesses, as opposed to what it more obviously was: a couched and perverted stab at him.

(My father, forgive me, was a man to toss homegrown insults around, and puppies, but never a factory-stitched ball.)

Malocchio

S tabs, perverted or no, he could stomach and even admire,
whether directed at his individualistic fat (now rendered) or
at yours. Guesses he would cock an atheistic eye (hole? pearl?)
at and pay no further attention to, so long as these could be
imagined (by a once imaginative brain, now simple salts and
vapors) to be, after the fashion then (which I hear tell is the
fashion yet again), "genuine." A couched anything, easily tolerated in his personal misbehavior, and absolutely prized in the
work of those "real" writers he referenced or read out loud to us
(through a vicarious vanity of his own, I imagine, or I guess),
tended nonetheless to confound him in any doing of ours, as if
both doing and doer were akin somehow to that overrun (or
was it already a granulated?) beachhead in his spine, which joist
(or which column, or which question mark) would shortly go
the same fiery way as all the meat that had dared to conceal it,
and all the flab that had hidden away all the meat, and all the
thinness of skin that might have encouraged, rather than hin-
dered, his turning a hot head around to cast one last melting
malocchio upon a stretch of oily back a-blister like a curtain
pushed playfully from behind by the company cutup and then
caused, by way of a single faulty footlight (*pop!*), too dramatically, if alas too tardo, to immolate.

The killer-log conceit he would dismiss as a Romantic sil-
liness: "The cure for that sort of thing is Ruskin. Ruskin's

really something. You should try Ruskin." (SON: *I like Ruskin fine. I just think the fun in it all may have eluded him.* FATHER: *Well, I doubt you'd get anywhere with Ruskin there. Ruskin always thought the problem through.* SON: *By half, maybe. Bathetic fallacy is more what I say. Wasn't he the one afraid of pubic hair?* FATHER: *Well—* SON: *You know, we ought to have employed a playwright here, if we couldn't afford the librettist. Sophocles? O'Neill? Synge?* FATHER: *Well, Ruskin tended to wrestle with his subject. You should probably give Ruskin a try.*)

The killer-God idea he would counter with a grunt, or a sniff, or a grunt-sniff, so as to demonstrate by this gesture how ontologically brave he was (and I will allow that he did die bravely: it was only his living that could have done with more panache), which would leave us here with but his "genuine" motivations to sift through, and his by now burnt-up rendition of the erstwhile sun-faded facts, and his eventual homing back in on, as the one worthy topic of talk between us (correct!), not the *meanness* I had meant when I implied that he both had and had not wished to see us killed by those wedges out in the yard but rather the *meantness* I had meant when I implied that neither one of us had necessarily meant to mean either.

Meanness, you see, came so easily to the earthly him that I would be shocked if his expirant too did not consider it almost a trivial subject, like breathing might be to those who have never known trouble breathing. (Deep inhale . . .) Meantness, on the other hand, or lung, gave him regular hiccups, and was a constant bellows to his own Romantic sillinesses, which blew across my childhood as delectably as did all those smelly little zephyrs bearing with them the news, if never quite the word, that a too-proud manse to the east of us (FATHER: *Wasn't Zephyrus the west wind?*), or else a too-ashamed shack nearer by, had the night before been consumed innard-outward by flame (and how unlike what will happen to humans!) on account of its having been occupied by "morons" with no idea how "properly" to "tend" a stove, which attitude presented even when the cause of the fire was clearly electrical (as our novice noses could readily detect and his, a guilded wirer's, surely must have), and which attitude could not then help but alarm us, given that our father had for years played the stooge to his too-well-tended Franklin (inventor of wood heaters and fire departments alike, the bastard), and had stuffed it so full of tar-drunk pine, and lead-painted boards, and anything else that would hotly and unsafely burn, as to send God knows what future incendiaries up the chimney to clutch at its innards like gargoyles and await their inevitable crack at revanche.

The worst of these Romantic sillinesses (my father's, I mean, or mean mostly) was a confused New Critic's conviction that whereas a log might be no more than a log, and a wedge might be no more than a wedge, and a childhood might be no more than a childhood, the same could not be said of "log" and "wedge" and "childhood" and "might" and "be" and "no" and "more" and "than" and "a," which totems he refused to accept for what they plainly were: descriptive (and therefore only proximate, and therefore ever maddening) *occurrences* that by eye and ear, or by ear and fingertip (thinking now of the blind), or by eye alone (thinking ever of the deaf), took a measurable, material form while fairly flaunting their refusal to make manifest those allegedly more "real" things, or imagined relationships between said "real" things, they were shaped millennia ago to represent, yes, but then were prophesied (Who did this? *Why?*) one day, impossibly, to become.

No, my faithless father (or was he, in this context, being oddly faithful?), unwilling to wait for the needless miracle that would make any scribble or scream of his as "real" as what he had physically done unto the trees, or by his backswings done unto us, sought to mortgage every word he encountered out into the future until it both was, in a legal sense (Romantic approach, early American variant), and was *not quite yet*, in

a logical sense (reasonable approach, late American compromise), half tantamount to its referent not just in these dumb
gists but, extrapolating one small step further here, its Twee-
dledee at least in a fatuous third, by which "log" is universally
understood as *indicating/becoming,* and therefore, what the
hey, *already being,* something more powerful than the mere
smudged stand-in for, or even the sharp-breathed reminder
of, what corporeal log awaited us at the edge of the corporeal
forest, the corporeal snake or spider beneath that log no
match, if you think on it enough (or too little), for what
venom awaited all of humanity beneath or because of the
non-non-noncorporeal word.

Which is only to say that my father held all words, and certainly all words of ours, which seemed real enough to us (and
were!), to be capable of a great and ghostly treason if not tackled and pinned down against their connotations by the proper
authorities, which by droit du seigneur always meant him,
whose own denotations were then left free to roam the countryside bare-assed until they stumbled upon, or transformed
themselves into (who can say how this happens?), such gross
apparitions as even he could not conscionably have believed in:

> . . . it seems to me not implausible to suggest that Seymour's
> enjoyment of foot-trampling is sexual and that his attack on
> Charlotte is motivated by sexual aggression. Admittedly,
> this is a suggestion that few Seymour fans, Buddy among
> them, would care to make . . .

this shy golem followed, a paragraph later, by the frumious
paradox of

> I hope, however, that it has not yet become an axiom of Sa-
> linger criticism that the author's intentions may not be sepa-
> rated from the beliefs of his characters.

What a lovely notion, I declare, this apartheid of "author" from "character," and "intention" from "belief," and "Salinger" from "criticism," and "axiom" from "hope," were words what my father suspected them of being and so ever demanded they be. But words are not demons, not yet, any more than they are seraphim. They are words, and thus wholly earthen vessels, and their morality (for all our faith in that particular vessel) will not alter with what company as they keep. Or are denied: I myself would wish it otherwise, would prefer that I could *mean* here rather than shuffle words around so that they but *appear* to mean, would be delighted if words could be arranged so as to *be meanness* rather than crudely describe and parody the stuff, for I am mean indeed. My father's actions, by wire and wanting word, made perfect sure of that.

Such was not my intention

J. D. Salinger died yesterday, up the country. Or was it the month before, downtown? Such was not my intention, nor even, initially, my belief. Had I but known this character still sucked air I would have butchered him 14 pages ago, so as to sync his death more poignantly with that of his coughing critic and unwitting, if unoriginal, creator.

My father mostly copped to having created me, though I doubt it ever occurred to him that he had also created, in the shadowy yet no less phenomenal realm of language (if only by accident, and if only for a secondary son), the character J. D. Salinger, so that I might reflect upon that, his creation of the character J. D. Salinger, in conjunction with his more problematic creation of me, and wonder, with the longer-dead but newer-wrote character Wm. Styron (whom my father always called a fraud), which one of us, if he had to, would he choose?

His was, I admit, a weak me (a worthwhile child would not have resorted to the Styron cliché), but was his Salinger not a touch too urbane to be viable here? He knew, I suppose, this Salinger, how to situate a young girl on a piano bench to smile and peck and flirt, and how to kneel her rival down on a beach towel to conversate and beg for a swim and be told a filthy story, but could he know how teenage boys not enrolled in fancy prep schools were sent out sullenly into southern yards to palm and fling frozen dog turds past the barbed-wire fences, so that they might trudge, these boys, around or through said turds toward a pile of impassable logs their father had decreed be fetched without vehicular assistance, since even a big Dodge truck's axle might be broken by ruts along the way?

We went in for Dickens at those times, not Salinger (nor Styron, nor Hardy, nor even the oddest Brontë, though we had plenty call to), and counted ourselves artful whenever our father went missing for an hour or two or three, and we could drive his cheap little sedan back across the field, and fill her trunk and passenger seats with what wood as we were expected to bear up bodily that day, betting rightly that he would think to inspect only the truck's tires and chassis for dog shit upon his too-energetic return. He would accuse us, of course, of having made use of the big Dodge anyway, which I swear we never once did, but I will barter this injustice of his for a happier one of our own: that on many occasions we accomplished his country work, and till his death he never knew about it, with that machine of his best suited to town.

My father is mostly gone now, with all his machinery, and good riddance. To the machinery, I mean, more so than the man, though some will say that by the very shabbiness of this disclaimer I aim to have it both ways here (they have my support, both the "some" and the "ways"), which must therefore constitute an intellectual cowardice on my part (support withdrawn), if not an ethical failure (injunction filed), and might even be considered a crime by and against our literature (charges brought), the local variant of this product recognizing but a single meaning meant per square utterance (judgment handed down), so as not to breach the implicit contract between potentially abusive producer and unfairly overtaxed consumer (firing squad convened).

I see no need for false civility here. Fathers write, and sons read, and sons then write, and fathers then die before they can read what their sons have written against them. It is a pity, pure, but unavoidable. My personal dead father, whose pearls alone I ever wanted to pore over this imitation coral made, chose instead at his drowning to try (try again?) Faulkner's *Light in August,* as opposed to the thinner and more buoyant *As I Lay Dying,* which joke all his read-up children made in their turn as they watched him get no further than a fur piece into September before it was finally asked, by simple human decency, that they feed him enough morphine to ensure that the first few pages of the first work would wash up at least sensibly against the last few pages of the last.

(All these Bills.)

With my own thumb I administered the crucial dose, or will swear that I did, though the hospice nurse claimed later (Sharon? Karen? Charon?), when I asked her about any legal exposure here, that we had stayed within all acceptable bounds, and that she had seen forty-pound "babies," riddled and forsook, take more dope in a day than our father had in a week and still suffer on, which explanation I accepted as a practical, if also a subversive (and therefore a perfectly American), lie, which lie then led me almost to love her, whose one great contribution to our cause (leaving aside all those catheter-bag lectures, and those seminars on ultimate (or was it penultimate?) bowel movements, and that advice on how to grind Ativan tablets down into a liquefiable powder, which tutelage I did not anyway require) had been to conduct us toward the truth that the only way around a death scored in ancestral screams and whimpers was to target and kill, without remorse, the slated and much-gossiped-about performer.

I had thought to fire him sooner

I had thought to fire him sooner, this diva, though out of conscience or convention I demurred. When he sent a southern
paw into my formerly northern yap over an infraction I and the
law had already agreed to forget, and split the right side of my
lip against its resident incisor, which ensured that my smile
would forever be altered, and I would never make a decent noise
out of my trumpet again, I might have done more than simply
grab and throw him to the floor, and kick his legs out from
under him when he tried to rise up, and lean over his huffing fat,
and promise that I would carve my hatred into his face as he had
just done mine if he did not apologize at once for the shredded
embouchure (which term he did not fully comprehend) and the
blood spilt down the front of my shirt (which term he fully did),
whereupon, ass-anchored and winded against the wainscoting,
he started in with the legalese, and professed that it was not yet
"permitted" in "the Commonwealth of Virginia" for "a child to
lay hands upon a parent," and that he was therefore "well within"
his "rights" to have me "committed to the courts," which I urged
him then to go ahead and do, since I was curious to know how
even a Goochland judge might rule, after an athletic young A-
maker such as myself had taken the stand, on the matter of
which one of us warranted a beating and which one of us more
properly belonged in jail.

Understanding that it was not the punch there but only the

legalese that had made me want to ponder patricide, my reader
should know that I first encountered this fey impulse several
years earlier, when our father abruptly installed, at his wife's
wet coercion, four units of baseboard heating along the house's
front rooms, which by chance included mine, these units finally
activated one gray and unprecipitate Christmas Eve so as to
coincide almost magically with the arrival of my mother's
pinched parents (and a schizophrenic scion), bearing with them
their boxed-up booze, and their bottled-up resentments, and
an open conviction that no daughter of theirs should have
dared to mate with so feral a creature as our father plainly was,
which conviction, and which resentments, and which booze,
made for costly eruptions in the kitchen, and an appetite for
vindication at the dinner table, and a wino knife fight that
began well before grace and stretched out entertainingly into
the hours and days before us, the one seeming rule here being
that no thrust by an adult in this fray should ever be so overt as
to allow a feral half-child to pick up on it, though of course that
was always the goal ("My God! They barely use forks!"), since
for whom else was all this intended, the swipes and the accusals
and the barbs, if not for those same little half-innocent half-
jurists who would scramble up out of their half-beds on the
half-bless'd Morn to discover a trail of comic books (we could
not be trusted, after all, truly to *read*) leading down each step
toward a father's poached and hastily hung fir (the haste there
being about as necessary as was the poaching), beneath which
awaited them what mall-bought toys and sweaters as the sotted
in their number thought fit bribes for a silence on the matter of
who, exactly, hated whom in this nativity set; and why, and to
what end (the Advent-calendar chocolate all eaten), their
mother would weep inconsolably as her parents' town car sped
away (hard-driven by the schizophrene); and how, and at what
price, her children would ignore both tire and tear to return to
a board game upstairs, robed as they were for once in an atmo-

sphere of comfort and joy, until at last they looked up to see a father's huge and hairy arm snake around the doorjamb to turn the thermostat on the wall above them back to zero, where by rights they knew it belonged, but why now? *Why just then?*

I might have sunk him for that, or for a thousand and one other slights, but in the moment, or those, I refrained, hoping I might eventually be gifted the chance to vouch him a hero in this report and not its abject suzerain. I made no direct move against him when he raised me up out of a smelly bag the night before a failed chemistry exam (or was it English?) to top off an already wood-drunk dragon whose sleepy burps would never reach the frigid corner where I myself lay dying, nor did I any-wise plot to kill him on that parentless, pointless snow day when his misguided firstborn, bored and possibly as crazed as I was by the work and isolation imposed upon us by a stupidly clever (or was it a cleverly stupid?) sire, wondered aloud, this future chem-ist of the language, what the result would be if he let some drops of his urine fall upon a stovetop he had seen make dancing and ephemeral beads out of our spit, which assay my sister and I begged him please to abort but could stay neither his curiosity nor his pee, whose instant, acrid stench upon the creature's hunched back (so much worse than my ejaculate had smelled!) drove us deep into the yard, nauseated and quickly ashiver, to stare at one another with a wild surmise over the scale of this calamity, which hours' worth of running back into the house, in shifts based on birth order (our breath held at first, then taken), to throw open a window and make it safely out to gag in the snow again (or else to toss heavy panfuls of gyroscoping water onto a devil we had never imagined had the means to do so pungent an evil unto us), could not dispel, nor could it prevent (given the surety of meltdown) our dragon from proclaiming, come dinnertime, that his lair was "too fucking cold" and that someone (staring directly down at me) royally stank.

Yet was this ogre-king, teched and repatriated by the Cold

War countryside, with its Potemkin charms and samizdat horrors, at all the same as the young czarevitch who had once traded sleep and sobriety to write, during a foiled escape to town (1965–1976: hunted by the land, ratted out by the in-laws), that Salinger's lovely "Hapworth 16, 1924," while not my father's ostensible subject in 1972, any more than it is mine today, seemed

> intended to be a demonstration of Seymour's genius and an indication that Seymour is fully versed in oriental religion and remembers well his former states of existence . . .

and was there really, if the answer is no, any harm in killing such a one?

What, then, will it win your occidental son to save him?

Past performances

I myself can recall but a few past performances, bleeding too easily into that singular sentence of childhood I try (partly) and fail (completely) to reconstruct (unfaithfully) here. Yet I suppose it at least conceivable that my unborn-again father, soon enough to present as mortuary smoke, might more accurately have remembered, and based his decisions about our future former selves upon, some several.

I suppose it likely as not that he stayed close pals with that boyhood him, who came to associate "farm" with "work," yes, but also with a kind of freedom, et into only when he heard his mother's screams from the fields abutting his wooded playpen, or from farther on up at the house, and knew then to run and fetch her into a vehicle he would by dial or happenstance steer, at nine or ten or eleven (his profligate father away at clocked work on the railroad), into the nearest approximation of town, so that she might there be delivered of a tenth or eleventh or twelfth child those fields could not feed, nor those trees hope to shelter, nor that encumbrance-hating boy ever bring himself fully to ignore.

He might have maintained a shy contact with that terrified teenage him, tossed too late into a town high school once his parents had concluded that their surviving children would not warrant the epithet much longer without infra-

structural assistance. The only fun to be had there was basketball, which an older him admitted the younger him had
played poorly. The college-bound him he would have admired and felt a sharp pang for, as I do now, not knowing
which response applies more properly to the farmboy mus-
cles, say, secretly acquired in town, or to the south-midland
accent dropped in favor of a Confederate professor's more
sonorous snarl, or to the "choice" to attend classes nearby,
when he might have gone anywhere, so as to hasten him home
each weekend to chop wood on the farm his parents had
since, in their stubbornness, returned to, with so many hungry children in tow that he was forced on those occasions to
sleep out on straw in the barn.

Even I would exchange Christmas cards with that him of
hims, were I at all the sort to exchange Christmas cards.

The remainder of my fathers I knew personally, with the
possible exception of his sportsfan ghost, and I assume these all
to have chatted incessantly: on how best, and how often, to
whip an unwanted child; on what it meant, or did not mean, to
whip an unwanted child; on whether the whipping of an unwanted child was proof enough, if only for the unwanted child,
of the nonexistence of God; on the ways in which *psychology*
might be used to explain away the need to whip an unwanted
child, just as *philosophy* might be used to explain the need to
whip away an unwanted God; on how *literature* (being what
psychology and *philosophy* would ever amount to anyway) might
provide any number of neat justifications for it: the whipping, I
mean here, not the deity, and certainly not the child.

I was just fiddling with one of these neat justifications
myself when our stove took Romantically ill, and although
tamped down for the night, and so shut of any unfresh new air,
could not contain what dispute had burgeoned within its belly
that day, and so sent great bursts of superheated gas up the

stovepipe in a forgivable attempt to relieve itself, which then lent holy succor to the creosotic rebellion that had clung to the house's butthole in a long and patient abeyance there.

I both welcomed and feared this coup, and asked that it succeed even as I instinctually fought against it, and crawled out onto the icy tin roof of the side porch, and steadied as best I could a ladder raised high against the roof beams, and helped my sock-footed brother scale those same rungs as his author had, and ferried up to him what pailfuls of water our sister, in perpetual prayer against the chimney's jet-engine whine, swung out the window to me, whose grip was uncertain, and whose faith in the enterprise slipped a little each time I saw my father, proud and erect above the flames, toss an empty down into the yard for his half-naked wife to dart out and retrieve, and fill once more at the tub's narrow spigot, and slop up those stairs her man had built because of and despite her, and deliver her load to a daughter who within the hour would play Juliet to volunteer firemen awash in her embarrassment, poking at this brick, and at that patch of siding, and watching where it was they stepped, until at last they had concluded, with no look up at her, that this fire had long since been joined and extinguished.

We tarried too in her skybox, and waited for the volunteers to make their smug departure, as if this had all been no more than another failed country tent revival, at which point our devil reawoke, and spat its orangey black up at the stars while all those lesser lights meant to save us disappeared around the bend. I remember that I scrambled quickly past her then, and set the ladder up much as I had before, and watched my father, and my brother just after him, climb heavenward to reinstate their hard tribute in water. Our mother went after those empties in the yard now with stronger legs, and with a calmer panic, and I got the sense that she was not acting anymore, or else had achieved some new level to her art: a "realistic" presentation of a woman wholly convinced just then that anything short of a full-on belief in her man, and by extension his miserable children, would surely result in the combustion of her matrimonial bed (being closest to the fire) and, given time, all our littler ones besides.

A velocity finally sufficient

I ought to have yelled up at him there, or beyond him up at her God, that I knew what they both were doing; that I had reconciled myself to the truth that Someone Else's hand might forever stay my own; that there were several on this planet, and at least One up above it, who had me figured for a pawn in their game, unworthy even of the modest bishopric I now played for (queen being quite beyond me by then), so that I might venture out catercorner of an evening to bestow my dull blessing, perchance to imbed a sharp blade.

Here is all I have left for a blessing:

My father, who beat me constantly at chess too, could not possibly have meant for his children to grow up so nostalgically enslaved to the countryside as he himself had been, and to long for it even as they tried and failed to fly its sucking gravity. He could not possibly have intended for his children to linger in that well for the threescore and change allotted them, unable to decide whether Earth's dumb trial was preferable, in this age of happy moonbounces, to the testy chatter available in town. And so he had resolved to make the tough call for us, in the only way he knew would excuse a wrong answer: He would hurt his children in the woods so as to force their eyes back upon devalued buttcheeks, rather than up at overpriced real estate in the sky. He would lead us not into temptation about the holiness of the trees, as he himself had felt (the temptation, not the holiness), but rather would deliver us, by means of a farm-bound misery, from the evil of thinking no good could ever come from town, where prior to his dying we were each of us ensconced, which then afforded him the defense of thinking that his hand, and our sorry hinds, had somehow achieved a velocity finally sufficient to escape the dirt he need not ever have returned to in the first place.

And if we slowed in that velocity, and sometimes let on about what harm town had lately done us, he would find himself comfortably within his rights (which was the goal here, after all, that comfort, and those rights) to look up at his exasperated wife, and wink, and say, "Well . . ."

Here, then, is what I retain for a blade:

I ought to have let that ladder go the second time I saw him climb up on it, yelling at me to hold the base steady and oathing that he would break my "scrawny fucking neck" if I failed to do otherwise. I ought, God help me, to have let that ladder go. If for no other reason than that the ersatz country boy atop it, so weak as to surrender every one of us to his personal torturer, and not man enough nearly to plot out the coordinates of a halfway decent escape, once opened a town essay by writing

> Since its publication in 1948, Salinger's "A Perfect Day for Bananafish" has received a large amount of critical attention, much of it concerned with attempts to explain the reason for Seymour's suicide.

Who would think to ignite a career so coldly? Or to extinguish one mixing memory and desire with disdain?

My brother, at least, might have survived the fall.

BOOK SIX

Horrid twist
(For those still keeping
    track)
My subterfuge began
A taste for Sousa
Americans about it
Good eating
Advocate
Cheerios
Wonder Bread
Fun story
A litany here
Want of angels
Is it possible
Redemption
My father's axe

Horrid twist

Weird county;
    Whose dirt was devoid of richness;
Whose humans were despoiled of sense;
Whose name could boast of no increase except in the multifold categories of shame;

Whose foundation of shifty gneiss, exposing itself characteristically near the men's state prison, so differed from the rest of Virginia that it was chipped at and pored over, this "Goochland terrane," by geologists who could in no way account for its origin or for its mysterious properties, thought by some to be related to the early formation of Manhattan (of all places) and by others to the breakup of a larger continent, long ago, that otherwise left no foreign elements secreted within our own;

Whose anomalous rock might have come from Mars, for all I care, or been donated by a passing comet, since I personally hold it to be no more, and no less, than the fungal big toenail of Lucifer as he kicks, across eons, at America from below;

Whose abhorrence knew full well what changes might be worked upon a human child who listens too carefully to the trees, and asks why they shudder and whistle and crack as they do, and seem always to be moving closer; and so turns for comfort to a "community" of peers who will lead it, with laudable speed, to accept bias and barbarity as down-homey truths, especially where they lead on to war; and so runs back to a mother who will come to regard it (not unfairly: she, too, is trying to fit in) as a simp and a secularist and a probable faggot; and so seeks wisdom, if no more understanding, from a father intending to workhorse his seed so hard that it will flee not only the land but also the simple notion that it might one day safely return there;

Whose product, I am convinced, and that great fungal toenail has always known, will rebel against nearly everyone in this scenario and will embrace the one apparent refuge left open to it, being unfortunately, and usually for keeps, its natural surrounds;

By which I can mean only Goochland.

Whether my father arranged this horrid twist in me, so that I might learn for myself how devastating even a sham attachment to the dirt would prove; or whether he merely allowed it, half hoping I might come at last (by way of a reverse *psychology*, which usually worked on the more emotionally disturbed JDs) to adore the dirt as he had always felt forced to; or whether he intended, this teacher of words and maths, only the first derivative (my rebellion against the dirt) and was therefore wholly flummoxed by the second (my rebellion against his plot to have me rebel against the dirt), and so slumped in his underwear and grew ever more despondent while his second son (and what of the first? *the first!*) pretended to pretend to be a country boy, and then just pretended, and then just was (or thought he was), I cannot say. Nor does it much confront me. I imagine that our continent has for ages now replenished its rural meatlocker by this same insidious snare.

I would ask my father to comment here, except that I killed him a few pages back, and no ventriloquism of mine ("Hold that fucking ladder or I'll . . ."; "Pay some goddamned attention or I'll . . ."; *"What in the hell is wrong with you?"*) will convince the reader that a pile of cool ashes is able, or willing, to puff straight answers out at anyone. I can only, then, try to be accurate about my own petty motivations:

Had our house up and exploded that chimney-fire night, and caught me out stuck to the roof, of a mind to jump off it but melted there by Judas soles, until the whole of my clothing took fire and I screamed in silence, my breath burnt away, and prayed to get out of those boots before I popped like a kernel and sent all my fluff up to God; had my devout yet town-hip mother been less apt to say, in those days of oaths and accusations (hers, mostly, the accusations), "Don't be so melodramatic," which hypocrisy I would gladly excuse, had that little "so" of hers, borrowed along with the rest of the phrase, not itself been so melodramatic (; had I but known then of melodrama's place in my melodramatic future); had I but resolved, all those decades ago, to remain forever a stranger to that corruptive county and never to allow myself, if only for a year or two or three, by means of a steady retreat down Jacob's unsteady stair, to be transformed into a proudly defensive, ecstatically religious, uselessly horny, country-smug moron, whose own parents would not have recognized him (though it cannot be said that they tried), we might have made an easier go of it ahead. We might have been able to sustain the fiction that a rhetoric of complaint is the one true path across memories of a perfectly ordinary American childhood, wherein delight and contentment, feigned at first, fine, but for that no less experienced, and no more given over to facile caricature than the complaint thus far has been, offer up their own loud and hair-raising hues.

(For those still keeping track)

(Do not reject me, please, for what joy I am about to express, or pretend to express (see above, and below), in Goochland's gross particularities. Is there a child born of woman who will not seek out pleasure where it can? Is there a child born to man who will not doubt that same pleasure?

(Do not discard me either as an ironist, for God knows I am nothing of the sort. Pretending to pretend I find no more honest, or dishonest, than pretending not to pretend, and neither of these masks will much, of itself, enhance the reality I pretend now to pretend not to pretend to.

(I am after, I hope, what lies beyond these two obvious choices, in that realm where I forever evade one possibility and forever chase after the other, or I guess am hunted, alternately or in tandem, and again forever, by both.

(Do also forgive, while we are at it, this late directness in me, which is meant primarily, if not exclusively, for those still keeping track.)

My subterfuge began

M y subterfuge began with the chickens. We had been reading Hardy in the high school, probably because our
teacher, who lived in Richmond's West End and I believe did
her best, thought the pastoral themes in his writing might at
long last "speak" to us. She was a close and clever reader of poetry, that I can recall, but she had fallen victim to the delusion
that novels were not constructions in the manner of poems, to
be clambered over and admired (if not always fallen for), but
rather were instructors, such as she imagined herself to be, of
how, and why (or was it really only whether?), to stay afloat in
the flood of life's tears.

Jude the Obscure stood at least a chance of scaring me up out
of the water, but it was *Tess of the d'Urbervilles* we were expected to grab onto, and that raft quickly capsized. We were
already familiar with the yeoman sort of naturalism, and betrayed by it, so there was no real news there, and we had learnt
from the land-puppeted fists of our peers what airs like Tess's
pa put on would get you. Yet our teacher, inferring from our *Yes,
and?* looks that most of us had failed even to open the book,
which was probably the case, persisted in her mission, and
made us watch *Tess* (1979) on a television set rolled in by a kid
from the disabled room whose every step held in it more drama
than the film ever could.

She then went on to explain, God help her, about the

symbolism at work here, and about how Tess, portrayed by the Kinski girl, whom we had all by then seen with a snake curled around her privates on a friend's sagging farmhouse wall, was clearly the prey in this situation, driven on every side by malevolent nature, but we understood about that too, and some of us even got that the reason our school emptied out at the start of each deer season was less about hunting than it was about feeling, if only for a day or two, or fourteen, less hunted oneself. This wisdom extended even to the gaudy orange garb those hunters wore: any uniform will make one feel momentarily like a cop, especially with a gun in one's hands, but in time the truth sets in that orange uniforms are worn far more often, and in vastly greater numbers, by the imprisoned.

I tried to be kind to this teacher, and not lash out at her as I did with most others, since I thought her both smart and pretty (not Kinski-with-a-snake pretty, but still) and only bewitched by the county's evil, as opposed to willfully ignorant of it, and because she was divorced and unhappy and hence (one can hope) sensitive to all those drowning metaphors of mine. (Some few of us had returned, in loud desperation, to the sea that had delivered our families to this haunted shore in the first place, and saw them off inland to be petrified there (I knew of a Goochlander who sat every day outside a gas station and in seventy years had never caught a ride into Richmond, even when I offered him one. (HE: *I wouldn't impose.* I: *It's no imposition, sir. I'm headed that way myself.* HE: *I wouldn't care for it.*) Williamsburg, and the great Oceanus beyond, must have seemed mere myths to this man!), though to be fair we ourselves approached it only with another family, more sophisticated than we were but in practical terms no better off (being similarly Catholic), so as to save money, and in tents sure to leak because it was sure to rain, as our guardians had elected to wait until summer was over, again to save money, and we ate cheese sandwiches for our sustenance, and what bits of sand affixed to the cheese and pooled in the bread's greasy chambers, and for warmth we played grab-ass in the deserted waves with a daughter from the opposite family whose father (our immovable own being planted back in Goochland) then gave us a speech about "respect," which by grabbing at her ass we assumed we had been showing her, though in truth we hoped primarily to make our intentions known to her older and more experienced sister up on the beach, sunning herself scandalously and noticing how we noticed not to notice her, until she saw her stiff Christian father jog waterward to lecture us, at which point she grinned and rolled over, as if to show us what an ass worth grabbing at actually looked like.

(I knew she would sneak out of her tent that humid night, and join us all down on the beach, around what fire my brother had built, and then presumably pissed on, out of what wood could be culled from nearby, though throughout the day she had shown little interest in our plans and our gossip. She might have come anyway, but I am guessing that my mother (who earlier that year had met with a teacher who inquired, as they emerged from their conference, whether her second son was liable to grow as large as the first, which elicited a harsh "No!" from my mare, unwilling to see a foal's waxing lust collide with a hag's waning sensibility (I only half mean to imply that this was the same teacher who had exposed us all to Hardy, or even that said teacher was a woman, but in either case my laughter throughout the episode was unwarranted and possibly unwise)) corralled this "mature" girl just after supper, and asked whether she would not mind keeping an eye on the kids tonight (she would have put it that way, my mother, "the kids") while the grownups gulped wine in their grownup tent and congratulated themselves on allowing their children this "important" and "formative" glimpse of freedom, secure in the knowledge that the oldest girl at their disposal, no matter how fecund, was sure to trade clumsy relations in for the chance to be treated, finally, by someone not a kid in this calculus, her actual age.

(And so she would come down to the beach, and sit cross-legged around the fire with the rest of us, in a sweatshirt because it was cold out but still bare enough below to hold our attention, and would not mind any scent of beer or pot she detected, since that was only what she expected anyway, and hours ago might even have encouraged (having been the first in our crowd, or so it was told, to find her way eastward into Richmond by moonlight, with who knows what in tow, to make contact with the riffraff there, and return with talk of new music and genitalia-friendly art films), though if anyone had anything on him that night he would not have brought it out in the presence of such a sudden and obvious adult, who smiled politely while a brother of hers played Beatles tunes on the guitar, keen (she, I mean) to what harmonies might indicate, from across the dune, a bikini bottom pulled off and a baby about to be made.

((I thought then, or should have thought, of that fun little church we all attended, in the fun little hamlet on the fun little hill to the west of our fun little county, and of how much fun it was when the old-lady organist there stabbed out at each note with three or more arthritic fingers, betting that one of these would hit the target and not worrying so much about the others, which ensured that even the most traditional hymn would morph into a modernist free-for-all, with the time signature generally chucked as her phalanges hunted after and failed to locate the melody, which the strongest voices in the chapel did their best to help out with, and also with the tempo, where they had not decided amongst themselves that this one was likely a wash. Now and then, in the midst of this mayhem, I could detect a high warble, not worried so much about the tune, or the beat, but only trying to make music with the crazy

A taste for Sousa

Of the many wonderful experiences I had in the natural world, pained though I am to call them that now (see above, and below) but damned if I will tolerate a convenient dishonesty here, none can rival my bond with the beasts of the air. There were those who sat on a telephone wire like quarter notes so that I might end their tune with a slug to the throat, and there were those who sang out even louder to insinuate that I would never destroy them all. There were those who hooted, or screamed, or pecked out their pentagrams on a tree too close to the house (a friend of mine kept a loaded shotgun against his dresser, so that he might raise the morning caws of crows outside his bedroom window with a more vigorous all-in; his aim was not to "learn" these birds, which had been my initial assumption, so much as it was to abolish the whole of their species: does that not qualify, somewhere, *somewhere*, as wonderful? did van Gogh not envision the same sort of thing before he abolished himself instead?), and then there were those strange little not-birds who gathered in such buzzing number on a classroom windowsill in early fall (or was it late spring?) that I had merely to spit in my palm to attract a candidate I could close my fingers upon, and with a sucked thumb work the tiny head upward until it was exposed, aslant and amazed, at which point I could fasten upon it a slip-knotted old woman, and I knew then that the eldest daughter from the opposite family had returned. From college? From after-college and dalliances there? I did not care: I cared only that she had returned to us with that mind and those lungs. She was considered by most a good sport rather than a good singer, but I knew different, and I suspect the old organist did too.)

(Despite our chaperone hearing no sounds of rape in the dunes that night, or because of it, she arose when she heard the F chord that all but guarantees "Yesterday" and summoned every girl to her bosom, not least my own sister, and lined them up by their differing lengths, and before she led them back to the tents, hand in hand, magnificently as I remember it, she counted them off by touching a comically bent claw to the top of each giggling head. Love, I sometimes think, is that witch finger, and any voice who follows after it.) The point I hoped to make about Tess is that both she and I kept chickens.

leash made out of a strand begged from the scalp of a serious girl who wished not to know what I wanted with her hair.

Hoping to commune with but also to profit from my environs, I conceived of a plan to market my harnessed houseflies as low-maintenance, low-grief pets, and so win the high-school business fair, except that there was no business fair. I planned also to coat myself in a "formula" comprising sugar and buttermilk and cow feces (or human: I had yet to decide), and then "command" these creatures to fetch me something light to which their strings had already been attached (the first-place ribbon, say), and so win the science fair, except that there was no science fair.

After I had learned that there were no betterment fairs at the high school, I tethered these flies to my wrists and shoelaces and even my own tresses, and walked those halls a pariah, whispered to be so evil, or so near death, that the maggots had already got a start on me. A year or two earlier I might have done so out of an anger or a self-pity; I acted now from a joie de vivre. (Around this same time I bet a friend five dollars that within twenty-four hours I could part these same students as if they were the Red Sea, and back them up against their lockers in awe of my passing. I put out the rumor that I had AIDS and by lunchtime the next day had pocketed his money: Tater Tots.) In the bandroom I tied most of these lovelies to the bottom of my music stand, so that they might feed upon what was let loose from the spit valve above, but one favorite I secured to the tubes of my trumpet, so that it might perform its aerobatics while I played, and by chance pass in front of the bell, to be knocked out by the decibels there, and so hang by the neck until it came to, and recollected its capacity for flight, and climbed the air to breach once more the purifying din.

We had lost our original band teacher, a beloved old mustachioed fat man with a taste for Sousa and pedagogical tricks (he dealt with gum chewers by saying that he had once seen a student choke to death on gum while playing "that very same instrument," giving us all the impression that hundreds of kids must have died on this man's watch), when it was finally discovered (we had known it for years) that he also taught band in that despicable county just south of the James, which the Rebs had wisely skirted when they fled Petersburg for Appomattox. Made to choose, he chose the despicable county the Rebs had wisely skirted, as it paid him more, and so we were stuck with a humorless young woman from Richmond who wanted to suck the oompah out of our operation entirely, and transform us into a concert ensemble more suited to her sense of self (based solely, that I could see, on Amy Irving's performance in *The Competition* (1980)), and would eventually, had I not acted at once, take notice of, and predictable exception to, my flies.

I convinced the trumpeter beside me (a recent recruit from shop) to cut his lip gruesomely on his braces and spend the rest of an afternoon spitting blood down into his mouthpiece. In time the teacher stopped us in our playing, and said that the trumpets sounded "gurgly," at which point we pushed all the music stands aside, so that she might properly see, and the boy sitting next to me opened his spit valve and produced a lake of crimson gore so large I was forced, as were several others in the vicinity, to lift my feet. Once the deluge had reached our stands, the flies tied to mine, already straining at their hairs, set upon it in dreadful unison. Our teacher flew out of the bandroom then, hand over her mouth, and did not return to us the following semester.

I must tell you, or tell someone, that at times in the process of leashing a fly the wings would come off and one was left, in the patois, with a "walk." This unfortunate was normally let loose to explore one's desktop until, say, a teacher tossed a graded paper down onto it—

"On *The Tempest*"

A–

Watch those run-ons, and please no more profanity.

—and realized what it was she had just seen (or *had* she?), and so turned back around, and lifted the paper, and out of human instinct used it to euthanize the pitiful thing that crawled underneath (would that *Lear* could have come to my aid there, with its "as flies to wanton boys" zinger, but we were not yet acquainted with that play, nor would we be by graduation), my profit on this being the demerits she then dramatically wrote out for me, which forced me to stay after class and explain that although I had admittedly done harm to the fly, and would have to answer for that in Act V (or *would* I?), I was at least willing to allow it what life was left to it, whereas she had robbed it even of that, and so of the chance (who can say?) to find a mate who did not mind the lack of wings, and possibly even found the look attractive, indicative as outer damage can ofttimes be of inner character, and had decided to make fly babies with this particular one, to the exclusion of all others, but could do no such thing now with the perfectly lifeless smudge we could each of us see before us, right there, on the lip of my desk. I continued along this line until she had torn up my demerits and was weeping so profusely I had to remind her to write me out a tardy slip for the period our intercourse had cut into.

But it is of the birds at home I now wish to speak.

Americans about it

True, I had succumbed at school, and happily, to the rural way, or perhaps it was only the southern, and could boast of numerous people repulsed by my actions there (such as when a principal sought to expel me for having shown my "rear" to a carload of honking Protestants riding behind my slow schoolbus: this man had said, during what he took to be our exit interview, "There's a time and a place for everything," which I argued was high school (time) and schoolbus (place), but he resisted this logic and insisted on a face-to-face meeting with my embarrassed mother and infuriated father (or was it the other way around?); I warned him that such a stance would lead on to trouble, to which he responded, "You bet it's trouble, mister, and you're in it," which then led me to explain that it was not *me* I was worried about, as I was already in constant and excruciating trouble at home, but rather a situation *he himself* might want to avoid, who had yet to taste the rhetorical wrath of a mother convinced that she alone had any right to judge her children or, beyond that, the narrative vindictiveness of a father seeking to win his wife to him by continual displays of violence against anyone his wife held to be worthless, who, I heard later, launched his sawdusted corpse-in-the-making (he is all dust and no saw now, I assure you: we may begin in earnest to sweep him away) across the principal's desk in an attempt to close forever the town man's offending throat, while my mother grabbed at, and pulled against, those same callused fingers she had perhaps that very morning scraped away from her delicate lap, hoping to beat out a last-minute compromise), but I had only then begun to assimilate at home.

The chickens were a help with that, the assimilation, and I thank them for it. I would also apologize, since there were moments when I sensed that their pleasure did not entirely equal my own. And, of course, because they are now all dead. It is silly, I know, to apologize to the departed with words so few of them made use of while still alive, but we do so anyway, apologize, or refuse to, if we are going to be Americans about it. My already condemned father stood too often at the side porch while the sun went down on him, declaiming (*he? it?*) against whatever after-school activity had lately kept me away from the stead (if I had come from a "sports-team practice" he would look about ready to disown me (from what? *from what?*); if I explained that I had just now been with a country girl, and had held her furry crotch in my dirty palm, and had squeezed it till et cetera, et cetera, I might enact a brief pause in his bitching while he gazed up at the purpling sky, and considered whether or not I was lying (invariably I was), or else reminisced (which is more what I was going for there), after which he would catch himself up and continue) when I knew full well that chickens would not eat by the light of the moon. Any child will become exasperated by this sort of thing (or inspired, is my overall point here) and will rejoice in the chance to teach its parent otherwise. I do, though, apologize to the chickens.

At first these birds appeared ruffled as the moon lit their dinner, and for a week or two they refused to lay, but I held fast to my schema and soon had them gathering in the coop yard to feed only when moonlight presented, and staying inside their shelter on those occasions when it did not, during which nights I threw feed down onto the coop-house floor, and shone a flashlight in through the mesh, so as to coax along what result

I wanted. My success in this experiment spurred me on to several others, hardly more scientific but every bit as fun.

The hens needed their wings clipped regularly so that they would not fly the hexagonal mesh that encompassed, but could not wholly hide from view, their grassless yard. Traditionally one cut the end feathers off the right wing and left it at that, but I wondered whether less standard dos might not produce more glamorous trips. I began to try out various shapes and depths of trim, on both or either wing, and with some rigor I vetted the hypothesis that a certain Bernoulli-friendly styling, accompanied by a hindrance attached to one foot or the other (after seeing my brother lift weights out in front of the house, and me do God knows what out behind it, my father asked what the hell I thought I was doing back there, and I told him my activities were of no concern to a petit-bourgeois arriviste (because a Parisian woman had after the war years married a Goochland farmer, mistakenly thinking she was doing something romantic, there were French lessons offered, if a tad sarcastically, at the high school) who did not even know that chickens prefer to dine by moonlight like everybody else, whereupon he took a step toward me, and I took a step toward him, with the clippers still in my hand, which may or may not have led him to stop, and to consider all the feathers strewn between us, and to say, before he turned and disappeared back into the house, "Those hens are *your* responsibility"), might produce panicked barrel rolls through the air, and desperate hover-bounces off the coop side, and flapping front backflips with a half twist (I achieved this once, or else the hen I conscripted and handicapped did: when she landed, facing suddenly back at me, she cocked her head and produced the second-best look of astonishment I have ever seen on a chicken), which even Wilbur and Orville (for whom I named most of the lady test pilots in my care) would likely have applauded.

Buttfucker the rooster I determined to mold into an assassin. His loss in single combat to that Rhode Island Red, and his subsequent not being eaten for it (see the second paragraph of the ninth part of my fourth attempt to end all this), had caused in him a confusion and, I suspect, a shame. I hoped to rectify that with a program of exercise designed to bolster, over many months, his self-esteem. My method here was to kiss and fondle his hens whenever I stepped into the coop yard, despite what sicknesses they might impart, until he showed even the slightest competitive spirit, at which point I would raise my foot and recommend his face to the clay. (Again, this was a very long-range plan.) In time he learned to attack me as soon as I came in through the gate, and his reward for this acumen was a quick boot to the chest that sent him flying back farther than any hen ever had. He kept at it, though, which pleased us both, and I once kicked my way through the Apostles before he finally stayed put, puffed up and heaving against the dirt, his claws folded under him, his eye a mucilaginous dot of odium.

Certainly my father took some notice of these experiments, but after our contretemps in the yard he made no direct reference to them, except when he returned with a rifle (or was it a shotgun?) slung over his shoulder, after sitting all day in a tree and waiting for a wild turkey to pass by (which normally I would have got after him for), and saw how I had the hood of a car up, and the air filter off and tossed against those cinder blocks he loved so well, and a hen perched precariously on the manifold, so that she might peck at a kernel I had placed on the carburetor's butterfly valve in an attempt to solve forever, via chicken, the problem of a flooded engine. To his eternal credit, he understood at once what it was I was up to and, leaving aside any complaint about corn down the carburetor, yelled out, just before I cranked the ignition key:

"If that car backfires you'll blow her fucking head off!"

To which I yelled back:

"She's been apprised of the risks involved!"

Good eating

So we have swallowed fried chicken we knew by name; and ground-up pig we knew by sight, and liked personally; and shreds of deer a-bounce in the bramble at dusk; and cubes of squirrel keeping cozy in the trees; and Lord knows what else we had no honest need of (the outlandish prices charged for outland groceries justifying gas-costly trips into town, yes, but never old goat meat for dinner); and after a spell it is good eating, you hardly notice it.

Advocate

I killed a pregnant lady once. She landed on a paragraph I was trying to construct (*Oedipus Rex*, I think it was, this time around: "On *Oedipus Rex*") and ambled across my lines from left to right. I shooed her away, but she merely rolled off the page, impossibly fat and slow, and I grew irritated by the distraction and smashed her with the heel of my writing hand. Which released, onto palm and desk and page again, a legion of tiny, squirming larvae I had then to scrape into a pile stage left and render into a motionless yet still somehow bothersome paste. To this day I do not know if I did right by that paragraph.

My intention here is not to advocate the misuse of God's clown airforce for human gain. I mean to say only that it was right for *me*, at that particular time, in that particular place. Earlier and elsewhere I might not have punched at those fireflies who invaded the yard on warm evenings, so as to aid along the subtleties of a nerd's self-defense, and felt such a pride when I popped one just right, and he arced off my knuckles like an errant spark, not blinking any longer but lit up now for good, until the grass at my feet shone with the vanquished and I was half entranced, swiping at the air all around me and able almost to ignore them that then faded in the blades below.

(Or else began to blink anew . . .

(And took miraculous flight . . .

(Though never to rise again, it seemed to me, any much higher than my bug-stinky fists.)

Earlier and elsewhere I might simply have caught these creatures up and smushed them, as American children will tend to do, and spread the now-activated goo in fluorescent bands across my innocent cheeks, and run down the driveway with the rest of the neighborhood, pretending with all my heart to be a Red Indian, as Waugh would have it, or Kafka's fornicating translators, perfectly aware that distally, four beats back along the proximal line, I actually was one. But then earlier, and elsewhere, and not surrounded by these objects (words, largely, and mold), and under worse conditions (cool enough tonight, I suppose, if a bit muggy), and not given what in the interim I have happily endured, I might have been tempted to lie. I might have been tempted to craft a cute little segue here between fireflies turning on rather than off when killed (or *were* they?) and my relationship with the Lord our Jesus, said Himself to have died aglow and then, in a blink, arisen.

I might even have made use of the fact that this metaphor will not hold unless Jesus is continually beat down again by the fists of men, since that would seem to be the Church's historical argument here, if not exactly its narrative, but in truth I acquired my faith not through metaphorical epiphany but by practical need. I was bored and lonely and afraid during my initial few years out there, and seeing folks on Sunday made me feel less lonely and less bored. (The afraid took somewhat longer.) Pre-rebellion against a gigantic atheist father, I could not fathom why these people would come together each weekend to celebrate the torturing to death of a self-absorbed Nazarene some twenty centuries earlier, even if He *had* once worked with His hands. Post-rebellion against a smaller threat, and working now gaily with my own hands,

I could not fathom why these people would ever do otherwise. I had joined them in a solemn acceptance of, and promised salvation in, the truth that all local life manifested, winged or not, and in perfect imitation of Jesus, a deathwish foretold and pounced upon.

Cheerios

The priests kept croaking, for one thing. Clearly they had come out to die among us, none of them being young or bright or worth all that much to the Church, and each of them forced to minister to the prisons all the workweek, which would have sapped even my own joyous spirit. Father X lasted longest. He was a bald zealot with too many ideas about Saint Paul. In time he was reassigned elsewhere, equally desolate, whence he sent weak epistles until his heart exploded. Father Y I saw some promise in. He was a mess with words, but his toe tapped regularly to the music, no matter how experimental, and his eyes had a tendency to roll back into their sockets, which trait I could not help but admire. He died of a stroke my sister described thusly: "He looked up into his skull and decided to stay there." Father Z was exactly what you might expect on the heels of X and Y: a short and effeminate wag intent on drinking himself to death by his tipple, which was scotch and milk. He achieved, I am told, a fatal infarction within a year or two's exposure, though by then I was fled from that plot and heard not a word about the martyr who sallied forth to replace him.

Father Y was the one I told about the flies and sundry, not sure if those were sins, really, but not wanting to chance it. He had no idea what to say but only scanned his frontal lobe throughout our encounter, looking for Jesus up there, I guess, or else for the vascular discrepancy that had first made him want to go fish. In time he came to and said that God loved me, which by then I needed to hear, and he gave me some prayers to say, which I suspect I did, and some penance to do, which was about as likely as my asking an eye-rolling priest if he honestly thought every being we encountered wanted to kill us, granted, but also to die, so plain was that notion to anyone who had persisted even a short time out there.

(You sad and forsworn country priests: cheerio!)

Ants liked to off themselves in the sugar bowl, which made sweetening one's Cheerios a challenge. The trick was to extract a spoonful of hardened sugar that did not include an ant dead from diabetic shock. I grew so adept at this procedure that there was some talk of my becoming a famous surgeon. Obviously that did not happen.

(You failed little country excavators: cheerio!)

Ticks hitched rides to hell on all five of us, especially newly enthusiastic country boys who ran around willy-nilly advertising themselves for rent (so that when a pig went missing its farmer might appear in the churchyard of a Sunday, just after Mass, and make inquiries, and offer a few dollars apiece, as my brother and I were said to be swift, and despite being Catholic still technically Christian, and unwilling to let a pig go any more than we would a human (and it was known by then that we had once apprehended a runaway delinquent in a field, hoping to make a name for ourselves in the bounty-hunting trade, and thus be availed of the millions we imagined were allocated to the retrieval of harder sorts who broke out from the State Farm every month or so, and fetched all those helicopters overhead, and left the shelter of the trees to approach small children, which dream went unfulfilled, as did my wish to become a repo man later on, when I worked as a teller for the local farmer's bank and thought I would be better put to collecting debts than to dwelling on assets, but we did catch that one little insult: asked where he thought he was going, the JD said,

"Home," by which he meant Richmond, and my brother explained that Richmond lay many miles to the east, through
those endless woods, whereas the JD was oriented north,
through *those* endless woods, and with any luck would reach
Washington within a year's time, to be picked up by the FBI, if
he were still alive, and beat on considerably, and sent back here,
or else he could come along with us right now, at which point
the JD started crying, and on the long walk back to the road I
explained that before he set off the next time he might know
how many phones were installed in his facility, and where said
phones were located, and then just prior to his escape might
unscrew the mouthpiece to each, and remove the resonator
within, and screw the mouthpiece back on, so that no one his
keepers then called would be able to hear anything about a
drug problem running through the woods with directional dif-
ficulties and dyed-red hippie hair), though I do remember on
one such occasion cornering an adolescent pig under the porch
of a farmhouse and behaving less than professionally with him:
we recounted the "Three Little Pigs," which seemed to agitate
rather than console him, and when he smelled bacon frying
brightly in the house above, and heard our stomachs grumble
in sympathy below, my brother pointed up at the smell, and
then at him, and he bolted and butted the smaller of us full-on
in the sternum, which sent me flying ass-backward and greatly
extended the chase (through crackly woods and still-dampened
grasses: how I miss them now!) until at last we realized that he
was playing a game with us too, and actually wanted to be
caught, and we formed a stratagem around this idea and
brought him in easily, though when we handed him over, wriggling and squealing with self-delight (can I not still feel those
precious ribs beneath his skin?), my brother took the farmer
aside and explained that this pig should under no circumstance
be eaten, as we had God's hard evidence that it could spell), till
word went round that these boys might get the job done, sure,

but were not so quick as was claimed, and were unorthodox at best in their approach, and perhaps even liberal, and should probably be confined to tasks that required less sense, or none at all, such as fetching more wood, or putting up more hay, or digging further postholes, or helping out your obviously insane old farmer ("What would you do if somebody pulled your nuts off? I reckon I'd shoot him. *And then I'd shoot him again!*"), whose niece, or cousin, or granddaughter, a cheerleader we had admired at the high school, once approached us in the parking lot and said that there was a truckful of wood in need of unloading, and the pay was fifty dollars because it was the bank president, and would we do it? and we said *yes we will* Yes (apiece?), and then discovered that the wood had been hauled in days ago on an unwashed fish truck, with the refrigeration turned off, which we managed nonetheless to clear, by means of rags strapped across our mouths and our noses, after which we ate crinkle-cut potatoes fried in butter by the bank president's looker of a wife and barely made it home before the worst of the vomiting began.

(You retchers into tacked-on toilets: cheerio!)

Ticks are famous, of course, for their propensity to swell up with borrowed blood and bust, leaving behind them, as vigorish, this or that ugly disease, but the majority I encountered in Goochland sought out a very different suicide upon me. In want of more dramatic assignments I had developed a sideline in the repair of barbed-wire fences, contemplative work I figured would at least impede the pigs and the rapists while I made a more intensive study of, and a healthier fellowship with, my surrounds. It was an easier job for two, but my brother had found steady employment to the east, with a twinkling farmer who encouraged him to drive the tractor along Route 6, even when there was no real cause to do so, in order that the tanned and shirtless young man might force to a crawl, and a familiar rage, motorists who otherwise took such political pride in the fact that they lived in a place where one had now and then to wait behind a tractor.

(You freeway cars and combines: cheerio!)

Wire and poles, then. Wood and metal. Solitude. The themes are familiar and the work relatively straightforward: one needed no more than a spool of barbed wire, and a wire stretcher, and some clippers, and a bag of bent nails, and a hammer, to remake all of America, which is known for its whitewashed fences, thanks to Twain and Rockwell (though these seem to have painted their pickets somewhat differently), but is more widely, and more accurately, defined by the wire. Still, I intend no abstract on American boundaries here: that has already been tried in our literature. Nor will I indulge my own vanity by making too much of the fact that my first attempt at "creative" writing occurred well within, and of necessity beyond, those exceedingly hurtful constraints.

(Really this was a trifle. Once I had repaired or replaced the strands along the road, cutting away the kudzu to do so, and hammering fresh or rusted wire into grayed posts that sometimes needed a hand up and help back into the ground, I reached a sharp corner and was forced down east into thick country pine, where the heat let up less than the humidity adhered, and my breathing shallowed of its own accord, and I began to see peripheral flashes of a red I at first thought presaged a stroke (did I in fact die in those woods? *am I lying there even today?*) but soon understood (I cannot overstate how real this was for me, at that particular time, in that particular place) to be glimpses of the Devil's own flesh as he stalked me from tree to tree.

(I hid in a depression behind a briar patch and shook, actually *shook*, in that hundred-degree heat, so country had I allowed myself to become, or willed myself to be (either way), sure that any moment I would look up and see Satan standing over me, until I remembered how Jesus had not cowered before this hindrance but rather had confronted him, and found him powerless, and had said to him *Get thee hence* (emphasis mine), who was not anyway painted red until much, much later, whereupon I resolved to rise up and approach him as any Christian properly should.

(My knees were at first uncooperative in this effort, and there were moments when I thought to shrink again behind the briars, but eventually I reached that point in the middle distance where I judged those flashes of red to have originated. What I saw there both eased my fear and inspired a lifetime's assurance of it:

(Tacked to numerous trees, beyond those stapled now with new or ancient wire, were red plastic ribbons, at about head's height, as if the forest had decided to commemorate something fully half its citizens refused to. This scene extended north for an acre or two, maybe more, and I could not help but consider its beauty, and its possible meaning, and estimate its odd outline, until at last I was able to ask my employer, ridden back toward me on pompous horseback, if he knew anything about the red ribbons, and he told me that his neighbor had paid a university man to tell him which trees ought to be chopped down so that the others might survive, which science he personally put no store in, preferring to leave such matters up to God, and he asked me how the fence was coming, and I said that it would be done on time, and he asked me was I sure, and I said that I was, and he asked me again was I sure, and this time I declined to answer him. As we spoke, or did otherwise, I do not think I took my mind for a moment off those brave and beribboned trunks across the way.

(I completed my repairs around that old man's property in a fever, kicking and cursing at his cows to get out of the way once I had made it up into the field, and when it was finished I found myself with a single carved-out weekend to spare, during which time I would be paid to haul my equipment down into those woods, claiming to be doing "touch-up work," and could hide said equipment in the dent behind those briars where I myself had previously hidden, and could flout the wire and re-assign those red ribbons to trees of *my* choosing, not a university man's, not yours, and certainly not God's, so as to spell out into the future, by means of a stranger's prophesied saw, a sentence the length of two football fields and readable, I prayed, from the vantage of the clouds.

((I will not be so crass as to transliterate that early effort here.))

At day's end I would climb up exhausted into the yard, and sit on the cinder-block step to the cluttered old side porch, and slop a lazy finger of kerosene into a rusted Campbell's soup can, and remove my boots and socks, and roll up my trousers, and use a pocketknife to shave my shins and calves clean of the ticks who had assembled there so thickly that I could not always see the blade's surface as I scraped it against the inner lip of the can. I hoped then that these beasts would at least be granted a final wish, and drown in the kerosene, before I had time to drop a lit match down onto their still-struggling number.

(You flames and far-off trepidations: cheerio!)

Wonder Bread

W as it the Word or only the Wafer that was meant to save me? For a stretch I believed it was both, and was pleased. A happiness to hear the Word; a happiness also to taste the Flesh, since I knew It at least by name, if not by sight, and had decided already, long before any Church-prescribed "retreat" to a half-defunct summer camp nearby (where some few of us had previously been day campers, to be lashed out at and spit upon by town kids whose parents lacked either the money or the intel not to board their angry issue out there, and one summer only after we had weatherproofed its failing cabins in the off-season, without having first been warned that what we slathered on the siding would raise welts and blisters where it touched our skin and then met sunlight, which it seemed almost to seek), to like It personally.

We were meant to admire the Jesus counselors because they were older, of course, but also because they took us all seriously, and thought us more "mature" than our parents ever gave us "credit for"; and because they played guitar, which our age group was known to "respond to"; and because they were not at all "uncool" about playing only "God's music" on their "axes" (and what a joy it was when we finally convinced that one counselor to play "Whole Lotta Love" on his, even though he did it wrong, and everyone, even the other counselors, joined in!); and because they were always "on call" for late-night "rap sessions" a full quorum of them might accidentally happen to attend, and then, with patient impatience (or was it the other way around?), continually steer the conversation back toward Jesus while the annoying teen in their trap refused to stop rhapsodizing about all the different ways rabbits knew how to kill themselves.

And the goats! My God, but the goats! I knew of a nanny who would position herself into death's grim profile whenever my friend, her ostensible keeper (or was he *my* keeper, and *her* friend?), took a dirtbike out into the fields that surrounded his toiletless home, and revved up the hillocks and jumped, only to find himself suspended, in air and in thought, looking down at a goat who clearly asked to be landed upon, her belly swollen with tumors (or else with a kid who for years refused to come out, as every vet she ever saw had concluded (and were they wrong, these experts? is the leap from *kid being born so that it might seek out ways to kill itself* to *kid choosing not even to be born* really so enormous? are our delays in this life, and prior to it, not explained by what awaits us beyond the vulva's tight grasp?)), until he threw his bike off to the left, and himself off to the right, landing each painfully so as to spare the goat, whom he then took to tying up by the neck in an empty hog pen, where one night she intrigued, by means of her bifurcate paws, to scramble over the southerly side and hang herself.

(The outer boards showed no evidence that she had ever tried to regain her confinement.)

A dog of ours (named by our father Wee Cooper O'Fife, after the Scottish folksong about the wife-beating old barrel maker, and because our part of the county was called Fife, and because that dog was monstrously large, even as a puppy) once employed this same method while tied up "for his own good" on the side porch, except that the barrier he made it over was shorter, or the rope was longer, and so, by this grace, or that devilment, he survived. He had tossed himself in front of a

Monte Carlo (which required real forethought, if you think about it, on a road less traveled by), though possibly it was a Gran Torino. The people inside it braked, and said how sorry they were, while the dog lay whimpering in a ditch, and asked was there anything they could do, he came out of nowhere, and I said, "No," and thanked them, *thanked* them, and they rolled up their window and drove off at the same suicide-heedless speed as before. Only our "melodramatic" pleas that night, and our "emotionally manipulative" tears, and our "frankly shocking" decision to part with a multigenerational coin collection we had cared not one whit for since leaving the Land of Lincoln, saved that dog from a self-consciously rural bullet to the back of the head and won him a town operation he little wanted and less deserved. After which he sought to hang himself on the side porch and then took primarily to murder.

Another dependent, Brown Dog (so stupid our father had decreed that she did not warrant a proper name), leapt in front of a Wonder Bread truck. Her usual method of curling up on a car roof and frying like an egg until she slid down and shook and barfed in the yard had been thwarted by our usual method of encasing her in a cold-water blanket, and tossing her into the back of the Dodge pickup, and driving her (with more laughter and radio, really, than concern) to the vet for an adrenaline shot. As regards the Wonder Bread attempt, we could scarcely believe that we had seen it, not because leaps in front of vehicles by Goochland's animals were at all abnormal but because Wonder Bread trucks were such a rarity out there.

Surely they passed by often, with their lively dots, or maybe only this one did, so as to restock the shelves of all those unjust but colorful little country stores, yet we ourselves never saw one without pointing and shouting, as if it were a disorientated celebrity. I cannot say, then, at this remove, that I paid less attention to the truck than I did to the dog's readying herself to jump in front of it, so as to bounce off the bumper's bend sinister and be ass-scooted across the gravel below our mailbox, after which we would fetch her up into the yard, and pet her velvet ears back, and pluck the shards from her lacerated haunches, and tell her what an entertaining idiot she had always been to us, all the while looking up and wondering after a turned town conveyance that had neither stopped nor thought to slow.

Fun story

F un story:
   Irish story:
   Eventually our mother used that same car, the one our silliest
bitch liked to scale and fry herself upon, to help an Irish setter die.
   This dog came at us in a flash of Muppety orange from the
right, and caromed off the grille, and landed absurdly far off to
the left, grinningly dead, in what we correctly assumed to be its
own yard. We braked and reversed and pulled up into the driveway and mounted the step and knocked, and as the screen door
opened we pointed at the blood-matted corpse on the lawn and
said how sorry we were, it came out of nowhere, and was there
anything we could do, and the lady of the house said, "No," and
thanked us, *thanked* us, and we waddled faux somberly back to
her driveway and headed home to what I remember now as a
perfectly pleasant evening.
   My brother drove us the rest of the way, to be sure, while his
mother sat beside him, her seatbelt melodramatically fastened,
and kept a moist eye out for any further life seeking to do damage to her car or to her afternoon. (Years later a big buck did it
in, this car, and himself, with our vanishing father behind the
wheel, but that is neither here nor there now, is it, the car or the
buck or the father?) My sister and I sat in back and discussed
the idea that the setter lady may have spotted all the paw prints
on our hood and windshield and roof, and concluded that we

had put them there on purpose, each one representing yet another dog slaughtered for sport along those lawless roads. Was she polite, then, the setter lady, merely as a way of shooing us off before we had time and opportunity (and motive? had not our angry Jesus granted us at least that?) to run down and saint a second sweet puppy of hers?

Our mother fidgeted beneath her belt over the simple likelihood of this. Our brother stiffened adventurously against the wheel.

A litany here

I might make a litany here of the higher self-death I heard about, or saw for myself, and in due time came naturally to encourage, since God's plan is God's plan, after all, and it is not every day, even in Goochland, that He gropes around in His trousers for a treat.

When that seventh grader diced his brains with a shotgun, believing he had just got his girlfriend pregnant, and we gathered in the cafeteria (to the east of our homerooms) and faced a small stage (to the north of our chairs) that had no architec tural right to be there (and upon which I would later lose, or had already lost, a spelling bee), and heard from our teachers what a promising (because a "silent") young man this had always been, and then heard them invoke the word "hero" (which I suppose he was, in the Hellenic sense, but still), I shut my eyes and tried to remember this champion but could conjure no more than his crisp polyester pantlegs, and those spotless if inexpensive shoes, and a desire to dodge his sharp toe on the playground, and an unbidden thrill at what violence he had done himself over so commonplace a seventh-grade worry.

When a friend's mom, it was rumored (always *rumored*), opted for a similar exit strategy, and timed her departure well or poorly enough that her son was able to see her off (the door pushed open with a child's innocent question; the loud and ruinous retort), I stared (without knowing, of course, and in no real position to ask) into those newly widened eyes whenever they neared, and sought out in them the truth: not of what had occurred with the mother, per se, but the *actual* truth, the *final* one. Having failed to find it there, any more than I could spot it in my narrower globes as I bent toward the bathroom mirror and pinched at all those bumps on my forehead, half aware that one day my own skull might fill up with ugliness and, by a tool worse than fingernails, pop, I began to avoid him. Having sensed in my ogle an indication that I was not after anything like the truth here, but only a vulgar entertainment, he began to avoid me sooner.

When the father of that boobless child we had been to the beach with (or would that be later?) set his drink down, and walked out of a bar along Route 6, and stood in the road and waited (for minutes? for hours?) until a tractor-trailer hit him, and bounced his meat up ahead, and caught it up quickly and dragged it, they say for miles (but who was there watching? *who took these measurements?*), all the while air braking and trying not to jackknife across the road, I made every attempt to spot this stain from a passing car window but could find no real easement there. Had it rained in the interim and washed all the iniquity away? I had thought myself luckier when that taxidermist blew his stuffing out near our home and, although the scene was days since dealt with, I ran to it and believed for a moment I had located a puddle of the dead man's blood, with some chunks of brain floating in it, though this turned out to be but rocks and clods dressed not in blood but in motor oil, which may very well have issued from the pan of an altogether different suicide.

When we drove to such sites (the crossroads where that van had met up with a maple, say, at eighty miles per, and had accordioned with all those drunken kids inside, only one of whom may have honestly wanted to die; that hill where a farmer we knew had "realized" that his brakes were out, and so had encouraged his son to jump but had remained seated himself, and so had perished in flame and metal when his truck collided with the obligatory freight train below), we were not unaware that our treks involved their own potential risk and reward. All road travel in that place was attempted suicide, after all (or homicide, depending: our instructional manual, *Defensive Driving,* served each and either need), and one was not considered much of a driver unless one had been in a "tragic" crash. Beyond that, no "tragedy" was considered much unless someone had actually died in it, and no death was considered much unless the deceased had been (a) "cut in half" or (b) "burnt alive" or (c) both. There were but a few exceptions to this nomenclature amongst the living and the left-alive. "Vegetable" bought one a piquant and so an almost respectable glory, as did "most of his face is gone" and, of course, "wheelchair."

When that paralyzed fellow, a graduate, I am guessing, of the high school, who retained his face but whose younger brother, a contemporary of ours, had seemed since the accident to have less of one, came to lecture us in the gym about the dangers of alcohol, and of arguing with one's parents about the dangers of alcohol, and of imbibing more of the dangers of alcohol, and of climbing behind the wheel of a muscle car one's parents had paid for in a misguided attempt to see one teetotaled out there, we scanned the stands above us, and sought out the shadow-face of the shy little brother, who laid back while the abstinence speech was under way, shifting only a little (in agitation? in hope?) when his precedent arrived at the God part, and said how grateful he was for the wreck, and the wounds, since without these he would never have been in a position (legs wrapped around his back, insensate toes pointed up at the welkin) to get off the dangers of alcohol and receive His love, which baffled a small but thinking minority out there (meaning me, mostly, but also, I prayed, the shy little brother), since why would a person praise the wheelchair for rolling him toward Jesus but not the alcohol for rolling him toward the wheelchair? Then, bless or curse him, he reached back and praised the alcohol too.

When he finished the segment about how his penis still worked, having described to his satisfaction (and our rapt disgust) the process of intimate massage that allowed him, theoretically, to defy the constraints of his injury and procreate, all became crystalline. Up through then the lines of his argument had been too various, and one could not tell where, exactly, he sought to collect the acclaim he felt himself owed by a gymful of deliberately suicidal country Christians. (Or were we a gymful of deliberately Christian country suicides? I suppose it cannot matter now.) He seemed proud of it all, really: the alcohol, the anger, the car, the wreck, the rehab, the getting off the dangers of alcohol, the cursing of Jesus before and during this trial, the humble acceptance of Him ever after, the weirdo sex stuff, the insurance-bought van in which he now got around to his various "ministries" better than any of us did, thank you very much. Personally, I was no longer looking for clear-cut answers by the time he started in on the slide show but only for a sign that he had not lost his sense along with the sensation.

When the lights dimmed, and his voice rose a fifth in register as he began to click enthusiastically from frame to frame, lingering longer on the Afters than he did on the Befores (*A*: the crushed car, so like all those others we had hunched around in our denim to admire at whatever gas station was nearest the crash site; a puff-faced him in traction, his short mom hugging a too-tall surgeon; he trying to do that parallel-bars rehab thing while an enormously fat therapist screamed at him; he leaving the hospital in a wheelchair and giving a feeble thumbs-up; he proselytizing before a congregation (his?), backed by a robed and beaming choir; the arrival in his driveway, with balloons, of the insurance-bought van; *B*: he smiling out-of-doors with comely and half-dressed friends, a can of genuine Budweiser beer in each hand; a half-empty (or was it a half-full?) bottle of Jack Daniel's in the bucket seat, "ironically" strapped in; a recently washed and waxed muscle car, black (or was it dark blue?), our hero installed behind the wheel, waving good-bye out the window (barely visible within, passenger-seated, the cautiously elated face of the shy little brother!)), I saw that this cripple had indeed held on to his sanity, and I wondered whether any of the administrators on hand were in a position to realize, if only by our wild applause at the end, that this presentation they had intended for a warning was in fact a well-built and powerful recruiting tool, at least as effective as what the Army and the Marines would later muster.

When, ages after (though in truth it must have been but a matter of months), on my way to sell cigarettes and maxipads to Richmond's West End, in what I recall (conveniently?) as a light rain, I found myself slowed by a state trooper and waved on past a wreck that reminded me, in a painterly sort of way, of a certain frame in that paralyzed young preacher's slide presentation, improved upon here by the addition of what looked to be a tall man's corpse thrown up high on the embankment and covered by a crisp white sheet just beginning to spot through now with blood, I found myself moved almost to tears. Not by what pain and fear this driver might have felt ere he died, nor by what would soon be felt among those who had thought that he belonged to them (and so thought that they belonged to him), but by the overwhelming sense of how *proper* death often looked against a country backdrop, and how perfectly beautiful its ugliness could usually contrive to be.

Want of angels

The line between death's admiration and death's desire thins considerably, or I suppose it may thicken, when one drives it at ninety miles per on a foothilly one-and-a-half-lane road, rising up out of mist for a weightless breath before diving down into it again, an unseatbelted sister beside one in the cab, screaming happily until she says, softly, "What the fuck is that?" and one sees, or thinks one sees (*does* one?), a faint flash of red (or was it only orange?) in the haze below, and so stomps on the brake, and then slides, and then spins, and then comes to a miraculous halt mere feet behind a car whose driver has decided to park on a foggy-bottom creek bridge so skinny one's peers have dubbed it "the eye of the needle." One gets out and walks back up the hill a little (why?) before turning and running down after the car (an old Continental, one insists it was) in a frenzy to *know*, or else physically to attack the knower, but stops short, as one's vehicle just had, and retakes one's place behind the wheel, and drives around and away from this fog-mine (one's sister spitting curses out her window), reflecting on the fact that upon stopping this murder-suicide had at least, unlike oneself, thought to switch on his hazard lights.

And so we have want of angels, those among us who wish to die, apparently, yet find ourselves unequal to the task. We have want of country-strong ones who will ride that gas pedal for us, and cut the brake line, and blow us straight to heaven.

Or else we have want of town-minded ones who will slow us down a smidge while they push that stalled Lincoln off into the creek bed below (or was it a Ford?) and convince us to take up Proust. Certainly we have want of higher beings who will help us decide whether we are country people at all or are only just pretending to be, under a hypnosis, self- or otherwise, and whether there exists a difference between these concepts large enough for us to consider it here. At minimum we have want of a passable excuse for the delay.

The chickens had to fetch me mine. Almost without my noticing, these fluffy and white little leghorn hens had formed themselves into the vibrant georgic community Mr. Jefferson had long ago promised and promoted, shooting eggs out their anuses at a pretty pace and gathering for jocular corn klatsches before and after each moonlit mealtime. True, there were set-backs: I began to find open sores beneath the wings again, which caused me to worry that I had made of their rooster too much of a brute, and I was helped along in that suspicion one moonless night when my mother sent me out to fetch a few eggs, and I kicked around the coop yard for my nemesis and, not finding him there, stepped in through the coop-house door and immediately felt his barb penetrate the outer knob of my right ankle to the bone. But in general these birds seemed to have adjusted quite well to their situation, and I observed that when not eating, or laying, or being raped, or volunteering for one of my aeronautic experiments, they banded together in an ongoing project of their own, such as I imagined might lead on to cathedrals.

Understandably, then, I watched them, and they watched me, and I saw them see me hobble out to take a peculiar pride in the constancy with which they pecked, *as a village,* at the wire just behind and to the east of their feed trough (being an oil barrel sawn inexpertly in twain, which required their jump-ing inside of it to eat, which resulted in an adorable defecation upon their own food), where I soon discovered that their team-work had loosened a flap of mesh I might easily have sewn back up (there was, after all, that remainder of correctional wire on the side porch), except that I wanted to see if these pioneers could succeed, partly out of a wish to be entertained, I will allow, but mostly because I needed to know whether an escape in (and from) our shared context was possible that did not de-mand a suicide's sarcastic surrender to it.

I might have gone to my mother then, and explained that I had experimented upon the rooster and, *as an unforeseen conse-quence,* had radically oversexed him, who was now using his hens so hard and so often that they were bleeding again, from where he "grabbed aholt and rode" (as I was myself, by the by, profusely at times, from the gouge just here on my ankle), and that the situation (to repeat, of my own making) had by all ap-pearances become so dire that the hens were at this stage con-spiring openly in an effort to free themselves from their side-yard prison and establish what I could only assume would be a vast underground railroad for chickens. That might have been the wiser course.

Instead, out of pride, or the fear that abides, I sought to solve the problem by less familial means: I shooed the rooster off any hen I saw him on, and I kicked him with my good leg as he tried to remount, and I kicked him even harder when it finally oc-curred to him to drop the pretense and come directly after me. No substantial lessening of assaults was achieved by this strata-gem, and if anything the offender's libido was only heightened. When next I tried to "flip the script" on this perp, and work *with* him as opposed to *against* him, in an effort to "establish trust," so that we might "make some progress here," and "transi-tion him back into society," he took all my pats and pets and coos to be signs of a weakness, and one evening, as I bent to pour corn down into the feed trough/oil barrel/chicken toilet, I felt him suddenly, and furiously, aholt at my back pockets.

Is it possible

*I*s *it possible, in all honesty, to rehabilitate a chicken?*
I say that doubts in this area will settle in after one of them attempts personally to rape you.

Is it moral to blame a monster for being a monster when you know that you yourself have made him a monster?

Well, that "know" there is debatable, I would even say highly, as is the "moral," and certainly also the "you" (either one), and our priority here, really, is to think about the flock and, moreover, our hero first responders (with their kicks and their corn, and their wounds and resentments, and their possibly put-on country pride), whose duty it is to protect the hens' sacred way of life and, theoretically, their one slim shot at democracy, which trust will brook no dissent or unseemly agitation.

By this route, or thereabouts, I reached the conclusion that I had no choice but to kill Buttfucker the rooster, and throw his carcass up onto the coop's tin roof, where all the dead things went in their time, to be disposed of by the enormous buzzards who were never long away from our property.

Redemption

I had come to think of these buzzards as dear friends, with their bald pink heads, and their crooked red necks, and that dingy black livery beneath the threadbare gray boas they insisted on wearing, reminding me always of queeny old butlers who had abandoned their posts decades ago but still skulked about the manor to pass judgment on anyone who disintegrated within. What a joy it was to watch them dine cooptop, in their immense silence, upon whatever frog, or mole, or turtle, or rabbit, or groundhog, or possum, or family of field mice, or neighboring cat, or barb-addled fawn, had lately come to be chewed to death by the dogs in the yard and wrested away from them once the sweet odor of redemption had become too much for our delicate mother to bear.

How the chickens felt about that scent, and the imperious visitors it brought to their roof, to perform whatever Parsee funeral rites were going on up there, I cannot say. They attended, these chickens, to their business, which was escape at all costs, regardless of any smell or looming betters, and I must allow that I drew some energy from their clucky resolve. A part of this energy (too much, by my current calculations) I spent worrying that the rooster's execution, while clearly called for here, might deprive his ass-workers of their initial motivation to flee, and so put an end to the Great Experiment altogether.

Also there were fewer of them. I first hypothesized this, or surmised it, one afternoon at the high school, during the discussion of a poem by William Blake (and what of his drawings? *why were we never shown the drawings?*) that landed on the fearful cheat-rhyme of "symmetry." Had there not been somewhat less of that in the coop yard of late (the rhyme, I mean, not the cheating), and so a lack of equilibrium (at least to *my* eye), which naturally I compensated for by remembering back to the first time those birds had been made to bleed, and why? This was a general impression, in that I had taken no roll call, but I became convinced that the flock was indeed diminished, and for a time my thoughts rose up and circled that possibility.

If rape was required for the eggs to come out fertilized, so that there might be made more chickens, was it not equally possible (by the old magic of *universal balance*? or by the much newer *conservation of energy*?) for a hen to be *mmped* away entirely? Not *mmped* to death, you understand (and left in the yard to be gathered around and laughed at, and pitied a little, and tossed up onto the tin for the buzzards to eat), but disappeared entirely? annihilated? gone? If so, by what right did I obliterate the obliterator, whose purpose it was to grant life while simultaneously destroying it? By Whose authority did I rank my experiment over his?

I had scarcely begun to keep count of the Orvilles when one morning I entered their yard to find them gathered at the loosened flap behind the feed trough, pecking desperately now to widen it, with even the rooster leaning in for some succor. They stirred but a little as I opened the gate and stepped in and shut it. Out of renewed habit, I raised my right shoe so as to stomp Buttfucker's beak down into the clay, but he only extended his feathered neck and gave my sole a pleading peck, by which I knew that something truly unholy was afoot here.

I searched the interior of the coop but encountered no more than orphaned eggs in the cantilevered roost I had built with my own glad hands, under the usual duress, against the wall where once had leant my father's books. (And was it not in the juvescence of the year that Christ the Tigger came? Why, then, do I remember this happening in late springtime, with too few of the trees pushed down?) Peering out into the coop yard, and finding the chickens still bunched together in the southwest corner, I was reminded immediately of a prize fight, which my father always relished on his television set, and I knew then to check the opposite corner, the northeast, for blood.

What I saw there, as I rounded the southern side of the coop house, hoping to come upon a compassionate Referee but resigned to the fact that He had not likely attended this match, was the usual revelation: A long black rat snake had slithered in through one of the hexagonal holes in the mesh and, with a young hen lodged in his dislocated jaw, could not well make it out the way he had come. Nor could he turn now and exit frontways through the infinite other holes at his disposal. I cannot swear that this was the same snake who had chased me away from the blackberries all those bushes ago, or who had entered my home to wrap himself around a fringed fagot while I paused in my chewing and hastened to look. His eye, though, seemed to indicate that we two were well acquainted, and so I told him, in plain American, to wait right there.

My father's axe

I ambled up to the side porch then, and fetched my father's axe. On the way back down I debated how best to solve the dilemma. The snake was currently out of sight of the chickens: I could halve him back there, and throw his carcass, and the hen's, roofward from that vantage, and the flock would be none the wiser. The buzzards would descend, and enjoy their meal, and their meal's meal, with the chickens never knowing that it was their *motivation to flee* being disposed of up there. The Experiment, that is, would continue. Alternately, I could yank the snake out into the coop yard and dice him up, still wriggling, in front of all the others, so that they might properly see, and be released from their fear and my science.

That I chose the latter in no way excuses the fact that it never once occurred to me to lift that blacksnake up, and swing him around my head for a turn or two, and toss him out over the wire, so as to let what was, after all, but a fellow gourmand go fed and free.

BOOK SEVEN

King

Two of my dead father's stories stand out for me today, due mostly to the animated pleasure he took in their retelling. He was not directly a character in them, that I can discern, nor does either bear much more than a loose analogical link to the tale I hope, yet again, to be quit of here. The first concerned a young man who had yanked every hair from his body, one by one, and so was urged to see a psychiatrist until he was diagnosed with the fatal brain tumor that had obviously been the trouble all along. My father took no interest in what the poor man had to say to the psychiatrist but wondered only *How long would that take, do you think, to pull out every hair?* The second concerned an experiment in hygiene conducted at a "famous university," in which volunteers' anuses were painted in the morning with a special dye, and then a fancy blue light was shone on these subjects at day's end, revealing their hands and clothes and faces to be absolutely awash in fecal matter. What my father wanted to know was *Can you imagine if that was your job—to paint all those assholes?*

In time, thanks to his no-less-indelicate ministrations, I had tales of my own to tell. (SON: *Girl I know just tried to remove her eye with a butter knife.* FATHER: *Which?* SON: *Girl by the name of ___.* FATHER: *No—which eye?* Your TRUE COUNTRY SON would have known to say, in that jam, *Well, she only ever had the one.*) Yet I must admit to being less clear on my point than he ever seemed to be on his. Long before I had reached my maturity I understood that the debate between town human and country human was as nothing compared with the debate between settled human and nomad. My father had chosen a stupid way to settle, is all, and then had spent the rest of his life on the trivial matter of how his children would choose to settle after him.

Those chickens, on the other hand, might well have been nomads. For all I knew, their efforts at the flap had been predicated not on a desire to flee the kingsnake at all (for that was what he was called now, suddenly, in his martyrdom, "kingsnake," who had clearly, and selflessly, warded off our destruction for years by eating the rats (*That poison doesn't really work; it just makes them angrier*), and scattering your more worrisome serpents (*The next thing you'll see, believe me, is two copperheads*), and patrolling the crops (*It'll be up to the dogs this summer, and you, to keep the deer out of the corn*), and guarding (was he talking about the deer again? or did he mean from mere humans?) those blackberry bushes not legally even on our property) but on an understandable wish to seek no place to begin with, and each place besides, and to map out by careful claw every nuance of their continent, and cluck forth its awful song, and claim an ownership over all and Nunavut, though perhaps I am getting ahead of myself here.

I paid little mind to the chickens after I had demised that snake to their roof, beyond feeding them, when I thought of it, and stealing their fetuses for the family to eat. Weeks went by before it finally occurred to me that by killing their killer I had done nothing to improve the cock-to-hen ratio in the coop yard, and had conceived of no plan, beyond beheading the rooster (who had already been granted two stays for crimes he did not commit, and was I country enough, really, to insist that he be executed anyway?), by which to lessen what insults a hen might receive beneath wings I no longer took much pleasure in grooming. Occasionally, of a weekend, I would hear a squawk, and would make my way back to the coop, there to discover a chick being disabused of the notion that those blue skies above were an apt metaphor where she was concerned, and I would slap the cock off her, and stand watch for a while, and quickly grow bored. To be blunt, these birds seemed less panicked, and so less banded together, and so of less interest to me.

Still and all, I would surely have said something at dinner one night about how we needed more hens, and been told that there were not funds enough on hand for that, and argued, despite a dispassion any town or country fool could pick up on, that there was clearly enough corn on hand to make a trade, and that even chickens deserved better than the septic death this ignorance condemned them to (and been told that I was exaggerating again, and agreed that I did have that tendency, and admitted that the hens seemed oddly less bothered by their sores this time around), had I not been preoccupied just then with the suppurative wound my right foot had recently sustained, in an increasingly common moment of distraction, from that same axe I had used to slay, and so rob us all of, the king.

Assumption

D o I lie here? It is possible, even likely, that I received my wound the spring previous, and so had healed, at least in the physical sense, by the time I betrayed all those chickens? Or had I yet to suffer this injury, and so possess no real excuse for my failure to stand between these birds and their oblivion? What else might I lie about here, or remember wrongly, which is anyway the same thing?

I recall that the trucks began to turn over around this time, one after the other, on the perfectly negotiable curve in front of our house, the inevitably drunken pilots inside seeking comfort in our grass and, where they could make it, the room off the side porch, while we called the volunteer rescue squad, and said who we were, and had no need to say more. Yet the apotheosis of these wrecks, as I recall just as clearly, was when an entire dump truck of state-bought sand tipped over in that very spot, and the stupefied driver climbed out the side window/sunroof, and we laughed and laughed because my sister had made a crack about how we now owned beachfront property, and that would have happened during the Ice, and the Ice had long receded by the time of the chickens.

These were the days as well of hunters parking pickups along the ditch to the north of our land, and setting up lawn-chairs and coolers in the truck beds while the short straw took the hounds around back, behind those woods that hid our father's unpurchased pond, and said something sad into a walkie-talkie, after which a whistle was blown to summon the dogs (our own being tied up on these occasions and evincing a touchingly desperate fascination with the scene), who then ran happily through the trees toward their masters, flushing does and fawns out into the field that fronted the road, all of whom were then laid low, along with the occasional dog, by gunmen who never raised, that I saw, one hemisphere of ass up out of those sagging lawnchairs.

But that also would have been in the winter months, and was too common a sight anyway for even a selective memory to assign to a particular year, let alone to a short span of months. And the Assumption (or that particular Holy Night I most associate with this period, when my faith and fervor were at their hormonal apices, and my unsanctioned communion with the land was at its most perilous height, and I had become humble where the land had wanted me humble, and smug where the land had wanted me smug, and abstemious where the land had wanted me abstemious, and profligate where the land had wanted me profligate, and I trusted more in Bible than in bile, though these were often enough the same thing): When did that occur? When exactly?

I know by my calendar that The Mother of God is sucked up into heaven each year on August 15, nine days shy of my birthday, except that it felt no worse than spring when those chickens (and I) suffered as they (and I) did, and we drove (short a disintegrating father) along the cool road to the west one starry night, and up the hill that held the hamlet, so as to park in the gravel parking lot and be astonished by the glow of candles stuck into the ground and shielded from the wind by white paper bags, which intrigue lit our path to the church door, where we were met and handed candles of our own, with doilies around them to catch the wax, so that we might illuminate by flicker the glorious cavern within.

Do I fabricate now what I felt then, with that soft candle in my hardened hand, as I climbed (briskly? painfully?) the stairs to the choir loft, where I knew there still to be seats, and looked up into the rafters above, and down onto the congregation below, and felt the Holy Ghost surge into me where before It had merely licked at my sides? Did I not wonder then why It had done neither that foggy morning when I went out to chop wood, and paid too little attention to my task, and let the axe glance off the rounded barkside of an already split segment and lodge, the far corner of the blade, so neatly in my shoe? Did I not stare down at where the axe had entered, near the tip, and pull on the handle and feel, admittedly, a tug but no pain? Did I not toss my implement aside, and kneel down to examine that tear in the upper? (Was this a boot? Was it a slipper? A boot, surely, but can that matter now, since said boot was not availed of a perfectly affordable steel toe?) Did I not pull the hole apart and look down into it, and was I not at once struck in the face by a warm geyser of my own blood?

I hopped up to the house then, and screamed to my brother that I had murdered myself, and this formerly prophetic being, who was by this point merely magical, and blessed with the knowledge that no matter what happened to the rest of us he and his seed would find a way to survive (which, I agree, is magic enough), responded that he was "busy" watching television. (Should I call him today (*he is bless'd still!*) and ask which program? *Should I?* I should call him.) In time he left *Good Morning America* and found me in the bathtub, which was by then painted red, to match my eyes, the second toe on my right foot split brutally from pristine nail to half-cloven metatarsal. "Wrap that up in something," he said, "and I'll drive you in." I thought he meant to Richmond, but he meant only to the county clinic, where a medic numbed my toe, and reconstituted the spread-out knuckle, and sewed the little piggy back up while my disinterested savior looked on.

I spent the next two months, as was ordered, with my foot elevated and kept dry, and we watched, late at night, *The Benny Hill Show* and, in the afternoons, *General Hospital* and, where we could get it to come in, *Soccer Made in Germany*. We also watched, because our Anglophilic mother always insisted, *Breakfast at Wimbledon*. (Vitas Gerulaitis! Or had he asphyxiated by then? And why was the breakfast not "made" at Wimbledon, as opposed to the soccer, in Germany? Might not this simple difference account for at least two world wars?) It was during this period, so late in our life together, that I learned my mother was the absolute best person in the world to watch television with. I have not encountered her equal since, and I expect I never will. Her comments hugged and enhanced the words from the set, and the gestures on it, and never once ran over either, and we watched all of *Brideshead Revisited* together (I suppose I could look up now when that first aired in Virginia, and be done with this charade of not knowing, except that I refuse to cheat where I might not appreciate the answer) while she explained, by her side notes, and her own delicate gestures toward the screen, and those throaty little laughs, what subtexts even a literate country boy (who had himself, quite recently in her memory, walked around with a teddy bear in his arms, and had just now done a ridiculous injury to his foot that demanded he be coddled and looked after, though our family could not afford to put up with that for as long as the Flytes) might miss out on: being, primarily, homosexuality among "creative" young types, which, she made it comfortably clear, she was open to having a frank and nonjudgmental discussion about, though how does one confess to one's mother that one wishes she had been special enough to produce something so interesting as a homosexual, one truly does, but this angel had passed over her, and her boy was but a boy, interested in homosexuality, as was Waugh (and as was she, if she only stopped to think about it), largely for its value as a literary trope (for which see the sixth through the eighth parts of my third attempt to end all this), and so was unable to grant her recourse to that convenient sin by which she might believably make her protagonist long for redemption via the joyous sacrifice of natural desire that was, and remains, her Catholic Church.

Which was the other great subtext at work here, and that Church, and her sense that I sensed how It might one day save me, even when we both knew It would not, so overwhelmed her watching of *Brideshead Revisited* as to make her gloss over those lovely, crucial speeches by the stuttering homosexual Anthony Blanche, wherein he warns against "charm" (the Flytes', yes, but then there are so many other kinds (and how akin was this "charm" to Holden's "phoniness," so important to both the atheistic and the worshipful elements in my household, and never once ignored there as was charm)), and this moved me, I think, her subterfuge (for my mother was, and is, a charming woman), and beyond anything she wanted me to notice in the episodes themselves sent me up into that choir-loft one Holy Night without television, with a candle in my grateful hand, to look down on the poor chiaroscuros below, and wonder what sins they had committed to gather them all here, and whether these sins could possibly be as bad as mine (and I would like to say that I pondered just then what Waugh or Salinger might have done with a scene such as this, but I am neither phony enough to claim it nor charming enough to pull it off), until someone down below leaned back on the light switch near the entrance and showed, in one ugly flash, our prefab chapel for what it truly was.

Tin and wood.

Faded felt displays.

Mail-order-catalog Stations of the Cross.

A decades-old course of industrial blue carpeting.

That light was shut off immediately, of course, but the Spirit had fled us, and for some It never returned. Most stayed until

Mass was over, out of phoniness, or charm, but few tarried after. I learned from the stragglers that a sibling of mine was rumored to have tripped the switch in back: both suspects had lingered there at the time, near my mother, and certainly *she* would have known not to do it. My soon-to-be-fugitive sister denied culpability, and I could see in her eyes that she would have been perfectly proud of the act. (She who would later steal a taxicab in the nation's capital, and drive around drunkenly taking fares, until a police roadblock was set up, and she was captured, and the offended hack said he would not press charges, and would even drive her home, by which the officers present must have known that he would then attempt to sexually assault her.) By those eyes I knew the truth. My brother, when I asked him about it, stared somewhat coldly at me, and for a moment I thought I was about to be punched, right there in the churchyard. Then he smiled and looked away, as if he had already forgiven me the insult (not of the accusal but of the sheer stupidity), and he put his hand on my shoulder, and his smile went away, and he asked me how that toe was doing.

Such is how I recall it, the loss of my faith (if never my fear), except that I am convinced now I was thinking, as late as ten paragraphs ago, about the Ascension, not the Assumption, if only mistakenly so.

Copperhead

1.

As I chopped weeds one Sunday, after my midnight escape from the Lord, in that corner of the backyard never asked to grow corn (nor to birth what other foodstuffs we would scrape after dinner onto the enormous pile of rotting garbage my parents told themselves was a "compost heap" and even the dogs would not go near), and swung a scythe through weeds that had caused even the tiller to choke and expire, I felt a garden hose pulled tight against my left heel. I looked back and saw there not a hose at all but rather a full-grown copperhead, rounding one foot and headed directly at the other. Why he (she?) did not simply bite the left, and save himself (herself?) the extra motion, I will never know; snakes, I suppose, make their aesthetic decisions too. I hopped off toward the tail, and he (she?) turned back around at me, and I chopped the top third of him (her?) away with my blade. This made him (her?) overly angry, or at least the top third of him (her?), and he (she?) continued to hiss, and to bare his (her?) teeth, and to inch my vulnerable way, until I had chopped that top third into an additional three pieces, after which his (her?) mouth remained open but mercifully silent.

I ran up into the house then, and told my brother what had happened, and he seemed honestly intrigued by my story this time around, though he did not, in the end, deem it worthy of his leaving the television set and coming outside to inspect my mess. That mess would have to be dealt with, of course, and soon, before the dogs got at it and one of them, chewing happily on the head, caught a lip or a tongue on a still-venomous fang. I threw the pastel meat up onto the coop roof for the buzzards to have at. The angry head I flushed down the toilet. Afterward I found it a terror to situate myself on that throne or on any other.

2.

The great black locust behind the house had finally died. No doubt this was due to desiccation, and heatstroke, and smoke inhalation, and all those pitiable burns; it had stood, the whole of its life, so very near the chimney. (For which see the second, seventh, and fourteenth parts of my fifth attempt to end all this.) My father felled it expertly, and it swung from left to right, as if waving goodbye, before landing, the top third of it, on the very spot where that southbound snake had turned and tried to topple me. Over the next few days we set upon it with axe and chainsaw, glad (my brother and I) finally to have firewood so near the home.

(Was this before or after my brother joined the football team, as the place had asked of him, and stuck with it just long enough to ask of a particular player out there, "How did you get so goddamned big?" So came the reply: "Hauling the motherfucking wood." By which we learned for how little a cord of stove-ready staves could be had, and one Christmas we gathered up our dollars and arranged, through this same player's family business, a whispery

delivery the night before, and the next morning we presented the stack to our father as if it were a gift for him
and not for us. I remember too well his effortful smile, and
his emasculated "Thanks," and the short-lived triumph, and
our long-lived shame.)

There was talk, and honest fear, that our father might
make us transport the whole of this treasure back across the
eastern field, to what wire bounded (and here and there did
physically bind) those trees that by this point spelt out God
knows what, so that when harsh weather hit he could command us to fetch it up the hill again, and haunt us from the
dry side of a farmhouse window while he told himself that
we would remember and respect him for making us so powerful. No male in the family, and I include poor vaporized
him, is today innocent of a town operation on his spine. I
suppose I can remember him for that.

On the second afternoon of the locust's agony, my brother
chopped into a cave made out of two branches: one broken
off against the trunk and one, by stubborn flesh, still held to
it. The grass was all but gone there, by the pressure of the
tree, and by his movements above and below it, and it is my
recollection that he slipped around a great deal in the mud as
he chopped away the roof of what had become home to a
large and coiled copperhead, which my brother, large and
coiled himself, chopped into pieces while his faraway father
turned the chainsaw off and yelled a *Stop fucking around over
there*–type sentiment and then heard, by way of a yell back,
what had happened, and so came over to inspect the scene,
after which he glared down at me as if I had just now nearly
cost him the better son. As this ghoul drifted off, and disappeared (*almost!*) behind the leafless branches at the top of the
tree, my brother stared after him and sighed. Then he picked
up some chunks of the snake and made for the coop roof. I

picked up some others and followed. I shared nothing about what I had done with the previous one's head.

Whether it was then or later I do not know. My brother turned to me and said, by that fading gray sky, or by the bare yellow bulb in our intestinal-pink bedroom, *The next thing we'll see is four kings.*

No truths here

I saw neither king nor copperhead in the yard after that. What I did see were rats, singly or in pairs, taking carefree constitutionals across a lawn they presumed, correctly, to be their own. The dogs mostly let these nature enthusiasts be: I would venture that the amount of d-Con rat poison coursing through their tiny veins had caused any dog who bit down on one to hallucinate and vomit and pray.

Snakes I saw plenty of, but these were always on the road, and I could never tell whether they hoped, by crawling out onto the asphalt, to depart this life for good or only that unconscionable county. Every snake I spotted seemed to be headed east, and it would not shock me to learn that all of Ophidia had voted to return to the sea, as the whales had long before them and we monkeys might just yet. Turtles, too, were hep to the highways. I once encountered a "box" variety on 250, turned a tad sideways (or perhaps he was only switching lanes), and as I swerved to locate him safely between my wheels I swear I saw him reach a little dinosaur foot out back to reverse himself, after which I felt his shell crunched at once beneath my right hind tire. Was this another suicide, or had he simply forgotten something back at home? Why did I miss so many of the elongated meat tubes I tried for but could not avoid this one cute lump of a fellow? To what truths are we ultimately beholden?

No truths here, I am sorry to say, mean anything any longer, except where they apply to the chickens; I have neither the time nor the patience left to swerve. Where once I had allowed myself to imagine these birds adventurous escapees, inspired by and inspiring me (*but which came first?*), I saw them now as complacent stay-at-homes I was not above pelting with their own eggs for boring me so badly, and for making me smell like chickens, and chicken feed, and chicken shit, as I sat friendless (I was sure) and Godless (I was equally sure) at school and talked about a sentence (or an equation) not even the teacher took much interest in;

Or on the floor of a Richmond Rite Aid, where my vacuum cleaner had just knocked over a maxipad display, and one of the boxes had come open, and I was yanking pads and carpet fibers out of the machine's wide mouth when a slim figure slipped around the corner, and stepped over the electrical cord, and snatched up one of the still-intact boxes, and hurried away toward the cash register, and I saw from behind that this was the very girl I was just then in love with, who would be pregnant so quickly, by another, that I might as well have scooped her up a free handful off the floor;

Or in the passenger seat of an adult I admired, as I asked him whether I should follow my brother to The University or should apply in secrecy to a college up north and in town (my parents had ordered me not to: they deemed the northern application fee an insult, or a hardship (I cannot remember which), and refused to pay it, thinking their hubris might at last put an end to mine), and this man had counseled me to do as I liked, though Virginia parents generally knew best, and he himself had received a fine education from one of the Atlantic Coast Conference schools, on a football scholarship there, and then he stomped on the brake, and grabbed a rifle (or was it a shotgun?) out of the rack behind our heads, and before I knew it had arced around the front of the vehicle, and jumped the ditch, and back-rolled over the barbed wire (I had not seen this maneuver before), and raced across the field after a wild turkey he had no honest hope of catching, and when at last he returned to me, and put the gun back up in the rack, his eyes asked a sympathy of mine that would prove as elusive as had the turkey;

Or in a booth at the McDonald's on Patterson, having passed on the way the burial of a child I knew perfectly well, some of whose bereaved, I knew perfectly well, would now filter in, all dressed in black, and await their turn to order Happy Meals and Big Macs, because they knew, perfectly well, given where they had opted to dwell and to die, how long it would be before they had another chance to eat at McDonald's;

Or on a couch in the still-usable half of our living room, trying to watch television and awaiting inspection by the parents of my brother's ambitious new girlfriend, who were visiting their ambitious girl and her new boy at The University, when we heard pressure on the gravel outside, and then a screeching of tires away, and my sister guffawed, and my mother collapsed into her melodramatic tears, and I remembered (how could I not?) that time I caught a ride home from a charitable girl at the high school, and pointed up at the house once we neared the curve that had famously bested all those drunks, and the girl drove right on past.

She assumed I was joshing, of course, and what pains me, in retrospect, is that I was. I meant only, by my pointing, that "here" was where I, and my little sister (who had recently been menaced by a boy at the high school and, before I could "have a word with him" (by which I mean attack him in one of those hideously tiled bathrooms I had avoided myself since at least the seventh grade), struck him in the face with a steel-toothed hairbrush she had ferried in her purse to school, reportedly with such force that it remained lodged in the poor boy's cheek as she turned back around to smile at the teacher whose job it had been, theoretically, to protect her all along; later, when inquiries were made, neither this teacher nor her charges would admit to having seen a hairbrush, nor to hearing any hypothetical screams), would be forced to sleep tonight, and eat our victuals, and do our chores, and compose a few paragraphs where such were asked, and set out for school the next morning worse people.

It was absurd to imply that human beings actually lived in that place. (*Philosophically*, there is no sound argument to be made that *anyone* ever lived there, or that the house itself ever existed, or the county, or the commonwealth, or the self, or that I in fact exist today, comprising as I can but these few paltry words (or are there too many?), which, again, seem real enough to me (see the fifth through the eighth paragraphs of the eleventh part of my fifth attempt to end all this), but what if I have that all wrong?) There was (*psychologically* speaking), for at least one of us in the car that evening, a visceral certainty (could we not smell it, the viscera, if not the certainty?) that chickens did indeed exist up there, next to a house haunted by an uncertain farmboy who half believed in that house, and in that county, and in that commonwealth, and who could not decide whether, to be free of his dragons, he would have to fly those birds or those birds would have to fly him.

Compass rose

I let my guard down, re the chickens. I see that now.
I took their quietude for serenity, when I should have taken
it for what American country quietude (or town loudness, either way) has always hidden: further subterfuge. So what if I
had seen them bunch up against the coop wire in seasons previous, and tear at the opening they had initiated there? By this
fuss they had wanted not freedom but snake blood, and by my
father's axe I had given them that. So what if they seemed
thereafter to want nothing? I was a fool to think the matter, or
themselves, the least bit settled.

One vernal eve, with the moon fat and jaundiced over Richmond, and the sky gone a gulp past grape soda, I stood and
watched a lone hen peck at the loosened flap behind the feed
trough/chicken toilet, and I wondered whether she had not
been driven insane. By fear, perhaps, and this was then an au-
tonomic echo of how she, and her kind, had dealt with insecu-
rity in more serpentine times. By grief, perhaps, and this was
then a senseless ritual: the pecking out of a passageway to the
afterlife for every sweet little sister she had lost to the king. I
wondered how she would react if I seized her now, and brought
her up into the yard, and laid the axe handle across her neck,
and pulled the body loose from its troublesome head. Would
the body run back down, past the asparagus patch, and ghost-

peck dutifully at the unfinished hole? Or would it die here in the yard, crestfallen, as the head already had?

Currently I have this hen figured for an agent, likely one of several whose work I was not meant to see, nor ever fully to understand. A week or so later, as I climbed the hill from our mailbox one ponderously green afternoon, having checked to see whether I had been asked yet to a college up north and in town (I had not), I saw in my periphery, laid out true across the front yard, a wide and fetching compass rose. The cardinal points of this compass were vacant, I will allow, unless you want to count nail-ridden boards and the odd rat lookie loo, but the ordinals there were well-enough represented: Brown Dog, as I remember it, held the southeast position; Ginger Snap, the southwest; Cooper held the northwest position and promised, by his quick musculature, that he could cover the northeast as well. That would have been Blackie's spot, had the pines not claimed him years before.

The center of this compass was a perfect bloom of leghorn white.

The chickens, by which I mean every one of them who had survived their captivity, and their sores, and the snake snacks, and my grievous experiments, now held perfectly still, and I had never seen them do that except when roosting on the diagonal lattice I had built, with my own unsteady hands, against the wall where once repaired my father's books. For a moment I thought, or hoped, that each bird was lost in an intense consideration of where it might like to travel next. To this day I sometimes think that, or hope it, when I flap past maudlin and find the alternatives too awful to consider.

Alternative One is that they had not thought the problem through. *Id est,* they were chickens, and so were, whatever their gifts of wanderlust and courage, inherently stupid. Hence they were bound to perish, in the American fashion, almost as soon as they stepped foot in a front yard so foreign to them it might as well have been another continent. (And has it not recently been confirmed that the colonists at Jamestown, from which sprang Richmond, from which sprang Goochland, from which sprang Jefferson, from whom sprang our country and western pride, once resorted to cannibalism, and gobbled at the flesh of a fourteen-year-old girl (and here I cannot help but think of the young Tanya Tucker: "Then a man of low degree stood by her side") so as to retain a foothold in this exotic lawn, and follow the sun across it, looking always for nuggets of gold, as opposed to animal crap, so that other little girls might be eaten along the way?)

Alternative Two is that they *had* thought the problem through, as they had all problems prior, and at last dug Old World claws into New World dirt in order to enact an end to the tradition that had sent so many of their cousins out west to comb the continent and die while the cocks who drove them onward grew richer and harder by the mile. (And how many frozen dinners were needed in those passes, Donner and otherwise, to ensure that we could hold and grow waxed Los Angeles, and hairy San Francisco, and pierced Portland, and damp Seattle, and tanned if flaccid San Diego? *How many?*)

Some of these chickens, in their unmoving attitudes, seemed almost to regard me; others, more generously, did not. For a moment I froze myself, in a personal regard of them. Then, gently as I could, I laid the mail on the gravel before my feet. (Another torture-gift, that mail, not invented, as is too often claimed, but certainly popularized by Mr. Franklin, and I would not be surprised if he had a hand in the American gravel business as well.) I made no discernable crunch by this action, but a single hen head twitched, near the northwest declension of the bloom, and turned suddenly from a disregard to a regard of me. (Or was it the other way around?)

That was all the dogs required. They collapsed upon the rose's center and began to kill. I ran into the midst of this mêlée and began yanking hens out of hounds' mouths, thinking not to save souls here (I confess it) but only livestock, which clawed containers of souls (or not-souls) I threw up one after the other onto the cool tin roof, and tried to keep a running count of, until I saw, peripherally, that these more elevated birds did not care to be detained from their trip and were willfully, even joyfully, jumping back down.

They leapt in pairs

I did my best to bat this Wilbur or that Orville back up into the air, but the jumpers soon overwhelmed me. They leapt in pairs, or in trios, and at least once I saw a quad, and then there were not enough of them left to make a quad, or a trio, or even a pair, and the last solo leap happened well back behind me, to be caught up and disposed of by Cooper, while near the compost heap I battled Brown Dog and Ginger Snap, who in turn battled each other, over the rights to a formerly fat fryer who had already become, by the nails and beaks among us, a torn and irredeemable corpse.

Our town mower, which I pushed later in a trance and a bother, was days in disposing of the evidence. It rendered the feathers into dust easily enough, but it had a tougher time with the flesh and the bone. The buzzards pitched in where they could, and did away with the occasional hunk of chicken meat and sorrow, or with an infarcted yard rat we would none of us miss, but after a week or so (was it the rat blood? *was it?*) we saw no more of these flying garbagemen. Buttfucker alone survived the cataclysm, by what luck or cleverness I will never know, and was allowed (by the dogs? by the family? by the fungus below?) to roam the yard as if he still had hens left to dominate. By his further actions, and inevitable demise, you would almost think he believed that.

Pace/Eggs

*P**ace* my fading father;
  Pace his infested yard;
  Pace what designs those chickens might have had for, or on,
their own little pecked-at lives;
  Pace what plans my father might have made for my personal
poor story, and I have since drawn out for his;
  Pace those lowly snakes;
  Pace the high-hat buzzards, and the suicide turtles, and the
doper rats;
  Pace the Lord our Jesus;
  Not everyone in this scenario needed to die.
  Not everyone.
  One morning, a week or so after the hens had flown, I got
it into my head to make eggs. I would argue that I was simply
hungry, but in truth it did not seem proper to me that anyone
else in the family should consume the last leavings of those
birds I had cared so incompetently for. I suppose that might
pass for a kind of hunger.
  I set some butter in the skillet to brown, and then, on the
lip, I cracked open the first of these eggs (or was it the last?),
and felt its innards glop through my fingertips as they waited
on a yolk they intended to cradle, so as not to see it burst in the
pan. What they felt instead was a sudden simple sharpness, and
I pulled the shell apart and took a step backward as butter and

egg white splashed out of the pan and onto the floor. I saw then, a-fry in the goo, not a yolk at all but a half-formed chick, pleasantly asleep on her side in this bubbling hell, and I think I stood and stared at that too long.

I took the skillet out back and flung its contents, still sizzling, up onto the coop roof. Then I threw the skillet up there too, and I cursed my mother, and I cursed my father, and I cursed the undead dirt I shook upon, and I vowed never to break another egg again.

A note on the text

This text was set in Christ knows what by who knows whom. I like for there to be a note on the text in the books I read, so that I might learn something about the typeface employed, if I enjoyed it (the typeface, I mean), and a little of its history, and possibly its designer's, though I tend to grow sad when it strikes me that the author probably did not write this particular passage (alone, perhaps, among all the others in the book), and so may have had no say whatsoever in the typeface, and the whole operation starts to smell like plagiary.

Acknowledgments, on the other hand, are most always written by the author, even if the rest of the book was not, and I cannot stomach them. Better to hate at the end of a book, I say, than to love. The one person I care to acknowledge here is that young man who said to me, long ago, "My dick don't get hard till it *sees* the pussy." If he does not greet me at the gates of heaven, or ferry me across the Styx into hell, then I cannot see how my efforts here have been of much worth. Your more discerning reader, *bien sûr,* will expect me to finger that father I last saw years ago, dying off obligingly in a town rancher (has it taken me this long to be rid of him?) and reminding me somehow of the last time I saw him (really *saw* him), years before that, as my brother and sister and I headed back to the pond, and he asked where we thought we were going, and we said to play hockey, by which anyone would have known that we intended only to slide around on the ice near the pond's fat lip, and whack at one another with what sticks as we had gathered along the way, but he insisted he come along too, and make sure it was "safe," and so we were forced to abandon our game and watch from the shore as he stomped out into the middle of the pond, and looked up at the whitening sky, and brought his sledgehammer down repeatedly on the ice all around him, each of us worried that he might sink himself forever and half praying that he finally would.

I will acknowledge this. I will also acknowledge that I asked the very earth below his dragon claws to open up and swallow him on that calm afternoon (strung now, forever, somewhere between a stolen country pond and a rented town hospital bed) when he called me on the telephone to acknowledge (not to praise, mind you, but merely to acknowledge) something I had written, whereupon he claimed, with too much pride in a failing voice, that he had "manipulated" me into becoming a writer, and I swore I could forgive him anything but that.

A note on the people

I feel obligated, all the same, to provide a note on the people: The people these persons put me in mind of I love a great deal. Those people, though, are not these persons. These persons are my personal inventions. Those people, if you ask them, invented me.

A note on the dogs

I promised a note on the dogs. (See the second paragraph of the fifth part of my fourth attempt to end all this.)

BLACKIE O'REILLY (1974–?). Our original town puppy, got from a sex accident on my paternal grandparents' Southern Illinois farm, after a cat we had from there, Hazel, named after a hideous television character my parents said she resembled, had become so suddenly and inexplicably feral that she was returned to the farm, which outpost itself proved too civilized for her, and we last caught sight of this beast, scraggled and enormous, splayed along a dirt-road ditch as we sped away from the countryside with the new puppy alert in our laps, though I may be compressing events there. (Is that what this is still called, compressing? I was so very young then.)

Adjusted well, this pup, and was an avid snuggler, as we all should be. Was availed of two littermates, that I am aware of: one called, unimaginatively, Snoopy, and given into the care of idiot cousins in whose company he would soon succumb to worms; the other called Tavish, for some reason, by our younger aunts, who encouraged him to run all around, as they themselves did, until he was caught in the woods one night and eaten by coyotes. Said to be part Chihuahua, of all things, on his mother's side; God knows what he was on his father's. Weighed a little more than ten pounds, eventually. Was for the most part black but sported a white chest and four white paws, which pattern he would later see repeated in our menagerie to his absolute horror. Had ears like a startled fruit bat.

Taken by my brother to a pet show being staged at a local town park. Sparked a small controversy when it was explained that pets needed to be registered beforehand to participate, whereupon the boy held his puppy up and asked what kind of pet show was this. Returned home, hard boy and triumphant dog, with jury-rigged award for "cutest pet." Slept always with his little head on a third of my brother's pillow. Knew his mealtimes, and became enraged when these were not strictly adhered to. Made the most religious effort I ever saw in a nonhuman to acquire language, so that all attempts at cleverness around the subject of food failed, as we sent one another the code f-e-e-d t-h-e d-o-g, or m-e-a-l, or a-n-i-m-a-l m-o-u-t-h, and then had to dodge the little fur missile, whose speed and vertical leap were by then legendary, as he hurled himself directly at our hands and our faces.

Was allowed after mealtimes to roam free, as we all were, which my town-caught father insisted was the natural order of things, his town-raised wife disagreeing, and while we formed our little packs and explored the town sewer pipes, never knowing what backyard we would pop up into next, our dog followed a different sort of scent, and soon half the town was abloom with his babies. If asked about this, we were instructed to blame the poorer family around the corner, whose numerous mutts were also black, with white on their chests and their paws, and to lie and say that these were born before we ever moved into the neighborhood.

Situated himself on the corner, when there was no heat on the air, and waited for challengers to come up the hill on Harrison, or to top the sad crest on Tenth, and gun their motors against him, after which he set off like a mechanical rabbit, holding to the sidewalk while the muscle cars and the motorcycles ran him down, the perpetual complaint being that just when they finally caught him he would leave off, self-satisfied, so as to remain, if but technically, undefeated. This brought, understandably, a certain reckless (one might even say a stupid) element to the street, and there began to be horrific crashes in front of our home. A car (it looked to me to be a Pontiac, though I might be mistaken there) collided with a large tree in the yard opposite, and I (and probably the dog) first learned the word "hematoma." Not long after, a motorcycle spilled into that same yard, and the stupefied driver said that a little black mutt, "the fast one," had come directly "at" him. He stayed locked away in our basement for the next two weeks (the mutt, I mean) while we more than once denied knowing him. Shortly thereafter we agreed, as a family, to move to Virginia.

Chased cows in Goochland, and was spanked by our father for doing so, which we thought was the funniest thing we had ever seen. Ran away from us then, and stayed away until my brother took out an ad in the local paper depicting what looked to be the head of a black devil-bat, with ears twice as long and pointy as the real ones were, above the caption *Have You Seen This Dog?* whereupon a local farmer returned him to us, gladly, within a few days. Stayed with us for a stretch after that, and bullied the puppies we had begun by then to accumulate, as country people will tend to do, with the obvious aim of teaching these mutts to respect him even after they had grown to two or three times his size. Must have known, on some level, that this project would fail, having been teased, and kicked at, and spanked, and picked up like a football and thrown out into the middle of a pond by a man who demanded respect from those all around him but would not receive it even from his tiniest dog.

Eventually made trips, on a daily basis, to a gas station roughly a mile off, behind which we had quartered when we arrived in that awful place. At first we assumed this was so that he might hassle the Holsteins along the way. They were black, as was he, with patches of white, and once, when spotted from the road by my parents, and fearing another spanking, he stopped suddenly and began to graze as if he were one of the cows: to this day I am not sure whether this demonstrated a mastery of perspective or a total misunderstanding of it. Soon became clear that he was not headed to the gas station on account of the cows, nor because he expected from the small commerce there a substitute for town, but because he wanted to huff the fumes, as the lower denizens of the station embarrassingly explained it to us, and we began to make regular stops to fetch him, goggle-eyed, home.

Sat like a human on the couch, upright, with his little hands and legs out in front of him, watching TV with one wandering eye and looking, with the other, to participate in our chat by means of his protovocalizations. Had the music of it right, toward the end, but he only ever made imperfect sense. Disappeared for good sometime in the early eighties, in search of what fumes we can never know.

Unclear whether he raced all those soon-to-be crumpled cars and trucks into the perfectly negotiable curve in front of our Virginia home.

BROWN DOG (1979–1988). The prettiest animal I have ever laid eyes on and also, by a wide margin, the stupidest. Given various names by my sister (I remember "Maggie" and, in a more desperate attempt, "Lolla-Lee-Loo"), all of which our father disallowed, arguing that a dog so stupid ought to be known only by some physical characteristic that distinguished it from the others. Became known, then, as Brown, or Brown Dog, when in fact she was spectacularly golden. I do not know why we never thought of "Goldie" for this sweet, furry shepherd-retriever collision.

Sat, out of fear, or ignorance, on the roof of a car in the driveway, like Snoopy on his doghouse, which may have spooked passing motorists, or at least distracted them, as they headed into the otherwise perfectly negotiable curve in front of our house. Caught heatstroke up there and gave us much joy in watching her shake and vomit in the yard. Survived, barely, an apparent suicide attempt by Wonder Bread truck, though later we wondered whether this had been, in fact, an attempt simply to race the vehicle, following after Blackie's faster example.

Was a big one for hugs and pets, and often, even after she was spayed, showed menses down the back of her pretty yellow haunches.

Sat and watched, mesmerized, as the deer roamed the corn rows and chewed, happily and unbothered by her, on the ears.

Died, suddenly and mysteriously, shortly after we had all left home. As our father explained over the telephone, "The bitch just up and died." Might have been snakebit. Was buried, unceremoniously, in what was left of the hole that had formerly been the old outhouse.

GINGER SNAP (1981–?). The product of a black-and-tan hound who had got loose from a hunting pen and impregnated a small, reddish housepet across the road from some friends in the eastern part of the county. Was unusually worried by, and about, herself. Fancied play, and the wedge-shaped boxes of d-Con rat poison my parents put around the place, but would go deathly still whenever I went out behind the house, of a quiet evening, and gazed out over the fields, and into the woods beyond, and gave a sharp yell to awaken, from every angle, the hunting dogs in the kennels all around. Then she would bark and howl back at them, and would look at me as if she did not know what was happening to her, and would not quiet down until I had taken her into my arms, and got inside a car, and shut the door against the world outside.

Asked always, by her eyes, about her true nature, but received no straight answer. Sat and listened, more than any other dog of ours, to the trees, and would jump if the wind shifted suddenly, and would snarl and snap at the air, but was perfectly happy again if you dangled a toy, or else a box of rat poison, in front of her. Was well liked, this dog, but misunderstood. We were never quite sure whether her agonized barks and squeals on the side porch, as her kin chased deer through the trees and into the northern clearing to be slaughtered, perchance to be slaughtered themselves, constituted an alarm so much as it did a cheer.

Disappeared sometime in the middle 1980s. We assumed she had been found in the woods, ours or someone else's, and taken off by a hunter to live and run and die with those kennel-bound cousins of hers. She had a good enough nose for danger, after all, and a loud enough bark, and she always chased the deer away from the corn.

JACKIE (1977–?). Not properly a dog at all but rather a gray tabby, come with us from Southern Illinois to teach us something about misery. Had free run of the place until she dared lash out at a puppy we had recently agreed, at our father's urging, to call Cooper, sweet and round, who climbed the concrete step to the side porch, looking to make friends, and had his left eye scratched by the cat. Was forced thereafter to watch said pup grow into an enormous and unforgiving beast, who more than once stood with a feline corpse in his jaws and glared up at where she now lived, on top of an old wardrobe on the side porch. Spent the rest of her life, that I know of, without once risking the ground again. When not on the wardrobe, or clinging to the mesh of a window screen, or in the leapt-to branches of the magnolia tree in the side yard, she sometimes vanished for weeks. It was rumored that she had managed somehow to access the walls of the house. On one occasion I was sure I heard her in the attic, as no assembly of rats could possibly have made such a racket up there. Whether she hunted these rats, and, if so, what their tainted blood might have done to a creature already mad with fear, I cannot say.

The time and manner of her death are unknown to me.

BUTTFUCKER (1981–1984). Was allowed, after the massacre, to roam the yard as if he were one of the dogs, which, henless, he basically was. The door to the coop yard remained open, in case he wanted access to his former manse and grounds, but I never once saw him go in there. When it rained he came up onto the side porch with the others and huddled in amongst them. Stuck to the side yard and moped when the pack went out exploring in the woods and the fields; had tried to keep up but was incapable.

Showed now only bursts of his former violence, though these were impressive wings-out/claws-forward affairs directed mostly at human visitors to the yard. Allowed me sometimes to sit beside him on the concrete-block step and pet his head, as he had seen me do with the dogs. Made little chicken noises all the while.

Never wanted for feed, with the hens dead, but was curious about what his peers were given for breakfast and dinner. Wandered over, one Sunday morning, to the communal dog bowl, where Cooper ate first, and then Brown Dog, and then Blackie (when he came around), and then Ginger Snap, and took exactly one (1) piece of kibble out of the bowl with his tiny beak, whereupon Cooper promptly killed him in a cloud of flesh and feathers.

B. F., he was generally called, in company.

WEE COOPER O' FIFE (1979–1992). Placed into my arms on the occasion of my thirteenth birthday, this mutt got from the union of a showdog housed briefly at the juvenile-delinquent facility where my parents both worked (said to have been designed by Mr. Jefferson himself as a waystation between slave-kept Monticello and his work in slave-kept Richmond, at which waystation once bivouacked Cornwallis's boys, on their way to Yorktown, and where later may have nightmared Sheridan's) and a giant of unknown origin. Popped, that is, too large, out of a tiny springer spaniel, which I suspect caused her later, dazed and damaged, to wander off into oncoming traffic in Henrico County and be flattened, which incident my father often made direct reference to when speaking with the sad little pup.

Caught and developed mange while in our care, and so we built a pen in the side yard to keep him isolated from the other dogs, and had him up regularly on the newspaper-draped dining-room table, to slather him with medicine, while everyone gathered around and worried, after which we placed him back in the pen, which he did not understand, any more than he understood why a tiny, massive dog of approximately his same coloring (black, mostly, with touches of white) leapt the pen's high walls on a daily basis to snarl at and ram him, who wanted nothing more than to make friends, just as he tried to when, let out of the pen one afternoon, he climbed, as we all watched, up the concrete-block step to the side porch and was met, in the cornea, by a tabby's hateful claw.

Almost died, on this and many other occasions, of infection or crush wound but refused and grew larger, which naturally he should not have, and grew stronger, which naturally he should not have, and in time there was no animal in the area who could match him for size and strength and simple deadliness. Earned, by that size, and that strength, and that simple deadliness, a respect from our father we children could not hope to match, since we never thought to greet the man in the yard with a turtle we were currently chewing to death; nor to lay before him the corpse of a groundhog or a cat we had no good cause to kill; nor to shove our snouts repeatedly into pond water after fish, always missing because we did not understand the principle of refraction; nor to jump up and bite viciously at airplanes, due to a possibly related issue with depth perception; nor to swim around and around, back at the pond, in a seeming schizophrenia, until it was noticed that we were chasing after a dragonfly we had no hope of catching until, suddenly, we raised up out of the water and (*chomp!*) it was gone.

Bounced in the fields whenever everybody, dogs and people, headed back to the pond. Was assumed for years to be bouncing for joy, he did so love the water. Eventually we learned that he was frightening field mice into showing themselves so that he might eat them. Throat-killed a deer, just before I left, and spent most of a day dragging it up into the yard. Had, nonetheless, a retriever's mouth so soft he once caught a too-low bird on the wing and brought it down to my father, who did not look until the dog got his attention with a "Woof," at which "Woof" the bird flew away.

Never bit a person, this dog. He may, for all I know, have murdered Blackie, and Brown, and Ginger, and Jackie, and all the rest, but he never did bite into us.

I last saw him many years later, alone but alive in the backyard of a Southern Illinois rancher. He was deaf and mostly blind now, and I did not think he would recognize me, but he did, and he gave me a bounce, and I said I was not a field mouse, and he licked me. I spooned with him in the grass for a spell, as we had when he was just a puppy, and then I let him be. Later, by telephone, I learned of his fate. My father, ailing himself by then, though we did not know it, had come across the near-dead dog in the yard and had gone to fetch a shovel. He began to dig, and by the time the hole was done the dog was ready for it.

ABOUT THE AUTHOR

BEN METCALF was born in Illinois and raised in that state and later in rural Virginia. He was for many years the literary editor of *Harper's Magazine*. He has since taught at Columbia University's School of the Arts and joined the *Lapham's Quarterly* editorial board. His writing has appeared in *The Baffler*, *Harper's Magazine*, *The Best American Essays*, and elsewhere.

Pine River Library
395 Bayfield Center Dr.
P.O. Box 227
Bayfield, CO 81122
(970) 884-2222
www.prlibrary.org